Praise for *The Invisible Life of Ivan Isaenko*

"*The Invisible Life of Ivan Isaenko* is told in the voice of Ivan. . . . His imagination may help him survive. And, as audience, we can only read about his life and allow our hearts to break more than once."
—*Psychology Today*

"Impressive . . . Stambach's surprising, empathetic novel takes on heavy themes of illness, suffering, religion, patience, and purpose, with a balanced mix of humor and heart."
—*Publishers Weekly*

"An auspicious, gut-wrenching, wonderful debut."
—*Kirkus Reviews* (starred review)

"*The Invisible Life of Ivan Isaenko* must be counted as a miracle of a book."
—*BookPage*

"An extraordinarily brave and original debut. Ivan is an unforgettable narrator, and his story ripples with intelligence, humor, heartbreak, and humanity."
—Carolina De Robertis, author of *The Gods of Tango*

Only a writer with considerable heart and imagination could transform a hospital for post–Chernobyl fallout kids into a captivating, complex, nearly magical world. Scott Stambach has done exactly that. And in the character of Ivan Isaenko he has created an irresistible narrator, just what one would hope for in a seventeen-year-old raised on Nabokov

and Dostoyevsky: by equal measures self-aware, hilarious, quick-witted, and profane. He is an original in every sense of the word, and his story is a marvelous one."
—Sarah Shun-lien Bynum, National Book Award finalist and author of *Madeleine Is Sleeping*

"It would be an easy injustice to spackle Ivan Isaenko with a bunch of clichéd praise: hilarious, poignant, heartwarming, heart-wrenching. While these are true, Ivan is so much more. It's an enchantingly acerbic and endearingly charming story about love, hope, and humanity in the face of death; truly a tender and thoughtful reflection on our universal malady."
—Bradley Somer, author of *Fishbowl*

"*The Invisible Life of Ivan Isaenko* is comic and staggeringly tragic, often both in a single sentence. . . . Ivan Isaenko is one of the most surprising narrators I have encountered— witty, adolescent, well read, at times quite vulgar, and confined to a life that seems nearly unlivable, until he discovers that even at Mazyr Hospital, love is possible. A grittier, Eastern European, more grown-up *The Fault in Our Stars*."
—Eowyn Ivey, author of *The Snow Child*

The

Invisible
Life
of
Ivan
Isaenko

The
Invisible
Life
of
Ivan
Isaenko

SCOTT STAMBACH

WEDNESDAY BOOKS
NEW YORK

THE INVISIBLE LIFE OF IVAN ISAENKO. Copyright © 2016 by Scott Stambach. All rights reserved. Printed in the United States of America. For information, address St. Martin's Press, 175 Fifth Avenue, New York, N.Y. 10010.

www.stmartins.com

Designed by Donna Sinisgalli Noetzel

The Library of Congress has cataloged the hardcover edition as follows:

Names: Stambach, Scott, author.
Title: The invisible life of Ivan Isaenko / Scott Stambach.
Description: New York : St. Martin's Press, 2016.
Identifiers: LCCN 2016007227 | ISBN 9781250081865 (hardcover) | ISBN 9781250081889 (ebook)
Subjects: LCSH: Teenage boys—Fiction. | Teenagers with disabilities—Fiction. | Critically ill children—Fiction. | Children—Hospitals—Fiction. | Belarus—Fiction. | BISAC: FICTION / Literary. | GSAFD: Love stories. | Humorous fiction.
Classification: LCC PS3619.T354 I58 2016 | DDC 813/.6—dc23
LC record available at https://lccn.loc.gov/2016007227

ISBN 978-1-250-08187-2 (trade paperback)

Our books may be purchased in bulk for promotional, educational, or business use. Please contact your local bookseller or the Macmillan Corporate and Premium Sales Department at 1-800-221-7945, extension 5442, or by email at MacmillanSpecialMarkets@macmillan.com.

First Wednesday Books Edition: September 2017

10 9 8 7 6 5 4 3 2 1

For Josephine

The

Invisible
Life
of
Ivan
Isaenko

Foreword

The following words were found in a children's hospital in Mazyr, Belarus, by an Irish journalist during the filming of a documentary. They were written on a pile of ragged papers, in a nearly indecipherable script, and stained with various substances ranging from coffee to borscht. A few years later, through a series of serendipitous events, they landed in the hands of an eager NYU graduate student, W. P. Kalish, who consolidated, edited, and typed them up.

The words on those pages were first written by a seventeen-year-old patient named Ivan Isaenko. For reasons that will become clear, Ivan can, and will, do a much better job of telling his story than we can, so we will leave that to him. For now, we only wish to make two points in order to help clarify the context of the story, as well as our role in its publication.

First, like most of the other children living in the Mazyr Hospital for Gravely Ill Children, Ivan was undergoing treatment for several medical conditions likely resulting from the catastrophic radiation released into the atmosphere following the explosion of a nuclear reactor near the city of Pripyat, Ukraine, on April 26, 1986. While Ivan's exact medical diagnosis is unknown due to a lack of cooperation with the hospital administration, consultations with U.S. doctors suggest that Ivan was born with the connective tissue disorder Beals syndrome, in addition to several other genetic abnormalities.

Second, while we have maintained the integrity of Ivan's original story and writing to the best of our ability, we felt it best to make a few minor changes where necessary. We have corrected errors in Ivan's grammar and spelling in situations where the intended meaning was obvious to us. There were also several instances where Ivan used a word that is unique to the Russian language or whose connotation has no direct translation in modern English. In these cases, we were careful to use the Russian word in the text, but clarify the meaning in a footnote. Occasionally, there were Russian idioms with no direct English translations. In these cases, we simply substituted the closest English idiom in its place or translated the sentence in an alternative way to preserve the meaning.

Before turning you over to Ivan, I would like to share an anecdote. I'm often asked at dinner parties and cocktail hours about the secret life of an editor. By now I have a canned response for this question; I pompously suggest that my job is Godlike. I help create worlds and decide which dreams of men are released into the cosmos to become woven into our collective consciousness. After years of making this comparison, I'm sure some part of me believes it.

Yet every so often a story finds its way to me for which the choice is not mine at all—to not package it, polish it, and let it flutter off into the world in its most honest form would be unforgivable. It would be unforgivable because there are corners of the world where voices cannot be heard; voices so tortured and yet so alive, so singular and yet so familiar, that they beseech the able for a path to hearts and minds.

Ivan's is one of those stories.

—*James C. Begley*
New York, NY
June 2014

PART ONE

The Count Up

Currently, the clock reads 11:50 in the P.M.
It is the second day of December.
The year is 2005.

I

The Anesthetization
of Ivan Isaenko

Dear Reader, whom I do not know, who may never be, I write not for you but for me. I write because I can't sleep. I write because Polina is dead.

Currently, I'm drunk from three capfuls of vodka on a three-day-empty stomach. I have Nurse Natalya to thank for this. She is the only one who knows what I've lost. She is the closest thing I've ever had to a mother, and I know she thinks of me as a son. Like any good mother, she watches over me. For the last two days, she's checked on me every fifteen minutes. She checked on me seven times tonight, and every time I was wide awake. On the eighth time, she discreetly entered my room with a bottle of Stoli.

"Open your mouth, Ivan," she said. "It'll help you sleep."

She poured a capful into my mouth, and I coughed and heaved. As she pulled away, I grabbed her arm and asked for another. Hesitantly, she produced another capful and emptied it down my throat.

"One more," I demanded.

She glanced at me menacingly as if to terrify me from asking again, but nevertheless sympathetically poured one last capful down my throat. Now I feel right. It's not enough to get me to sleep, but it is enough to help me write.

I need to share this place with you, Reader. I need to share my friends who I would never admit were friends. I need to share with you my beloved, whom I would never admit I loved. For if I don't document our world right now, on this ambiguously stained paper, with my fading pen, in my delirious left-handed penmanship, we will risk fading into the foam of history without mention. Reader, I hope after this you understand that we are entitled to more than that.

II

Spectrophobia

I'm seventeen years old, approximately male, and I live in an asylum for mutant children. I first learned of the name of this hospital—the Mazyr Hospital for Gravely Ill Children—from spying on random documents lying around the Main Room, but I wouldn't be able to find it on a map if you asked me. I only know it is somewhere in southern Belarus in a city that is most likely called Mazyr.

I've never met my parents, but as far as I know, when I squirmed out of my mother's nether parts, she took one look at the abomination that had been cooking inside of her and dropped it onto the doorstep of the nearest church in fear that she had fallen victim to the Soviet curse that she had heard so much about on the radio. Incidentally, this was the same curse that resulted in the random explosions of horse thyroids and in Eastern European fauna enduring more hair loss than Gorbachev.

I, for one, am hideous, and consequently, I've developed a crippling phobia of reflective surfaces (and anything else that reminds me of what I look like). But I will bravely face this fact for the sake of my story and describe to you what nature dealt me. My body is horribly incomplete. I only have one arm (my left), and the hand attached to the end of it is deficient in digits (I have two fingers and a thumb). The rest of my appendages are short, asymmetrical nubs that wiggle with fantastic effort. My skin is nearly transparent, revealing the intricate tapestry of my underutilized veins. The muscles in my face are only loosely connected to my brain, resulting in a droopy, flat affect, which makes me look like an idiot, especially when I talk. Of all my privations, this one has come as an advantage, since it helps me to feign a comatose state, which has allowed me to remain largely undisturbed by my doctors and peers whenever I'm uninterested in interaction (which is most of the time). Mostly, I choose to leave the hell of my surroundings in favor of the slightly more palatable hell of my mind. At least there I can create fantasies of the lives I'd rather have lived, such as King Leonidas, the Dalai Lama, Miles Davis, Oskar Schindler, Wilt Chamberlain, astrophysicist Carl Sagan, Larry Flynt (pre-wheelchair), any Russian who's ever written a book, and Confucius, to name just a few.

III

The Day I Came Online

Not many people have the luxury of recalling their first memory. I know this because I've asked Nurse Natalya, Ridick, and my eleventh therapist, Dr. Dubov, but none of them can remember. My first memory, however, is like glass—I came online with a swift slap across the face, which resulted in at least one tooth flying across the room, which I never found. I was four years old, so luckily it would grow back. Before that, there was nothing. Not even blackness. Just nothing. Nothing and blackness are different. Most people don't understand. I, for one, prefer nothing over blackness.

"Take them, Ivan! Take them now!" she hollered while squeezing my cheeks so hard my mouth popped open like an origami change purse. Into it she tossed a few white Soviet-mandated pills, which I spit back into her face.

"Ivan, you *hui morzhovy!** Take your medicine!"

Apparently, I was a menace even before I was old enough to choose to be one. I don't remember what kind of pills she was trying to feed me or why I resisted (it was my first memory). I only remember the look on the face of the nurse, which spoke so many things.

It said, "I hate menstruating."

---

*   Roughly translates from Russian as "walrus dick."

It said, "I've come to hate other things too, but I can't draw a line between what I really hate and you."

It said, "What the *fuck* is the meaning of all this?"

It said, "I wasn't born this way."

It said other things too, but you probably get the point.

I hated that nurse. In my opinion, no one with all her parts in all the right places deserves to have any of those thoughts. Before I even got to know her name (I nicknamed her *cherny pukh* after the hairy mole on her upper lip), she died after falling off the hospital roof in near-hurricane-like weather during a smoke break.

Coma Boy

Most of what I know about the world outside of these walls comes from the images that flicker across the antique black-and-white TV mounted in the Main Room. However, when I'm not watching TV or gazing through the barred windows scattered throughout the institution, my favorite pastime is to act catatonic and eavesdrop on conversations among nurses and doctors. This feigned obliviousness disarms the adults into lengthy streams of uncensored talk; it's the only way I can get accurate news and information. Anything they speak directly to us or around us is either nonsensical baby talk or lies crafted for the purpose of making things appear better than they really are. Despite the smallness of my world, I'm able to mix my observations with a bit of imagination into compelling story lines in which I star. I will play anything from the hero to the villain, but at no time am I the observer, because that is what I already am, every minute of every day. I appreciate the freedom; I learned a long time ago that there are no consequences to the things that happen inside my mind.

Early on, Nurse Natalya caught on that I was faking my comas and gently made me aware of her acuity in a way that resonated perfectly with her. She put a picture of a famous (and very naked) Russian actress in my field of vision and said tauntingly:

"Pretty girl, huh, Ivan? Such a beautiful naked woman, eh?"

And then while my attention was firmly embedded in that picture, glued by every ounce of my helplessly horny, adolescent, sex-deprived being, she yanked it out into my peripheral. Inevitably, my supposedly comatose eyes lustfully followed the image, and my game was revealed. But, before I even tried to explain myself, Nurse Natalya understood the psychology behind my game. So instead of shaming me, as any of the other nurses would have, she sat me down and interrogated me as to my interests. When I told her I had none, she flapped her hand and walked out. The next day she returned with an old paperback copy of Bulgakov's *The Master and Margarita*. I devoured it in three days and asked her for more. Since then, Nurse Natalya has scoured libraries and used-book sales to feed my habit. On the days in which I'm too sick or overmedicated to read, she tells me stories on a variety of esoteric topics ranging from Tollund Man's peat bog to

Saint Ursula's cathedral of bones to Cleopatra's seduction techniques. I once asked her how she knew so much about the world despite being almost as stuck in this place as I am.

"I'm a few chapters away from a Ph.D., Ivan," she said. "But it turns out universities are even lonelier than hospitals."

One day, Nurse Natalya gently suggested that I should try writing down the scripts that played through my pseudocatatonic head. She thought that it would amount to some sort of therapy.

"Where are you when you leave the hospital and go into your head?" she asked me.

I smiled asymmetrically, shook my head one and a half times, and looked away.

"Sometimes the stories play right in your eyes, Ivan," she continued. "You should write them down."

She paused for a second and smirked.

"If you wrote your stories with the same chutzpah you use with the nurses, I'd give you two years before you're the world's most despised Nobel laureate."

"My stories are for me," I replied.

"You say that now, Ivan."

And then she smiled, and when she smiles, it means that she knows that we both know.

She would revisit the topic once or twice a week every week for the next few years. As always, she was right. Actually, I'm not sure Nurse Natalya has ever been wrong about anything.

One day she asked me, "Do you know how the Buddha became enlightened?"

"I don't believe in enlightenment."

"Perfect, Ivan. The Buddha wouldn't want you to believe in enlightenment."

"Aren't you Orthodox?"

"The Buddha makes me a better Christian."

"So how?"

"How what?"

"How did he become enlightened?"

"He sat under the Bodhi Tree and promised himself not to move until he solved the whole puzzle of human suffering."

I suppose I currently bear a striking resemblance to that Buddha under the Bodhi Tree.

Currently the clock reads 1:55 in the A.M.

I've been writing for two hours.

It is the third day of December.

The year is 2005.

I closed my eyes and fell asleep for the first time in
   three days.

But it only lasted for three minutes.

I saw you, Polina.

But I saw the you of three days ago,

not the you of three months ago.

V

One Day in the Life of Ivan Isaenko

Every day is exactly the same. The episodes on the antique TV in the Main Room may change. The nurses' moods may oscillate according to the details of their lives and synchronized menstrual cycles. The menus might switch up by an ingredient or two. But, in every other way, every day is exactly the same.

My experience of the first sixty seconds of every day depends entirely on whether I wake up in one of the months between April and October. During the summer months, the sun rises at 4:00 in the A.M., so when the internal alarm clock I've honed through the years starts trumpeting, my eyes open to the soft sunlight flowing through the black iron bars covering my window and onto the cold linoleum tiles, which incidentally warm just enough to make the crawl to the bathroom tolerable (the urge to urinate is too urgent to take the time to get into my wheelchair).

In the winter, however, the sun rises as late as 9:00 in the A.M., so I wake into a dark, cold room, which feels like being born into the primordial loneliness from which I originally came. Waking up in the dark fills me with existential dread, and it isn't just because of the cold crawl to the bathroom. There is something deeper and darker to it, something that comes from a place that I'm not sure I will, or could ever, understand. But someplace familiar all the same.

After my mentally programmed alarm clamors, the first thing I do is pull off the covers in the hopes of finding all my body parts are actually in all the right spots and that the last seventeen years have all been a dream. When I realize that I'm still incomplete, I empty the contents of my freakishly small bladder and then move on to dressing myself, which includes some combination of the three T-shirts, three sweatshirts, three shorts, and three sweatpants I have on rotation.

When I turned four, the nurses became irritated with the obstinance I displayed during my dressing ritual. After several futile consultations, they transferred the responsibility of dressing to me. One day, Nurse Greta, the nurse formerly tasked with concealing my naked body every morning, simply dropped a bag of clothes onto the linoleum and said, "Well, then, have at it, Ivan." For the next year, my dressing ritual turned out to be the most frustrating part of my day. Reader, if you care to step into my shoes, please put down the papers in your hand and try to put a shirt on with one arm and two nubs for legs. I'll wait before moving on . . .

Now that you understand, I will reveal that after a year of flubbing through my ritual, I eventually discovered a new technology that I affectionately call "the worm." It involves laying my shirt facedown on my bed and squirming my body through the bottom until my head emerges from the top. Once in this configuration, I'm free to pop all my truncated parts through their respective holes. Dressing like a grub allows me to conceal my God-given nudity in under a minute.

If all goes well, I'm prepared for the two-minute wheel-chair ride to the cafeteria for breakfast hour, which is from 8:00 in the A.M. to 9:00 in the A.M. Once there, I take my spot at the long table, which is the same spot I've eaten at three times a day, every day, for the last seventeen years. At any given time there are between fifteen and twenty-five patients living at the asylum, and they all have their regular seats, not because they were assigned but because that's just how things are. I've held mine the longest, so far as I know.

As we assemble, the nurses drop plates in front of us with food that I'm not sure I've ever tasted. This is because I rush through my plate too fast to taste anything, mostly due to the eating habits of more than half of my comrades, which make me physically ill, as does the sloppy way the nurses feed the other half. That said, I'm not entirely sure I would be able to taste the food even if I made an effort to taste each bite. A typical breakfast invariably involves some combination of bread and cabbage. The taste and texture of the bread most closely resemble those of plywood. Not only are the loaves not baked fresh but they are shipped in from remote wholesale bakeries in countries like Greece and Tajikistan. According to our director, Mikhail Kruk, this is because most of our local state bread-and-cabbage facilities are either defunct or run by *gavnoyeds** since the year 1991.

After I finish my breakfast, with sweaty cabbage juice still running down my face, I return to my room to read until TV

---

*   Translates from Russian as "shit eaters"; however, it also carries the connotation of those who are cheap or stingy.

hour. To this day, no nurse or doctor employed at the Mazyr Hospital for Gravely Ill Children has ever been able to explain to me why TV hour is only an hour long. I spent three months lobbying Nurse Natalya to have the TV on all day. I provided written documentation to help promote my position. In the end, she returned with a one-sentence-long written memoranda from the Director, Mikhail Kruk:

At the Mazyr Hospital for Gravely Ill Children, there is one hour of TV in the morning after breakfast, one hour of TV in the afternoon after lunch, and one hour of TV in the evening after dinner.

So, until further notice, I get to watch TV for an hour every morning. When the hour is up, I return to my room, where I read some more and fantasize about ways to leave. Options for escape include slipping outside the front doors of the hospital when no one is looking or, in the middle of the night, squeezing my tiny body through the bars that line my bedroom window. But all of these options end with me slithering away at an embarrassingly slow clip, followed by someone catching me with grass stains and mud all up and down my nubs and dried tears caked to the side of my otherwise transparent face. After years of thinking it through, there is no viable plan for escape. Even if I managed to get to a major road, they'd look me up and down and take me straight to the nearest hospital, which is, of course, the Mazyr Hospital for Gravely Ill Children.

That's when I begin to think of other, more permanent

methods of escape. I've gotten as close as breaking a jar of mayonnaise and picking up one of the jagged pieces, only to realize that I hadn't thought through the fact that I only have one wrist, which, incidentally, is connected to my only hand, making wrist-cutting a violation of the laws of physics. Also, I'm terrified of blood, which makes throat-slicing impossible. The thought of my last sight in this life being two to five violent red spurts leaping out of my neck is simply too horrifying to entertain. And sadly, using other, more obscure, entry points would be difficult due to my limited knowledge of human anatomy. So, in the end, I usually just masturbate for the first of what is usually twice daily.

By the time I finish and mop up, it's usually time for lunch hour. Lunch is typically better than breakfast because it is usually warm and involves some sort of meat, though the particular variety of meat is questionable. It is too red to be chicken, but too white to be beef, so you can understand the dilemma. I once made the mistake of asking Nurse Katya:

"Is this pork?"

To which she replied:

"Ivan, have you ever seen me eat the lunch here?"

To which I answered:

"No."

Then she stopped saying any more words.

After lunch, it's time for the second TV hour of the day. As much as I enjoy TV hour, I occasionally use this time to fake a good coma because I realized that it would be entirely too obvious if the only moments when I was *not* catatonic were moments when the TV was on. This concern led me to what I now call the *two-three rule* (i.e., every second, then every third, day, I pretend to be catatonic during afternoon TV hour). This schedule provides enough of an illusion of randomness to avoid other nurses catching on that my comas are actually acts of award-winning drama.

I tend to wake up from my coma just in time for dinner, which is usually a cold, leftover version of lunch. At this point, I look around the table and note that although I'm no leading man, I'm also the only one of this gang of misfits who can remember my lines. I once asked Nurse Natalya why I'm the only mutant at the asylum who can spell his own name. She said that I should just be grateful for the fact that I could spell my own name. I said that if I was going to be stuck in a hospital for the duration of my life, I'd prefer to be mentally deficient (the word *deficient* is incidentally quite hard for me to say). She said that my self-awareness makes life worth living. I said that my self-awareness makes life lonely. She said that as long as she worked at the hospital, she would never let me be alone. I wanted to say that she didn't understand, but couldn't bring myself.

After dinner, I head back to the Main Room to watch my third hour of TV for the day. By the time TV hour number three is over, there is no more light coming in through the windows, and all the other misfits have been locked away in their rooms. I sit for a minute in the stillness with my skin basking in all the fake lighting and only a few residual howls and groans reverberating through the halls. Then I wheel myself back to my room and read until I'm tired enough to masturbate again. Then I masturbate until I'm tired enough to sleep. Then I wake up the next morning and start all over.

V I

The Children of the Mazyr Hospital for Gravely Ill Children

I have nothing to compare my hospitalities to, but from what little I know of the outside world, I am fairly certain that my comrades and I live in hell. For most of us, the hell is in our bodies; for others, the hell is in our heads. And there is no mistaking that, for each of us, hell is in the empty, clinical, perfectly adequate, smudgy, off-white brick walls that hold us in here. In spite of my intelligence, I'm forced to accept that I'm one of the lucky ones. But for you to truly understand, I will have to introduce my comrades.

Polina

Polina comes first, even if she is the only one of us who never belonged here. I've been sitting impatiently for thirty-seven minutes trying to write her into life, but nothing comes. My hand shakes at the thought of sharing her imperfectly, especially since this manifesto may be the only elixir that keeps her alive and, even then, only in your mind, Reader. Understand the gravity of your part in all this—you're in control of her immortality. You preserve her, even if by accident.

The only consolation I have in my failure to bring her to life is the belief that despite my love for words, they are actually rather useless and undeniably fail to capture the essence of anything at all, let alone a creature like Polina. Consequently, if I ever meet her again in a different place, I can blame my shortcomings on Russian vocabulary and not on my inattentiveness to her details. With that said:

There is *no* doubt in my mind that if I hadn't met Polina here in this desolate place, I would have met her one night, years from now, moving gracefully across the antique black-and-white TV in the Main Room. She would have been Belarus's leading lady, captivating the love and lust of every man in Eastern Europe and setting a hopeless bar to which every woman and girl would hold herself. Similarly, there is no doubt that I still would have become addicted to her, falling every bit as in love as I did here while sitting next to her fading body.

Let me make this perfectly clear: Polina was objectively beautiful. She wasn't beautiful because I was a revolting invalid whose desperation for companionship dictated that he reduce his standards of beauty to a level that was practical for obtaining such companionship. Even as Polina lay pale, emaciated, and on the verge of death, she would have won any pageant in the world. With this clarification, I can go on to tell you what she looked like.

She had long brown hair besieged with curls and ringlets persisting in the face of her ongoing struggle—a struggle that forced her to abandon all modes of regular feminine hygiene. Her skin was a perfect tender porcelain with rosy undertones. Yet she had a simple, modest beauty mark on her right cheek, which made her just imperfect enough to be real. The structure of her face was exotic. Each turn and curve was slightly exaggerated, giving her face an instant edge over every other feminine face in the world, rendering Cleopatra unassuming, while intimidating the breath out of me every time I laid eyes on it. Her body was long and slender, yet adorable little breasts bloomed from her chest and would trace the contours of her respiration right up until her last breath. Reader, can you see what I'm dealing with?

And while you pull me to stay here with you,
I need to build our world.
You, of all people, would understand. *

Max

Max is two years old and shaped like a sickle. His head and heels bend back in a perennial struggle to be the first to reach the other. His lips are blue, thin, dry, and chapped. His face is altogether taut, and his eyes bulge with exasperation and

---

* This note was not written within the body of Ivan's original text. Rather, it was written in the right-hand margin of this page. Nevertheless, we thought it worth including.

panic, as if at the tender age of two he realizes that his eyes are the only way he has of communicating. Sadly, no one will ever know what Max is trying to say, but I'm sure we all have a pretty good idea.

When Max was only a few months old, I began watching him every day with an intensity that was admittedly creepy. Perhaps it was the fresh new life sitting in a drab crib. Perhaps it was my inability to recall any suffering that looked deeper than his. Or perhaps it was a morbid fascination with his tightly drawn skin, which looked like it could snap open at any moment, revealing a loom of striated flesh and gizzards. I doubt I have the psychological insight into the ongoings of my head to know for sure. But what I do know is that in those first few months of meeting Max, I stumbled onto a new emotion, which I can only imagine is the feeling people call empathy.

Actually, it was more of a cousin of empathy because it included a sense of responsibility. Maybe it was an inbred, collectively unconscious, evolutionary impulse, a paternal drive to nurture and protect due to the fact that before Max, I never held anything worth protecting. Nor did I ever consider the marginal possibility that I would ever be in a position to protect. In fact, it is entirely possible that any tender emotions I felt toward Max were totally selfish and rooted in a desire to feel a fraction less freakish than the baseline level of freak I lived with.

At first, this had the counterproductive effect of making me feel *more* freakish. But I've had enough time to watch the behavior of normal people to know that they're not any different. I listen to the conversations between the nurses as they help each other pick up the pieces after any one of them finds out that her husband is leaving her for a nineteen-year-old ballet dancer with blue eyes and feet that are distinct from her ankles. Or when their Crohn's gets so bad that they can barely get off the toilet, and if they can barely get off the toilet, they can barely work, and if they can barely work, they can barely make money, and if they can barely make money, they can barely survive, and if they can barely survive, then . . .

I'm an invalid with no natural instinct for human nature. And yet I can see the twinkle in the eye of Nurse Lyudmila when she pats Nurse Elena on the back and explains that all will be well: the nineteen-year-old dancer is vapid and the husband will come running back, the diarrhea will lead to other more fulfilling jobs in an office in Minsk, and so on. The truth is Nurse Lyudmila (the youngest and newest of the nurses here) is an invalid in her own head, and I know invalids well. She will stuff a box of *ptichie moloko** into her slightly out-of-proportion mouth in about ten seconds and then sneak away to the bathroom to regurgitate it. I know this because I sneak into the bathroom after and see the residue of the foamy chunks floating in the water. So when Nurse Lyudmila gets the chance to tend to anyone, she feels less broken. And when I get to tend to Max, I feel less broken.

Max's most primal survival needs are met through machinized feeding. However, there are some needs that the

---

* A famous Russian dessert better known as "bird's milk cake."

machines can't take care of. For example, Max needs to shit out the food that is pumped into him through the long plastic tubes. On most days, this happens into a disposable diaper. I once asked Nurse Katya (who is the only black woman in the whole Republic of Belarus as far as I know) if I could change Max's diaper. She took one hard, excessively long look at my one arm, with its see-through skin and digitless hand, and asked, "Child, have you lost your mind?" Despite having had fourteen years to come to terms with the epic cataclysm I have for a body, it still hurt. So I did the only thing I could think to do. I asked Nurse Natalya if I could borrow a few diapers. She looked at me quizzically, and then her face twisted in such a way that made it clear she didn't even want to know the reason for my absurd request. Then she walked off to a supply closet only to return a few seconds later with three baby-sized diapers.

The first one I tried on myself. The fit was snug, but luckily my frail pelvis was compact enough to accommodate the squishy fabric. There are two things I've learned over the years about my limits: (A) I can eventually, with enough time, sweat, and sometimes blood, learn to do just about anything with only one arm (the only exception to this rule is cutting a hard-boiled egg), and (B) if there is a God, then I should thank Him for my thumb, since it is the only thing that makes (A) possible.

While patiently waiting for the urge to defecate, I played with my diaper's tiny adhesive tabs. I was getting comfortable with the mechanics of the contraption, finding the subtle tricks required to get a single thumb and index finger to attach and detach the various flaps with ease, exploring the necessary tension required to keep a diaper in place. I've found that after about eight hours of practicing just about anything with my flimsy hand, I can become good enough at it to put a rare smile on my droopy face (incidentally, before the eight-hour mark of proficiency, don't touch me—I will simultaneously snap, beat, hiss, gnash at you; Nurse Natalya calls it my *d'yavol** face).

Luckily, eight hours is also a sufficient period of time to build up an adequate urge to defecate. In other words, by the time I mastered the art of the diaper I was ready to fill it. I cringed as the warm paste spread over my *zadnitsa*.†

I removed the diaper, which, by now, I could do quite easily, and used the towel in my room to clear out all the chocolate pudding that managed to coat every crack and contour of my backside. This proved far more challenging than I had expected, and I immediately wished I had more towels and diapers. In my stubborn obsession, I had also not really thought through what I would do with the leftovers. Nor did I fully appreciate the speed with which the smell would make me expel that morning's cabbage.

The soiled towel was the easy part. I just let it soak in my bathroom sink for the night so the next morning I could ring out all the supersaturated brown water until the towel was reduced to the traditional shade of antiquated off-white of the typical hospital towel. The diaper, however, would be more

---

*   Translates from Russian as "devil."
†   Russian slang for "ass."

difficult. After considering several possibilities, I eventually decided that the best option would be to wait until the Director (as well as the majority of the nursing staff) left to go home for the day and drop off the soiled diaper behind the leather sofa in his office. At least half the days of the week he left his office unlocked so Nurse Lyudmila could casually let herself in for late-night erotic activities. Years later, I still imagine the carnal things that might have happened on that couch, directly above that diaper.

At this stage, I had one more step to mastering my diapery. There was an old (and by old I mean Stalin-era standard-issue model) baby doll buried in a bin of useless toys in the TV room. Unfortunately, rummaging through a crib-sized box of chaotic toys goes far beyond my current level of athletic ability, so I had to reduce myself to asking Nurse Elena if she could dig it out for me (Nurse Natalya was off-limits, as she was very close to her critical mass of suspicion). Nurse Elena was equally baffled by the request, since I had not asked to hold the creepy, odd-smelling doll in my entire tenure at the asylum, but she gave in nevertheless.

Somewhat disgusted, somewhat excited, I wheeled myself back to my room, laid the doll (whom I lovingly named Rebeka Rebokov) on my bed, removed its tattered outfit, and tried to slip the diaper onto its androgynous pelvis. Then I slid Rebeka Rebokov under the covers of my bed and fell asleep next to her.

The next morning, I initiated another eight-hour session. On and off, on and off, on and off with that diaper. All morning. Then lunch hour. And then again all afternoon. During one particularly awkward moment, Nurse Natalya had come by to change my sheets (in my fever, I'd forgotten it was sheet day, which is the third Tuesday of every month). When I heard the knob turn and the door open, I craned my head back around my shoulder to find her staring wide-eyed with a stack of linen in her arms. After three or four unbearable seconds, in which both of our sets of deer eyes were locked into each other, she simply turned around and walked in the opposite direction.

"I'll come back. Perhaps by then our doll will be ready for a bottle," she said.

By the time my eight hours were up, I could change a diaper in ten seconds, which I find impressive for an invalid with one arm and three fingers. I had one diaper left—the one I saved for Max. I waited till the lights went out and the hum of the hospital died down to approximate silence and the daytime nurses left for the night, and which made it easy to slip into the Yellow Room, which is the room that holds all the children under three years old.

Max is not exactly a flight risk, so his crib doesn't have a high-gated perimeter. It is actually something between a crib and a cradle. He lives his shitty little life in a tiny blanketed tublike dwelling with walls on either side that are at most a foot and a half high. Lucky for me, this is a height I can scale.

I wiggled my way out of my chair and maneuvered myself into the tiny padded nest in order to arrive at Max's tiny meniscus of a body. This was the first time I'd ever seen Max at night. My first thought was that Max makes the same face regardless of whether he is awake or asleep. I've watched enough faces on enough sleepless nights to know that faces soften when they sleep, regardless of what thoughts and demons torture their minds when they're awake. Max, however, looked equally desperate in the stillness of sleep.

I had no idea what the status of Max's bowel schedule was, so I gently pulled at his diaper to see if it was brimming with the characteristic heavy brown slop I'd become so intimate with. At the moment, we were pudding-free. So I sat. And waited. And attempted to sing to him in whispers. I sang Russian nursery rhymes like "Brother Ivan" and "The Hare Went Out for a Walk." I sounded wretched, probably like the ghost of a chap who died at the peak of puberty, but it helped pass the time.

Then it happened: the aroma of fecal particles diffused into the air. The most intensive training never really prepares you for the reality of the moment. Max's odd sickle-shaped body made the removal of his diaper far more formidable than I had expected. Eventually, however, I was able to slip it off, but not without leaving fecal streaks throughout his bungalow.

A part of me panicked, most likely because my reputation was on the line, my pride, my proof that I could, at the very least, tend to another being enough to change a shitty diaper. So I did what I could (with a mixture of saliva and my own sweatpants) to eliminate the streaks of chocolate from Max's warm linen.

I could be crazy—actually I most certainly am—but I do believe I saw Max's eyes ease a fraction when all was said and done. I doubt his dirty diaper had ever been changed with such gusto and love (typically the nurses toss him around like a bag of onions). After I completed my mission I stayed with him long enough to croak out "Granny Ate Peas" and then remounted my chair and disposed of Max's soiled diaper in the Director's office en route to my room.

The next morning, I woke before breakfast hour and wheeled myself back to the Yellow Room and waited smugly for the nurses to make their rounds. Eventually, Nurse Katya arrived at Max's crib and checked the status of his undergarments. I watched as she manhandled his stiff, bent body, rotated his torso until he resembled a city arch, and opened the flaps of his diaper only to find it empty. Katya closed him up and then opened him right back up again for a second look. At which point she confirmed his clean diaper and scanned the bed frantically for alternative signs of waste. When she found the chocolate streaks, it only enhanced her bewildered look, leading her to scan the room in a panic, while I bit my inner cheek to the point of blood and thought about dead puppies in order to suppress the laughter. When she turned to me, I simply looked back with the remnants of a dirty smile. Then I fell into a coma.

On that day, I basically adopted Max. At least in my own head, where I don't need papers or legal documentation. And after the diaper incident, I did my best to play the part. I would sneak into his room after lights-out with a stolen book or two. Some were age appropriate, like *Special Clothing and the Electrician*. Others weren't, like *Lolita* and *Notes from the Underground*. Probably not a word makes it into Max's head, and even if it did, the look on his face tells me he has worse things to worry about than Russian literature. But then there is a part of me that believes that he is being groomed to be a scholar. So when Nurse Katya asks me what the hell I'm doing reading Nabokov to a frozen toddler, as she often does, I respond with one simple word: *otyebis*.[*]

∾

Currently the clock reads 4:57 in the A.M.
I've been writing for five hours.
It is the third day of December.
The year is 2005.

According to the clock, I slept for twenty-two minutes. I don't remember my dreams, but I do know the vodka wore off, which means that I now can remember the green file folder with my name on it, which is currently hiding under my bed and overpopulating my (now) sober brain with irritating thoughts. I can't bring myself to ask her. I would either choke on the words or choke her to death.

She hasn't appeared since the last time she poured vodka down my throat, which is unfortunate, since I'm in need of more Stoli. I decided that a reasonable remedy would be to take the standard-issue metal bedpan they keep next to my bed for emergencies and beat the similarly metaled frame of my bed. So I whacked away incessantly, until Nurse Lyudmila opened the door.

---

[*]   Roughly translated from Russian as "fuck off."

"Ivan, what in the hell do you want?" she asked.

Now that Polina was dead, Nurse Lyudmila was back on nights.

"Natalya," I said.

"Her week is over."

Which was true. There are four nurses at the hospital, and four weeks in a month. Each one of them gets to work a week of nights every month.

"She said she would stay for me," I said, but that was a lie.

"Tell me what you need, or I leave."

"I need Natalya."

"Not happening," she said, and she initiated the process of turning toward the door. So I started beating at the frame of my bed some more. In response, Nurse Lyudmila turned back, ripped the bedpan out of my hand, and threw it in the corner of the room. By the time the bedpan stopped ringing, a tired and haggard Nurse Natalya, with her nurse's belt noticeably off center, her hair swollen, showed up at the door with a face that condemned the both of us.

"I can take care of this, Lyudmila," she said.

"What are you doing here?" Nurse Lyudmila asked, fairly flummoxed, but Nurse Natalya ignored the question. Instead, she took a few seconds to seethe at me, during which I stared back resolutely, at which point Nurse Lyudmila just stomped out of the room.

"You don't have permission to be an asshole," Nurse Natalya said.

"Lyudmila is an asshole," I said.

"You're both assholes."

"I need more."

"More what?"

"Vodka."

"Uh-uh, no, Ivan. I'm not letting this turn you into a drunk before your eighteenth birthday."

"You and I both know I'm too stubborn to be a drunk."

"Yes and no. You're stubborn for certain, but I've met plenty of stubborn drunks."

"It's the only thing that helps, and I don't want to stop writing."

My gamble was that sympathy would work. I lifted my notebook and fanned through the filled pages, several of which were wavy as a result of the salt water that had leaked onto them from my face. When she saw the waterlogged pages, she sighed, walked out, and returned with a flask a few minutes later.

"It's full," she said, while setting it on the table next to my bed. "Don't even think about asking for more."

Spasibo, Natalya.

Then she knelt down and kissed my forehead.

"You stayed for me?" I asked.

"Maybe."

She combed her fingers through my greasy, unshowered hair, and I let my head fall to the side, feigning sleep. When she left, I took one long, hard sip, waited a moment to evaluate its effect on my brain, and then took another.

Alex

Alex looks almost normal from the nose down. However, at his temple region, his head blossoms into a veritable melon at least three times the diameter of the rest of his head. I once asked Nurse Elena why his head was so big. She just said:

"That boy's dome is just one big water balloon. Don't get too close, Ivan. It may pop one day."

It is entirely obvious to anyone within a hundred meters of Alex that his center of gravity resides at the tip of his forehead. Consequently, it's no surprise that balance is a luxury for the boy, making it nearly impossible for him to hold up and control the colossus. As a result, he is constantly bonking his head off furniture, doorframes, and medical equipment.

Apparently, all that water resting on Alex's brain results in a variety of neurological disadvantages, including an inability to formulate any words with his mouth except for *shoko,*[*] severe limits in the range of motion in his legs, and spontaneous outbursts that have become part of the melodious soundtrack of this institution. Fortunately, his love for *shoko* often negates whatever irritation is causing his tantrum. At any given time, we are likely to find charming gobs of chocolate smeared all over Alex (primarily on his cheeks and elbows).

There is a bright spot for Alex, when he is not tantruming, he is smiling. It is an idiotic oaf-like smile, but it is a smile nevertheless, and to be perfectly honest, it is a smile that I

---

[*] Presumably, a mispronunciation of the Russian word *shokolad,* which means "chocolate."

would love to have if only my weak cheeks could muster it. Why Alex smiles, I do not know. Maybe it's the weight of all that water applying constant pressure to the smile real estate of his brain. Or it could simply be one of the more innocuous consequences of the brain damage he suffers due to repeated head collisions.

Alex once had a mom and a dad. When he arrived a few years ago, they visited him every Sunday morning. Shortly after church hours, the duo would arrive with blank, stoic faces and spend an average of eight minutes making small talk, to which Alex responded with various varietals of *shoko*, some deep and boomy, others abrupt and shrieky, to which the parents responded by feeding him bar after bar of chocolate. When they were out of chocolate bars, the mother would violently wipe away the chocolate residue from his round cheeks, and you could almost hear the water in his head slosh around.

The father, who peeled the wrappers off all those bars, was a tall, imposing, and quite fat man with a serious, almost fierce face. He dressed sharply in expensive suits tailored to fit his monstrous stomach perfectly. The mother, who scrubbed the chocolate off Alex's face, was quiet and aloof and looked like she might have suffered some brain damage herself. She wore frumpy, conservative church dresses, which made it impossible to tell what hid beneath them.

In all the years of their visits, I don't believe I ever heard them say a word to each other. Sometimes the nurses would try to say a few cordial niceties or ask questions, but the parents would never respond. When their time was up, they would pack their coats, scarves, and assorted other belongings (faces just as blank and emotionless as when they arrived) and walk out. No hug, no emotional good-byes. And yet they never missed a Sunday.

"What's with Alex's parents?" I once asked Nurse Natalya while she arranged giant cans of cabbage in the pantry.

"They remind me of my parents before they died. To them life is all about duty. They are just two tiny pieces of a big machine, and machines don't smile, Ivan. It's a souvenir of communism. Old folk wouldn't know how to give it up for a lifetime of *sbiten*."*

This was their ritual for years, until one day, one tiny detail changed. The suits that once fit Alex's father so precisely began to look off. At first I couldn't pinpoint the difference, but as the weeks passed by, I kept watching from across the room, and luckily, they were too oblivious to notice.

After a few weeks it became clear that the suits were beginning to hang off the old man like the Soviet flag. And eventually it appeared to me that you could fit two of Alex's father in one of his suits. While I was puzzled by how this out-of-touch, gruff old man could have the combination of discipline and vanity required to lose so much weight so fast, I found myself secretly applauding him. For a while, he looked like he could model for the Communist Party of Belarus. But, eventually, the fat-shedding went too far, and it was abundantly clear that the transformation was not his

---

* Traditional warm Russian drink made from honey, spices, and jam.

choice. His face turned gray and gaunt, and his suits (which he somehow didn't replace) began to swallow him. The makeover made the man look even more unforgivingly stern and fierce than he already did. Eventually, he began to slow down, and every movement looked like it took his entire will to live to complete.

As he wasted away to nothing, Alex continued to smile dumbly, while the mother's face continued to look aloof and mildly brain damaged. Honestly, with the exception of the father's facial structure becoming more crisp and the ever-increasing drape of his suits, nothing seemed to change in these weekly episodes. The family carried on normally as if it were business as usual. Judging by the nurses' faces, even they were baffled by the absence of emotion.

One unimportant Sunday morning, another tiny detail changed: Alex's mother arrived alone. And despite all the fluid resting on Alex's brain, disrupting all of Alex's natural mental processes, it was easy to see that Alex knew his father was gone. When his mother sat down next to him and peeled off the wrapper to his chocolate bar (a job that had been reserved for his father), the idiotic smile fell off Alex's face, and he broke into an unprecedented tantrum, screaming, "*Shoko! Shoko! Shoko!*" while batting the chocolate out of his mother's hands. His mother responded by grabbing the boy's cheeks and pushing a piece of chocolate into his unopened mouth. As she did, Alex surrendered and chewed sadly while his body slumped and his eyes filled with glass.

When I was young, I had this naïve notion of karma. I believed that there was a set amount of bad to be distributed to all people and that each person received the same amount. If it were any other way, God would just be too much of an asshole. Or maybe it was my own flavor of communist conditioning bleeding through the hospital walls. Either way, this notion of cosmic justice helped me get up in the morning. Because if this were true, then that would mean that my entire lifetime of bad things had already been dealt to me. I was born a hideous mutant, abandoned by my parents, and relegated to a dreary hospital. This, I believed, was my full lifetime's allowance of misfortune, leaving a windfall of good for the rest of my life. But on the day I saw tears roll down Alex's bloated, chocolate-stained cheeks, I had to let go of my theory. Alex, like me, had been born with his entire lifetime of bad things, and still, with not a prospect of good in sight, he was getting steamrolled with more.

After a year, Alex's mother stopped showing up too. I asked Nurse Natalya what happened to her.

"Cardiomyopathy, Ivan. Some call it broken heart syndrome."

Sometimes I spend too much time wondering what Alex might be like if his brain weren't supporting the weight of a koi pond.

The Heart Hole Children

Enju, Dasha, Vlad, Alexa, and Nick all have holes in their hearts. Apparently, this is the most common affliction at the asylum. These kids are relegated to the Red Room (it's actually a scuffed-up pink), where they all lie in an assortment of beds and cribs with plastic wires that leave their chests and arrive at machines whose cold and impersonal intelligence fills me with existential nausea.

The heart-hole children don't last here for very long, and certainly not long enough for them to reach an age where they've developed a deep enough sense of personhood for me to see them as human beings. Actually, they feel more like a miniature alien species with humanoid features than actual people. And, contrary to conventional wisdom, the heart-holes' brief tenancies are *not* due to cardiac arrest but to a miracle of God. Within ten months, their hearts are fixed, and they are released back to their families and out into the world, presumably to live a normal life filled with candy, sex, and voting.

Actually, God is not responsible for fixing any heart-holers, so far as I can tell. I used to wonder why He, if He were to exist, wouldn't make it easier to know it's Him doing all the fixing. Then I realized that it's probably because we would also blame Him for all the rest of us, who, incidentally, are much less fixable. So until I have some evidence that God is the one making the heart-hole children better, I will give all the credit to Dr. Ridick.

When I was about eight years old, Ridick started showing up in Mazyr with an entourage of assistants carrying boxes of medical supplies. Included in these boxes were a few pieces of technologically advanced medical fabric, which are apparently the perfect substitute for heart stuff. Currently, Ridick visits about twice a year, once in June and once in December, and during his stay, the good doctor sews up as many hearts as he can. The newly patched heart-hole kids wake up the next morning with a smile that comes with the feeling of their hearts beating properly for the first time in their lives. I know this because I've camped out and waited patiently to watch their eyes open. Then, two days later, an unfamiliar vehicle rolls up to the front door and picks up one of the newly patched kids. The child saunters down the front steps and wobbles into the backseat and then drives off into a new life where he eats real food cooked by a mother who takes proper credit for birthing him and makes friends who are capable of uttering words and courts a mate whom he can learn to love and copulate with.

For most of my life at the Mazyr Hospital for Gravely Ill Children, I've resented the heart-hole kids, but this has changed recently. Not because my situation is any different but because I've met Ridick.

Like most people, I hated Ridick at first. The first few times he and his entourage arrived, they were accompanied by a team of cameras and audio equipment that followed around the good doctor as if he were, in fact, the God of Old Testament notoriety. They filmed the bloody open hearts of the heart-hole kids, careful not to omit any detail of the carnage, for the enjoyment of thousands of faceless viewers who wanted to feel warm and gushy over the prospect that happy endings are real. I observed from a good safe distance as Ridick, and then the nurses, and then the newly functional heart-hole children were interviewed by glib international journalists. It's not that I wanted the attention (maybe I secretly did). It just lit my mutant fuse to see the cameras put a pretty ornate frame around the affable doctor and happy heart-holers as if they were some island isolated from the rest of us. One abrupt 360-degree panoramic revolution would expose the fact that we *all* have a story here. But I quickly learned that Nabokov was right when he said the world needs happy endings, no matter how unethical.

As a cripple confined to a wheelchair, and consequently severely limited as to my means of releasing anger, I typically resort to prankery as my primary method for expressing difficult emotions. So, one gray day, the kind that leaves even a whole person questioning the meaning of life, I found myself caught amid the dreary mood I was already in, next to an interview between an Irish journalist named Nigel—whose accent I found like sandpaper to my *Hui**—and Ridick. Though I did not understand a word of the English they spit back and forth, I found myself wanting to tear both of their heads clear off their necks. Logistically, this was an impossibility, once again, given the limitations of my physical body. So instead I took one of the ketchup packets I had stolen from the pantry earlier that day, opened it up with my teeth, and squirted the contents into my mouth. Then I whisked the mixture up with my tongue (one of my few perfectly functioning organs) until it had a nice homogeneous consistency, which could easily be mistaken for blood. Then I started convulsing like I was possessed by Caligula's ghost.

As I expected, the good doctor leaped over to me while the carnivorous cameras panned over to the spectacle. In an effort of heroic proportions, Ridick pulled me out of my chair,

---

* Popular Russian slang for "dick."

laid me flat on the ground, and leaned in to protect my thrashing head. And as soon as his furled brow got close enough, his eyes poring over me, searching for a clue as to why my body had just turned into a Mexican jumping bean, I coughed the pseudoblood into his face. The cameras got in nice and close and caught everything like sick little robots. Ridick, who I expected would run for the hills, continued to hold my thrashing head as the cocktail of ketchup and spit dripped off his chin and into my agape mouth.

Then the cameras disappeared, and all the thrashing turned into a vibratory hum in the background, and it was only his eyes and mine. It occurred to me that his priority was protecting my spastic head, and not the repulsive fluids that were spreading over his face. At that moment, I remember hearing Frank Sinatra singing "As Time Goes By," which he once sang during TV hour. Perhaps all my thrashing jostled that particular memory loose. Eventually, the ambient sounds of the room fell away until nothing was left but the song and Ridick's own Sinatra-brand blue eyes. As if it weren't even my choice, my convulsions slowed and eventually stopped altogether, until my head fell to one side and I started to sob. Two parts shame and one part self-pity, it was the only time I felt loved by anyone besides Natalya.

At some point, Ridick must have smelled the ketchup, because his vise grip on my head softened, and he wiped the spit and tomato from his face. He could have left me on the floor crying like an idiot. He could have left me in a cave of shame. He could have called a nurse to have me subjected to a battery of psychological evaluations. Instead, he continued to hold me, which made me blubber mercilessly.

The cameras caught everything. It is entirely possible, Reader, that you have already witnessed the scene I just described. You would be sitting on a couch with your loved one(s) in front of a TV in the comfort of your pasteurized living rooms. The scene would end and the program would cut to commercial, and the awkward silence would prompt you to turn to each other to say words about me. I often muse about what those words might be.

At some point, I must have fallen asleep, right there on the cold floor, because I woke up the next morning in my bed. After wiping away my dried tear crust, I found a white ball with red stitching next to my bed, signed with indecipherable squiggles. It was resting on a note written in very poor Russian, which intended to say:

Dear Ivan,
This baseball was signed by Reggie Jackson. He was my favorite baseball player when I was your age. Not sure what you know about him, but if you want, we can talk baseball sometime.

Your friend,
Ridick

Later that day, I worked up the courage to find Ridick, disinfect his face, and return his gift, which I could not accept, though I wanted to. However, I was informed by Nurse Elena that he had already left for America.

"Perhaps that will teach you to be a little *govniuk*[*] then, huh, Ivan?" she said.

To which I said:

"At least I need to pretend to be one."

To which she mumbled some ignorant shit and turned to walk away.

I waited 188 days for Ridick to come back to the hospital to fix up more hearts. When he finally appeared one day, camera crew in tow, I had built up an elaborate six-month apology, teeming with various acts and scenes, but by the time my mouth opened wide enough to start, he tossed me another ball, which I dropped because I only have one arm, with two fingers on it. Then he picked it up and put it into my hand. This one was signed by someone named Tom Seaver.

Ridick taught me about baseball for three hours that night. From then on, he brought me a signed baseball every time he came to patch hearts. Currently, I have twenty-two baseballs with names on them like Mike Schmidt, Johnny Bench, Pete Rose, Jim Palmer, Steve Carlton, Carlton Fisk, and Catfish Hunter.

⌒⌒⌒

Currently, the clock reads 11:47 in the A.M.
I have been writing for twelve hours.
It is the third day of December.
The year is 2005.

---

[*]   Roughly translated from Russian as "shithead."

Nurse Natalya came in a few moments ago with a
    change of clothes.
"You haven't changed in four days," she said.
"I'm fine," I said.
"I can smell you in the hallway.
And so can everyone else.
Do us this kindness."
"Leave them on my bed."
She stared at me for a few long seconds,
and in that time I was close
to asking her about the green folder,
but the vodka had me sufficiently numb.
She tossed the clean clothes onto my bed.
"I'll be back in an hour to pick up your dirties."
"Make it two."

Dennis

Dennis is an enigma.

He is unique in that he is the only one of us whose mother
also lives here at the asylum. Living, however, may be a bit of
an overstatement. At the moment, Dennis's mother is a vege-
table kept alive by the machines in the Red Room. Her fate
has become a subject of controversy here at the asylum.

Dennis and I arrived at the hospital within days of each
other. Back then, as now, he was, quite simply, an enormous
mass of catatonic flesh, spending forty minutes of every hour
rocking in a wheelchair that is too small for his six-foot-

eleven-inch frame. The other twenty minutes he is perfectly still and unresponsive. Doctors have kicked, prodded, zapped, jiggled, burned, and slapped Dennis during these twenty-minute periods, but these efforts never elicit anything close to a response. To add to the mystery, Dennis rocks with an astounding regularity. One day, in my boredom, I counted the number of undulations per minute during each forty-minute rocking period. I discovered that, invariably, Dennis rocks seventy-six times every minute. This was a complete puzzle until two days later when a nurse inadvertently locked me in the Red Room. In my escalating nausea, I noticed that the machine hooked up to Dennis's mom (which I presume maintains her heart rate) was set to seventy-six beats per minute.

When Dennis's mother first brought her child to the Mazyr Hospital for Gravely Ill Children, she was looking for help. She loved the poor lump of skin and bones to death but needed an explanation as to why he never cried, babbled, crawled, played, grabbed, kicked, or ate. After the first few weeks of consultations and dozens of neurological, physical, and mental examinations, the doctors concluded, quite simply, that Dennis lacked a soul. All the bits and pieces of a person were there, all connected and wired in the way that God intended, and yet he was lifeless (in those days Dennis hadn't yet developed his habit of rocking). The medical team of the time, which included three nurse practitioners and a doctor with a degree from an unaccredited medical school in Lithuania, decided that no other conclusions could be drawn.

As the days went by, Dennis's mom became more and

more desperate, which registered primarily in her face, which was crumpling like a Coke can, and her hair, which was turning gray in real time. She insisted on a regimen of experimental procedures that could put the soul back into her son. The roomful of medical specialists took one long, hard look into her desperate eyes and very disingenuously told her of some new cutting-edge research at the frontier of medicine, knowing full well that there were no promising methods for putting the soul back into a child.

At this point in the story, a little background is necessary. According to hospital folklore, Dennis's mom had been born to be a mom. She expected nothing more and nothing less from life. But despite her destiny as a maternal provider, the poor woman lost eight fetuses before finally giving birth to the lifeless bag of bones she named Dennis. Moreover, the eight fetuses that came before Dennis were conceived by the same man. Unfortunately, that man lost his patience after the eighth attempt and apparently left the woman—and Belarus—altogether. Her last and final attempt was allegedly with a drunk soldier in a dark alley during an inebriated walk home from a pub on Leninskaya Street. Apparently, drunken sperm tend to be more viable. So, in this context, you can imagine the disappointment when the child she finally birthed after all eight attempts entered the world with a heartbeat and nothing else. Hence the dramatic display of emotion when Dennis's mom challenged the doctors to fix her baby.

In an unusual show of pity, the doctors performed about

six months of experimental treatments to reconnect Dennis's soul. They did so with earnest faces, knowing full well that the boy would never change. And when all diagnostic theories were tested and the doctors could do nothing else to convince her that there was any chance that some life might jump back into the child, they offered Dennis a permanent spot at the hospital and let it be known that they could care for the child, could monitor, stimulate, and examine him in a way that would be impossible for her alone. Dennis's mom responded by packing up her child and walking out of the hospital.

Two days later, she was back, an unbearable, terrible, tearful mess, charging through hallways, frantically looking for anyone in a white coat but settling for a nurse, to whom she handed the baby before locking herself in a bathroom. Then came the thud that could only be one thing. By the time the three on-staff nurses and a security guard were able to break down the door, it was difficult to tell if more blood was streaming from her wrists or from the laceration on her head that happened when it slammed into the tiled floor.

The doctors were able to stop the bleeding both from her wrists and from her head. They were not, however, able to fix the fact that she was now just as lifeless as her son. Dennis's mom was brought into the Red Room, where they connected her to machines that have kept her alive ever since. I sometimes wonder if Dennis's mom lost her soul then too. One day, I found Nurse Natalya folding some linens and asked her if she thought Dennis's mom would ever wake up.

"Never," she said. "Her brain is mostly dead."

"Then why don't they just unplug her?" I asked.

"Ivan, this hospital is funded by the church. She'll be here as long as we are." And with that, she shook her head at an invisible deity and returned to folding linens.

I, for one, have a special appreciation for Dennis. Not because I sympathize with his story or feel any deep primal connection. I appreciate Dennis because he unintentionally serves as my timepiece. Three sets of rocking from breakfast and I know it's time to make my way to the TV room for *Nu, pogodi!*[*] Six sets of undulations from lunch and I know it's time for dinner. Two sets of undulations from dinner and I make my way back to the TV room for *Chetyre tankista i sobaka.*[†] Four more rocking fits and it's lights-out.

During one of our semiregular power outages, resulting in the failure of every clock in the Main Room, I was even able to keep the nurses and technicians abreast of the local time by counting Dennis's undulatory episodes.

Everyone deserves a purpose.

The Ginger Twins

Mary and Magdalena are eleven-year-old ginger twins. Their long ginger hair is not the bright red hair of model notoriety. It is the dull red hair that inevitably comes with a nondescript homely face and freckles that verge on scar-like. Their skin is whiter than ivory, even whiter than mine, if that's possible,

---

[*] A late-1960s Soviet/Russian animated series produced by Soyuzmult-film.

[†] A popular Polish black-and-white TV series based on the book by Janusz Przymanowski.

and perhaps with a hint of lavender, as ginger skin often is. Their faces are spotted with freckles, and their eyes are green like what I imagine the color of seaweed to be. I would almost find them cute in a sexually specific sort of way if not for the way their peculiar aura wilts my *Hui*.

I'm not sure why Mary and Magdalena are here at the hospital. They have all their right parts in the right places. They are able to take care of themselves and have a grasp on most major hygienic rituals. By all standard societal measures, the duo appear normal. Actually that's a lie. They are so devastatingly abnormal it is difficult to think of them as fellow human beings. So far as I know, they have never spoken to *anyone*. And yet, if you asked anyone here, he might tell you that they speak to each other every moment of every day, only not out loud with words. Everyone here believes they talk to each other, and only each other, with thoughts. Understandably, Reader, you require evidence: when either Mary or Magdalena decides it's time to stand up and rummage through the box of toys, they *both* decide. When either Mary or Magdalena decides that it's time to jump to their feet and run laps around the Main Room, they *both* decide. When either Mary or Magdalena decides it's time to move to adjacent bathroom stalls to empty the day's waste, they *both* decide. Everything the ginger twins do is in synchrony. There is not a fraction of a moment's delay between the time one makes a decision and the other follows. And yet, not one nurse, not one doctor, not even Nurse Natalya, with all her clever antics and maternal tones, has ever been able to elicit a nod or a wink or any body language at all that even suggests that they are aware of the world outside their own two heads.

Once upon a time, even I, the poster child of unsociability, made a heroic attempt. Obviously not to cultivate any lifelong friendships—I was just bored. It began with innocent enough banter: *Who's your favorite nurse, Mary? How about you, Maggie? Can I call you Maggie? Do you girls really read minds like everyone says? So, what am I thinking?*

(All said with my slow, offbeat droopy drawl.)

Unsurprisingly, no reaction whatsoever. And yet I wasn't rejected either.

This was my gateway into a game I could only play with myself, which, incidentally, is my favorite sort of game. A game of challenging my mind to develop a sufficiently provocative display that would force the duo to react to other human beings. In my head, I imagined the celebrity I might become around the asylum if I was the first to open them up to the universe.

I kept my first attempt humble. As per usual, the duo were playing *Durak** on the cold tiles of the Main Room. I rolled my chair within inches of the twins, close enough to smell their clinical shampoo, and parked myself on top of their game. As expected, the twins continued to deal their cards without reaction. So I nodded off into one of my well-rehearsed comatose states and let the drool that typically accumulates in the corner of my mouth drip down my cheek in

---

* A Russian card game that is popular in post-Soviet states. The object of the game is to get rid of all one's cards. At the end of the game, the last player with cards in his or her hand is referred to as the fool (*durak*).

a long molasses stream into my lap and then onto their cards. For the next half hour, the ginger twins carried on with their game as the puddle of my spittle gathered into a small pond. When Mary (or maybe it was Magdalena; I never bothered to learn which was which) shed her last card, the duo synchronistically stood up, collected their blankets, and shuffled off to bed, not taking care to avoid my puddle of drool. Both happened to step through it, leaving little liquid footprints leading to their door. Clearly, I would need to try harder.

Everyone needs to excrete waste. That, at the very least, is unavoidable. *What goes in must come out* is the most sacrosanct law of human biology. Here at the hospital, every room for a long-term resident has a bathroom. There are very few frills in this place, but at the very least we all get a bathroom. One of the design flaws of our bathrooms is that they all can be locked from the inside by pressing a small button on the doorknob and then closing the door. It is entirely too easy to lock yourself out of the bathroom if you happen to be on the outside and accidentally press the lock due to limited control of your extremities (clearly the case for 97 percent of all hospital residents). I know this from personal experience; I've accidentally locked myself out of my own bathroom no less than six times in my tenure here at the asylum. This scenario made my next attempt low-hanging fruit—I would reproduce this "accident" in the ginger twins' bathroom. My theory was that with a locked bathroom and nature pounding at their door, the duo would have no choice but to hunt down one of the nurses to unlock it.

Though the gingers are the most unpredictable and spontaneous residents at the hospital, with no set daily regimen or schedule, you could at the very least depend on their being immersed for hours whenever they were engaged in a competitive game with each other (perhaps winning is the only way the twins have to distinguish themselves). I waited all day in the Main Room until I caught the twins absorbed in some hand-clapping game, which apparently required extreme concentration so as not to lose the sequence, count, and rhythm of the claps. I figured this would buy me twenty or thirty minutes at least.

So I took the opportunity to wheel myself into their room discreetly, then into the bathroom, where I pressed the button on the doorknob, then back into their room, where I closed the door behind me, then out into the hall, unnoticed like the world's only wheelchair-bound ninja. Then I waited. First, for twenty-four hours. Then for forty-eight. I didn't take my eyes off those twins (except, of course, during the moments in which they slept behind their closed door). And nothing. No ginger twins running out to a nurse with flailing arms. I didn't even hear them rattling the bathroom door. Not a sound.

After the third day, I learned that while peeing is unavoidable, peeing in a bathroom isn't. Inundated with curiosity, I waited for another high-intensity game of cards to do some investigating at the Ginger residence. Sure enough, the bathroom door was still locked. This left two options: the twins had managed to hold their bladders for three days, risking infection and rupture, or they had found another way to relieve themselves altogether. So I frantically wheeled around the room, searching high and low for an alternative. Eventually, I found it hiding under their beds. The twins were stealing their breakfast, lunch, and dinner bowls in order to fill them with pints of their own urine and waste. I deduced that the nurses would soon find them too, check the bathroom door, and unlock it (i.e., another failure).

Attempt number three: the next night, I waited until the duo went to bed. Once I was convinced they were sleeping deeply, I wheeled myself into their room armed with a flashlight and a pair of scissors I'd stolen from Miss Kris's desk. I put the blades of the scissors right up to their long red locks and snipped away. I chopped and chopped at odd angles and dissonant lengths. I gave them the Ivan special. And with the wasted cords of hair I tied their little legs together for good measure. Then I wheeled myself out and returned the flashlight and scissors, leaving no evidence of my hooliganry.

It was hard for me to imagine any two human beings, particularly female ones, no matter how pathologically anti-social or psychically confined to each other, not reacting to the fact that their hair had been removed from their heads and used to bind them to one another. The next morning, the sisters emerged from their room with their hair looking like it had been through several rounds of chemo. Their faces, however, were perfectly buoyant. The duo synchronistically shuffled to the breakfast hall as if it were any other day.

Nurse Lyudmila was the first to comment:

"What in the name of Saint Alexander did you two girls do to each other?"

I thought the question was more rhetorical. But she continued anyway:

"If there was ever a time I need you two to talk, it is right now."

The gingers continued to chew their cabbage. This inspired Nurse Lyudmila to shake them violently, which resulted in cabbage flying from their mouths, but nothing else. This is when I gave up and Nurse Lyudmila took the reins.

It was the first night of Lyudmila's week of nights. Much more diabolical than I, she realized that the most effective way to torture the twins was to lock them in different rooms (brilliant!), thereby severing their psychic umbilical cord. So that night, she cleared out two heart-holers from their respective rooms and dragged one ginger into one room and the other into the second. Unfortunately, she made the mistake of selecting adjacent rooms, which allowed the ginger twins to communicate with each other through some combination of telepathy and Morse code, which they tapped to each other all night long through the connecting wall. On the next night, Lyudmila, in her serpentine way, would leave nothing to chance. She pulled Dasha from her room in the girls' wing and replaced her with Mary, and Dennis from his room in the boys' wing and replaced him with Magdalena. That night, no one at the Mazyr Hospital for Gravely Ill Children slept. We were kept wide awake by the shrill and grueling screams of two eleven-year-old girls.

VII

The Bleeders, the Non-Bleeders, and Polina the Interloper

I heard about Polina before I ever saw her. This is because I spend most of my days alert, ready for new intelligence, which I can then use to mentally prepare for any changes in my daily world that might upset my delicate equilibrium. A little reconnaissance also helps me predict the moods and general dispositions of hospital staff. For example, I know the precise day (and time) of the month on which all the nurses initiate their in-sync menses (the third at approximately 2:55 in the P.M.). Some experience worse menses than others (Nurse Lyudmila), so it is nice to know when in order to keep a vigorous distance from her. To ignore this information is negligent behavior. Two decades of observing human nature have revealed a few notable differences between the way men and women approach conflict: men will knock each other out and then hug it out, while women tend to leave deep, unresolved scars on the souls of their victims. I suppose this makes sense from an evolutionary point of view—women were forced to develop their own effective brand of violence to compensate for their disadvantages in size and strength.

One of the benefits of my espionage is that I quickly learn of all pending intakes. If I'm holding aces, I can glean important information about the newbies (age, gender, race, clinical diagnosis, personal and family history, demographics), which

I can then use to predict how they might affect my day-to-day life. I am an expert at reading doctor-nurse body language, and this alerts me as to when important information is about to be revealed. Usually, it begins with a quick and nervous survey of the room as the doctor attempts to create the appearance of confidentiality. This is typically my cue to appear increasingly drowsy and bob my head until I nod off disingenuously. Within minutes, the disarmed doctor begins spilling his guts, giving the nurses orders as to how to attend to the new patient, while I take notes in the notepad of my mind.

Historically, this has been very helpful, since there are some new intakes I try to avoid completely. The most notable category is those who require me to have any visual contact with blood. This is because I have a deep, abiding, and existentially catastrophic fear of blood (there is no need for me to fake catatonia when I see blood). Over the years, there have been several new intakes who, without advance warning, would have caused me to pass out and vomit all over everything in a two-meter radius. I call these patients the Bleeders.

Alyona was a Bleeder. She had a three-year-old festering wound in her neck because she couldn't help herself from picking at it in spite of varying states of infection. Had I not used the intelligence I gathered to hide from Alyona, I'm not sure I would be here to write this story. Fortunately, she didn't last very long at the asylum, for she died tragically as a result of complications arising from picking at an infected neck.

My most feared Bleeder was Georgiy, whose blood ran through plastic tubes into a machine because his kidneys didn't work. I'm not sure I would have escaped Georgiy alive if I'd had to face his blood plumbing. Fortunately, early reconnaissance revealed the extent of his blood woes and alerted me to keep my distance.

Most new intakes to the Mazyr Hospital for Gravely Ill Children are Non-Bleeders. These include characters such as Max, Alex, the ginger twins, and most of the heart-hole children. When I gather enough intelligence to determine that a new intake is a Non-Bleeder, I breathe freely and return to reading my book or imagining Grace Kelly's breasts. If evidence begins to point in the other direction, I flee straight for my room (or a stairwell, depending on which is closer).

Then there is a third, more esoteric category. These patients are not likely to set off any blood-related triggers, but they do pose a potential risk to the consistency of my day-to-day life. These patients are called Interlopers. Mostly, Interlopers are patients who just require more time to fully understand. For example, the ginger twins were Interlopers before they became your standard boring Non-Bleeders.

Interlopers and Non-Bleeders are best distinguished by their IQs. In a place where the average IQ doesn't rise much above sixty-five, anyone of standard or superior intelligence poses a risk to the consistency of my daily life. These risks include competition for hospital resources, World War I style power struggles, or the possibility of having to face the anxiety of interacting authentically with a person. Which brings me to my point, Reader—Polina was an Interloper. Actually, she was the worst kind of Interloper, the kind that didn't belong here.

I first heard the name Polina as it was being screamed from the lips of the Director during a phone call with someone who was probably the director of another hospital. The Director was angry, and you could see the spit mist off his mouth as he screamed Russian obscenities to the man on the other end. Here is the intelligence I gathered from that conversation: (1) the man on the other end was trying to get the Director to accept a new patient into long-term care; (2) the new patient had leukemia, which implied strong Interloper potential (since both smart and dumb people can get leukemia); (3) the Director insisted that our hospital didn't have the room or the resources to treat her and that it would likely be a death sentence; (4) the new patient had recently been orphaned and there was nowhere else for her to go. It was obvious to me when the Director slammed down the phone that he had lost the argument and the new patient would be staying at the Mazyr Hospital for Gravely Ill Children.

At that time, the only information I had regarding the new intake was her age (sixteen) and gender (female). So I did with her what I would with any Interloper. The next morning, I parked my chair close to the brown double doors at the entrance of the hospital and waited so that I could assemble the rest of her picture. In hindsight, I should probably have been more concerned about the fact that a young girl of the human species was coming to a hospital to die a long and slow leukemic death, alone, without the comfort of her recently deceased parents. Instead, I was more concerned about what her posture, hair length (if any at all), pace, and stride might tell me about the potential duration of her stay at the hospital.

It was 9:17 in the A.M. on the fifth day of October when I first saw Polina. She was wearing jeans and a T-shirt, and her flip-flops brought in a single autumn maple leaf from the outside. The jeans had a small rip in the left thigh. The T-shirt had a picture of a beam of light entering a blue triangle and coming out as a rainbow (which I later discovered was the cover of an album by a singer Polina liked called Floyd Pink). Reader, could you imagine anything that belonged less in this particular hospital? If your answer is yes (?!), then I've failed at telling our story.

Admittedly, there was a moment I felt sympathy. She had no idea where she was or what she was getting into. This place crushed the souls of sweet sixteen-year-old girls with pretty brown hair, blue eyes, and Floyd Pink T-shirts.

But mostly I hated her.

I hated her because she wasn't supposed to be here.

I hated her because even in her first three steps I could see that she obliterated the edges of my world.

I hated her because her presence alone taunted me.

I hated her because she forced me to see how easy it was for me to hate.

Twelve steps. That's how many steps she took from the front door to the Director's office, where she would complete her paperwork. I was able to feel that much hate in twelve steps.

That was the last time I saw Polina in jeans. After leaving the Director's office, she walked to the front desk and traded them in for a pair of gray sweatpants. They also handed her a hospital gown to adorn her during rounds of chemo, which is known to make patients spontaneously lose control of their bowels.

By the time she left the front desk with her new wardrobe, she was already a different girl. When she walked into the hospital, her back was erect and her shoulders were square, like she was actually walking into a prison, ready to break the nose of the first person she saw in order to establish alpha status. When she left the front desk holding her cancer uniform, her shoulders hung forward and her chin fell slightly no matter how hard she fought to hold it up. She also looked like she might have lost three kilos in those three minutes. And, suddenly, Polina was less threatening.

The next morning, I waited until breakfast hour was over and cautiously rolled myself out to the Main Room. I've never once eaten breakfast during the first twenty-four hours of a new Interloper intake. The situation is entirely too assailable. I need a few days to gather good, solid intelligence, and quietly observing anyone for three days reveals enough infirmities to knock even the most indestructible Interloper off his pedestal. Moreover, the thought of unprepared conversation with real people scares me like blood scares me.

When I first saw Polina that morning, she already had a bag full of chemical therapy plugged into her arm. It's a sight I've become rather familiar with over the years, especially with leukemia kids. What I wasn't used to was someone of *Polina's* pedigree getting pumped full of poison. I remember moving my eyes from the clear bag over to her brown hair, which hung almost all the way to the base of her spine. It was thick, with waves that verged on curls, and I could almost see my reflection in it. In a month it would be the scraggly wisps of a corpse. In two months it would be gone altogether.

Whenever I spy on a new leukemia kid, I can't help imagining what he will look like without hair. Besides enjoying the challenge, I find that it also mentally prepares me for the downhill wreck that is about to transpire. The first time I watched a leukemia kid lose all his hair, I was only eight. I bluntly recommended to Vladimir, the fifteen-year-old leukemia kid, that he put us out of our misery and take a razor to it before it got any worse. He told me that I would need much more than a razor for him to feel like he didn't want to heave cabbage every time he saw me.

Touché, Vlad.

But this time, for the first time, as I watched Polina's medical bag slowly drip chemicals into her bloodstream, I couldn't picture a leukemia kid without hair. Maybe I just didn't want to. Maybe I had already fallen in love with her but was too clouded by fear and trembling to notice. All I know is that no matter how hard I tried to put a bald head on Polina, the image wouldn't come. But my inability to imagine her without hair was hardly a problem. What really twisted my intestines in a bevy was when I slowly moved my eyes from her head down to her hands and saw that Polina was reading *Dead Souls.*[*] Reader, patients at the Mazyr Hospital

---

[*] The satiric 1842 Russian classic by Nikolay Gogol about a man who tries to trick landowners into buying their dead serfs.

for Gravely Ill Children do *not* read Gogol, unless their name is Ivan Isaenko. And, upon further consideration, it occurred to me that no one at the asylum even *possesses* Gogol unless his name is Ivan Isaenko. Which meant that I was no longer the sole and exclusive recipient of Natalya's gifting.

Later that day, I decided to approach Nurse Natalya on the matter, not so much begrudgingly but more to make my curiosity known. While she was chiseling several species of mold from some bathroom tiles, I asked:

"How'd the new girl get *Dead Souls*?"

"How should I know? She probably brought it in with her."

"Impossible. I watched her walk through the doors with nothing but a notebook and various cosmetics."

"Maybe you should stop being so suspicious of new intakes."

"I'm more suspicious of you."

"Well, I'm innocent. You're the only one I've ever given Gogol to."

Which, of course, made me curious. So I promptly wheeled myself into my room, and then into my closet, where I rustled past copies of Dostoyevsky, Chernyshevsky, Goncharov, Bulgakov, Lermontov, Turgenev, and, of course, Gorky, but no Gogol. Which could only mean one thing: *I had been burglarized!*

This presented a novel quagmire (so to speak). I was rattled, but not in the way you would suspect. It wasn't the sense of personal violation that spooked me, though in almost any other set of circumstances I would have been raising holy hell. It was the unsettling unfamiliarity, which I typically only feel in the presence of insects and news anchors. She was not a Max, or an Alex, or a Dennis, or any of the two- to three-year-old kids with holes in their hearts. She was a different genus. She was the hospital void. The missing demographic. A beguiling blend of cherub and imp. She was a puerile Goddess in enough want of proper Russian literature that she stole from a convalescent. Which meant that she was someone who could see my reality and reflect it back to me. She was someone who could make me feel like I was not just a ghost haunting hallways. I was used to playing with chimeras, not equals. And what's worse, she wasn't an equal, she was a *greater*. She didn't belong here. She was the true Interloper. She was perfect, and perfectly awry. She was supposed to be the queen of somebody's two-person kingdom. And I knew nothing of fairy tales. I only knew about Gogol and the side effects of benzodiazepines.

After a few moments of mounting anxiety, I returned to reality and wheeled myself back to the Main Room to take another look, careful to check my proximity and exposure in order to see if I was at any risk of getting caught. I shifted slightly away, wheeled myself a few meters toward the north wall to make it look like I was watching TV, and looked back at her again, but only from the corner of my eyes, which now left her hands and moved down to where her legs grew out of her hospital gown. They were soft and foreign and prohibited, and I found it adorable the way her calves were swallowed by her pink socks. Then I returned to her face, which didn't betray any of the fear that I was sure she was feeling or the nausea that was building as the chemo started marching on the cells that lined her stomach. She only read intently and calmly, like someone might read a book on a Tahitian beach, free from worldly concerns. Her face was so calm that I got lost in it for a minute, like getting lost in Mona Lisa's smile, and I forgot that I was staring at her at all and probably had a dollop of drool gathering at the corner of my mouth. She must have felt the infrared heat of my eyeballs, because she lifted her head away from the book and toward my face. I, quite predictably, panicked, unlocked my chair, turned myself around, and wheeled myself away as fast I could, which, of course, is not that fast because I only have one arm.

I saw Polina once more that day. Usually when I need to hide away, I go to my room and shut the door. But occasionally, I cannot sit still, in which case I roam the halls of the hospital until I've used up enough energy to pass out somewhere. Sometimes, I wheel myself into stairwells only to hum and chant gibberish because I like the sound of reverb. On that morning, I tried to go back to my room but was too muddled to stay put. So I spent the next few hours wandering the lesser-used halls. After four hours, I ran out of hallways and decided to move into stairwells. I love the second-floor stairwell most because, owing to whatever laws of physics, the reverb there is most like a nineteenth-century Russian Orthodox cathedral. This time when I opened the door, I detected the reverbic sounds of suppressed crying coming from the floor below. Of course, I knew who it was. Not many people here had enough function in their tear ducts to cry like that, and by now I knew the lachrymal fingerprints of most of the nurses. Which meant it had to be Polina. I listened for a few minutes, thinking about what I might say to her. Then I turned around and went to my room.

That night, Polina stopped being an Interloper. True Interloper status is reserved for robots and psychopaths. She had inadvertently arrived in a new unnamed category, which was far scarier than the others.

VIII

The Three-Monthers

In my seventeen years at the asylum, the most important piece of information I've gathered from faking comas is that the children here fall into two categories: six-monthers and three-monthers. This is because medications are prescribed in either six- or three-month supplies. For the vast majority of us, six-month supplies are prescribed, since they are cheaper and require fewer prescriptions. We are, of course, the six-monthers. However, when a doctor deems that there is little chance that a child will make it more than a couple of months, one final three-month supply is ordered to cut down on costs. In the tatters of an Eastern Bloc economy, every penny counts.

When you live in a place where nothing changes, even morbid change is entertaining. Thus, one of my favorite activities is guessing three-monthers before med day. One of the few things I pride myself on is how good I am at this game. In fact, until a month ago, I had correctly called every new three-monther over the last fifty months.

The more spiritually inclined nurses have argued that my radiation poisoning gave me psychic powers pertaining to death, but I reject this because it would violate the Three Tenets of Ivanism (see below). The simple truth is that after seventeen years of watching kids die slowly, I have gotten good at picking up all the telltale signs. Every disease has its own classic omens, a fingerprint of mortality. For example, the leading cause of death here at the asylum is thyroid cancer. When a thyroid kid is still a six-monther, he looks just like any other cancer patient (i.e., bald-headed, pale, thin, frequent trips to the restroom, a bit spacey—also known as chemo brain). But when he becomes a three-monther, you can expect an onslaught of much more interesting symptoms. I got so good at recognizing these symptoms that Nurse Natalya once asked me to create a diagnostic assessment document (DAD) for the other nurses, in the hopes that it would streamline care and also make me feel useful. Here are a few sample pages (as you can see, in another life I would have made an excellent diagnostician):

A thyroid kid is a three-monther if he/she exhibits four of the following five symptoms:
(1) His/her neck swells up so big it looks like the kid swallowed a rabbit, which then became lodged in his/her throat.

(2) It takes him/her thirty minutes or more to get through a single bite of food.

(3) When he/she asks for an injection of Aloxi and it sounds like his/her vocal cords have been replaced by an Apple Computer–style voice generator.

(4) He/she keeps the entire hospital up all night coughing.

(5) His/her ordinary breathing sounds like a fat kid after walking ten flights of stairs.

A leukemia kid is a three-monther if he/she exhibits any five of the following six symptoms:

(1) His/her smile looks like he/she flossed with barbed wire.

(2) Every one of his/her standard white hospital T-shirts is stained with blood from daily nosebleeds and eye bleeds.

(3) His/her bones ache too much to walk.

(4) He/she begins to resemble Olive Oyl from famed American cartoon *Popeye.*

(5) He/she stops showing up to breakfast hour, lunch hour, and dinner hour.

(6) He/she begins sleeping through his/her favorite Russian TV shows.

A Marfan syndrome kid is a three-monther (more like three-dayer) if any of the following events take place:

(1) His/her heart stops, he/she has a heart attack, or his/her heart otherwise explodes.

(2) He/she is blind.

An amyotrophic lateral sclerosis* kid is a three-monther when:

(1) His/her face becomes droopier than mine, and

(2) He/she is poor (for some reason the rich ones seem to hang around longer).

A diabetes kid is a three-monther if:

(1) Two or more of his/her appendages have been amputated, and

(2) He/she is blind.

These are just the diseases that have names. There's an abundance of maladies that make their way through the halls of our hospital that stump the best in the medical profession.† Still, I'm clairvoyant when it comes to these blokes' three-monther status. After a while, I can just smell when a kid has given up because something in his body tells something in his brain that no amount of fighting is going to keep him alive. In the end, calling any three-monther can be reduced to two simple symptoms:

---

*   Better known in the West as Lou Gehrig's disease.

†   In the interest of informing the general public, the editors have deemed it important to clarify that there was a spike in the following conditions during the time period in which Ivan was at the Mazyr Hospital for Gravely Ill Children: fibrodysplasia ossificans progressiva disease, progeria disease, Dupuytren's contracture, juvenile rheumatoid arthritis, Parry-Romberg syndrome, collagen II gene disorder, multiple sclerosis, and most forms of cancer.

(1) A light leaves his/her eyes, and
(2) He/she has a posture that looks like someone stole half his/her bones.

Nurse Katya (not known for her tact) once asked me if I thought I would be able to tell when I became a three-monther. My first instinct was to tell her to fuck off. My second instinct was to tell her that she would be a three-monther living alone in the Mazyr Hospital for the Gravely Old long before I was ever a three-monther. Nurse Katya (also not known for her wit) did not have anything clever to say back to me, but once the satisfaction wore off, I actually started to think about whether I would be able to predict the day that my own three-month bag would be dropped in front of me. Then it occurred to me that I would never let myself become a three-monther.

IX

The Staff of the Mazyr Hospital for Gravely Ill Children

Polina, myself, and the other misfits are tended by four nurses at the asylum: Nurse Lyudmila, Nurse Elena, Nurse Katya, and Nurse Natalya. It is their job to read our blood pressure, change our sheets, wash our clothes, clean our toilets, take our blood, change our diapers, clean our asses, cover our wounds, deliver our meds, serve our food, forge our prescriptions (there are no permanent doctors on staff), turn on our TV, take our temperatures, and diagnose viral versus bacterial infections in order to determine antibiotic needs.

This is where the job description ends for the nurses at the Mazyr Hospital for Gravely Ill Children. The more optional traits of a good health care provider, such as empathy, humanity, honesty, respect, professionalism, and human decency, are not mandatory. I know this because I've made it a point to eavesdrop on every nurse interview in the last eight years, of which there have been two, in order to feel like I was a participant in the hiring process.

Nurse Natalya is the one exception, of course. One day, while she was scrubbing my toilet with bright pink rubber gloves, I asked her:

"Can we talk about the elephant in the room?"

"I'm not sure what you're talking about. There are many elephants in many rooms at this hospital," she said.

"Exactly," I said.

"Ivan, are you trying to stir up muddy waters?"

"The water is already muddy."

"It is, but I'll never admit it."

"Just tell me why I love you and I hate them."

She stopped scrubbing, pulled off her pink gloves, and hugged me awkwardly because I'm in a wheelchair. This was my third hug ever and second from Nurse Natalya (the first came from the narrator of an American documentary, who seconds later wiped her arms of me).

"You know my husband is dead, don't you, Ivan?" she asked.

"No, you never told me. How would I know if you never told me?"

"Because you figure everything else out."

"When did he die?" I asked.

"Eighteen years and nine months ago."

"That was a year before I met you."

"We had just decided to have a baby, and then he died."

"How?"

"Guess."

"Some variety of uncontrolled cellular reproduction?"

"Yes."

"Obviously."

"After he died, I had a choice. I could stay faithful to him for the rest of my life, or I could find someone else to give me a baby. I tried to find someone else, but I couldn't touch another man. So I became a nurse, and now I have more babies than I ever wanted."

And like a sweet cosmic revelation, it occurred to me that while the other nurses were just curmudgeonly women, Natalya was a mother.

"Are you happy?"

"Yes."

"But we're all so wrong."

"You're exactly what you're supposed to be."

"Why can't they at least pretend?"

"Ivan, you lose your patience over cold cabbage. What kind of nurse would you be in this place?"

Touché, Natalya.

X

The Jungian Archetypes

Carl Jung, the esteemed psychologist and protégé of Sigmund Freud, is the only man who could tell me something I didn't already know about my own head. Like every other author I read, I challenged every point, mostly because I'm clinically stubborn. In his book *Archetypes and the Collective Unconscious* (1969), Jung argues that every person is made from an archetype or hybrid of archetypes, which are basically cosmic personas that existed well before you or I were born. I spent the first fifty pages deconstructing and demolishing his thesis sentence by sentence. By the hundredth page, I couldn't argue anymore. Currently, Jung's archetypes are the only method I have for understanding the characters who populate my world. A few of my favorites include the Trickster (clearly my dominant), the Mother (Natalya), the Child (Max), and the Goddess (Polina).

The rest of the nurses have their archetypes too. Nurse Elena is the Addict. By my current count, there are seven bottles of vodka of varying brands hidden in cupboards and sofas throughout the hospital, though I'm not sure why she even hides them anymore, since the Director and every nurse at the asylum know where they are. Luckily, alcoholism is a widely accepted vice in Belarus.

Nurse Katya is the Bully. She is large, imposing, and highly black. She is also an unhappy woman with eight kids and only a half of a husband (and I mean that literally—he lost both of his legs in an industrial accident; I know this because he comes to the hospital every few months to have fluid drained from his stumps). Carl Jung would say that Nurse Katya uses her size and exotic appearance to exert control over a world that often leaves her feeling out of control.

Nurse Lyudmila plays the part of the Insecure Vixen (I prefer Bulimic Adulterer, but Jung failed to coin that term). She is also the Enforcer, since she rigidly and uncompromisingly adheres to the rules, even in an environment where rules hardly matter. Furthermore, while the nursing staff of the Mazyr Hospital for Gravely Ill Children includes its share of dubious characters, she is the only one who inspires a deep, abiding fear in me. This is because she is a complete sociopath, and I'm fairly certain that, like Dennis, she was born without a soul. To dispense with the obvious first, she is engaged in a long and nauseatingly sexual affair with the Director, Mikhail Kruk. I know this because the hall often smells of erotic play on Tuesday and Thursday mornings and also because Lyudmila can't remain quiet during orgasm. But her maleficent ways extend far beyond the Director's office. The only reason she works at this hospital is because she was transferred here five years ago from a mental asylum after one of her old patients shot himself in the head. Apparently, he was playing a game called Russian roulette with several other patients. Furthermore, during her tenure at the hospital, I've seen her steal money from every nurse, take a bar of *shoko* away from Alex only to toss it in a trash can seconds later, and systematically cut her inner thigh with a collection of kitchen knives she hides behind the laundry detergent. There was also a patient named Dimitri, who I was almost friends with because he was almost as smart as me, but Nurse Lyudmila psychologically tortured him until he left the asylum without saying good-bye.

There is one more character in my story worth mentioning: the secretary, Miss Kristina. She spends her business days filing paperwork and robotically greeting nurses and patients as they pass by. She plays the part of the Submissive Servant, though I prefer the Pincushion. In seventeen years at the asylum, I've only ever seen her follow orders. The Director and the nurses bark, and she moves. Jung would say that early experiences with an emotionally absent father and an unpleasant mother conditioned her to believe her only value was service. I know this because her mother is Nurse Elena.

Currently the clock reads 2:08 in the P.M.
I've been writing for more than fourteen hours.
It is the third day of December.
The year is 2005.

I hadn't even known I was asleep until I felt Nurse Natalya shaking a nub.

"Ivan," she whisper-yelled.

"What?"

She sniffed my breath and shook her head disapprovingly. "You gave it to me."

"I have some news."

"What news?"

"There will be a funeral."

"What?"

"Yes."

"A religious one?"

"Yes, Orthodox."

"I thought there wasn't any money."

"The city will pay for it."

"The city has never paid for someone to be buried."

"They want to make an exception in this case given the circumstances."

"What circumstances?"

"Her youth. And her dead parents."

"You're paying for it, aren't you?"

A silence that answered the question for me.

"You don't have money."

"If I didn't have money, there wouldn't be a funeral, would there? But there is a funeral, so I must have money."

"You're doing this for me."

"And her."

"We *all* deserve to be buried."

"Since when are you moved by moral arguments?"

"Since now."

"I'm taking you with me."

"No."

"Yes."

"I won't go."

"I thought I couldn't either when he died. But I did."

"Why?"

"Because if I didn't, it would be like dropping a big turd on his grave."

"I'm not going."

"Stop making this about you."

"She's dead, so by definition nothing is for her ever again."

Then I rolled over.

She got up to leave.

"Three days, Ivan. Be ready."

Dr. Mikhail Kruk, the Director

Mikhail Kruk is the perfect composite character. First, and foremost, he is the Thief. His job amounts to accepting money from the Orthodox Church earmarked for fixing kids, but in reality, he spends less than half of it fixing kids. I know this because when I'm catatonic the nurses rant on about having to make adjustments to his accounting reports.

He also plays the part of the Casanova. Twice a week, he has secret sexual rendezvous with whoever is the youngest— and typically largest-breasted—nurse on the staff, in spite of having your standard wife and three kids.

He is also the Most Mediocre Man in the World, which I

suppose makes him the Everyman too: he is smart, but not too smart. He has charisma but only enough to run a rundown hospital. He is fat, but not preposterously so. He is mediocre in the worst possible way.

I've spoken to the Director twice in seventeen years: once about my penis, and once when I was drunk on his vodka. After twelve years of watching him get drunk from behind the curtains, I just got too curious, shakingly so, and resolved to take my first sip. I snuck into his office on his next scheduled late-night rendezvous with Nurse Nika, the youngest largest-breasted nurse of that year, and opened the desk drawer he always pulled his bottle from. I removed the bottle, and underneath, I noticed a picture of his family standing outside by a lake, with rolling hills covered in evergreen trees in the background. For the most part, they looked happy, and Mikhail smiled innocently. Incidentally, I could see why Mikhail copulated with women who were not his wife. Objectively speaking, she resembled a proboscis monkey I had once seen during TV hour.

When you're used to consuming tasteless cabbage on a daily basis, a sip of vodka can be quite shocking, so of course I spewed my first mouthful all over the Director's desk, leather chair, and pen jar. I spent the next hour using toilet paper to soak it up from every corner of his desk and the insides of two of his pens. When the mess was gone, I conjured up all the gumption in my gut and resolved to take another sip, only this time I swallowed it so fast there was no time to spew it out.

My first thought was, why would someone ever put

himself through this? But by the time that first thought ended, the ethanol hit my blood-brain barrier, and I had my second thought, which was, why doesn't everyone do this all the time? So I took a third sip, only to realize that I weighed approximately thirty kilos and didn't have all my body parts. This meant that I had already consumed what would amount to half a pint for the average Belarusian, and my world and words started to swirl together in a cosmic dance. So I quickly put the bottle away, which made me see the picture of Ole Mikhail's family again, which made me want to get to know him, which was perfectly convenient because just then the doorknob turned and the Director himself walked into the room. Before he could say hello, I picked up the picture and told him he had a beautiful family. Then I vomited all over his desk. The next thing I remember was waking up in my bed with a note on my chest that said:

Let this be the last time.

—Mikhail

XII

My Therapist, Dr. Arkady Yakovlev, M.D.

(and also Dr. Leonti Ivanov, Ph.D., Valery Lagounov, M.S., Ph.D., Roman Pavlov, M.S., Dr. Vitaly Maksimov, Psy.D., Igor Polzin, M.S.,

*Anna Sokolov, M.D, Dr. Mikhail Anders,
Ph.D., Dr. Lazar Vasilyev, Ph.D., Dr. Naum
Berkinov, M.D., Dr. Daniil Trotsky, M.D.,
Dr. Alexey Konstantinov, Psy.D., Dr. Marlen
Dubov, Ph.D., and Tikhon Andreev, M.S.)*

Ever since declaring its independence from Mother Russia in the year 1991, the government of Belarus has been generous enough to pay for a psychologist, psychiatrist, and/or social worker to come once every month to try to fix our heads. In my seventeen years at the asylum, I have had a total of fourteen different mental health specialists assigned to me. I was seven years old when I had my first evaluation by Dr. Leonti Ivanov (or Dr. Leon for short). Our first conversation sounded like this:

> **Dr. Leon:** Good morning, Ivan. I'm Dr. Leon. It's good to meet you. How are you this morning?
>
> **Me:** Bad.
>
> **Dr. Leon:** Why are you bad, Ivan?
>
> **Me:** Because I'm in a hospital. Because I'm ugly, and no one here talks. And because I don't have any parents.
>
> *Dr. Leon looks genuinely uncomfortable as I share these things.*
>
> **Me:** Are you okay, Dr. Leon?
>
> **Dr. Leon:** Yes, of course, Ivan. So what I hear is that you feel bad because it's lonely here?
>
> **Me:** Yes, and for the other reasons I said.
>
> **Dr. Leon:** What does loneliness feel like, Ivan?

Me: It feels bad. Just like I said.

Dr. Leon: Can you tell me more about that?

Me: Have you ever felt bad?

Dr. Leon: Of course, Ivan. Everyone feels bad sometimes.

Me: Well, it feels like that. Except all the time.

Dr. Leon: Where does it feel bad?

Me: In my head. Actually pretty much everywhere.

Dr. Leon: You feel bad in your toes?

Me: I don't have toes.

Dr. Leon: Of course. How long have you felt this way?

Me: I always felt this way.

Dr. Leon: Well, that doesn't sound very good.

Me: Can I ask you a question, Dr. Leon?

Dr. Leon: Yes, Ivan, anything.

Me: How come you're old but it seems like your first day?

Dr. Leon was my therapist for the next two years. Every meeting sounded approximately like the one above. After Dr. Leon, I had a therapist named Miss Lagounov. Our first conversation sounded like this:

Miss Lagounov: Hi, Ivan. I'm Miss Lagounov. How are you?

Me: I'm bad.

Miss Lagounov: Oh, that's not good. Why are you bad?

Me: Because I'm in a hospital. Because I'm ugly, and no

one here talks. And because I don't have any parents.

Miss Lagounov: And how does that make you feel?

Me: It makes me feel bad.

Miss Lagounov: Oh, I see, Ivan. Let me see here . . .

Miss Lagounov begins typing into the computer in front of her that was recently donated by a local Belarusian tech firm named Belanuv.

Miss Lagounov: Would you say that you also feel angry frequently?

Me: Yes.

Miss Lagounov: Have you lost interest in the things you love?

Me: There are not many things that I love.

Miss Lagounov: And you can't stop feeling sad.

Me: Yes, like I said, I feel bad.

Miss Lagounov: Here, Ivan, look at this.

Miss Lagounov turns the computer monitor in my direction.

Miss Lagounov: Ivan, this is the Internet. We can learn a lot from it. According to this Internet site, it says that you have depression.

Me: Doesn't that just mean I feel bad?

All of them missed the only thing that I was ever looking for—someone who could make me forget for a second that I was talking to a shrink about being stuck in a hospital. By my fifth therapist, Dr. Polzin, I decided that I could do much better on my own. So I started asking Nurse Natalya (who was always good at making me forget I was talking to a nurse) for every book on clinical psychology she could find. Currently, I consider myself at least as educated in the therapeutic process as any of my therapists. Moreover, when I look back on the long line of carnival freaks masquerading as psychologists, I'm almost certain that at least ten of the fourteen were more psychologically damaged than anyone here at the Mazyr Hospital for Gravely Ill Children. I have a strongly held belief that most therapists enter the field to fix themselves and later get sidetracked trying to fix other people. By the time I reached my sixth therapist, it only made sense to perform the altruistic service of serving my therapists.

My first project was Miss Anna Sokolov, M.D. When I looked into Dr. Sokolov's eyes, I noticed that she lived about three inches behind them. Her shoulders slumped forward, which, as I learned from a book on the Alexander technique, meant she was submissive. She also dressed like the wife of a priest, spoke too fast, almost never looked me in the eye, and could not get out the door fast enough after each session, which I later discovered was so that she could light a cigarette. The impassioned way in which she took a drag reminded me of what a baby might look like when it attached itself to its mother's teat after being starved for a day.

In summary, Dr. Sokolov needed some fixing. During one session, she was in the middle of a sentence that may have sounded something like, "So, Ivan, have we made any progress on your communication style blah . . . blah . . . psychobabble . . . blah?" when I interrupted her:

"Do I make you uncomfortable, Dr. Sokolov?" I asked.

"Umm, no, Ivan, of course not. Why would you ask me that?" she said in her characteristic whisper.

"I notice you never look me in the eye. Didn't Carl Rogers[*] say that eye contact is the key to establishing trust and rapport during the therapeutic process?"

"I make consistent eye contact with you every time we meet, Ivan."

"See, just then you tried to make eye contact in the beginning, then your eyes drifted over to your hands. I make you uncomfortable; don't be afraid to admit it. You said yourself we need to learn to trust each other."

"Ivan, I promise—"

"Have you thought about why?"

"Why what?"

"Why I make you uncomfortable."

"Ivan, this is my job, I promise—"

She paused to take a sip of tea, which gave me time to interrupt her again: "I make you uncomfortable because you want to have sex with me."

Dr. Sokolov spit out her tea, and I continued:

"I'm not judging you, Dr. Sokolov. Not in the least. I'm sure there are many understandable reasons for your paraphilic attraction to the disabled."

"Ivan—"

---

[*]   American psychologist (1902–1987). Founder of the humanistic movement.

She desperately tried to regain control of the conversation, but I continued:

"I'm guessing when you were a child you were rather plain, if not ugly. You felt isolated and alone. I'm guessing your father was emotionally abusive and fortified your feelings of inadequacy."

In reality, I was only about 60 percent sure of anything I was saying.

"Ivan, this is inappropriate, and just . . . wrong. Let's get back to you."

Even in her indignation she could hardly rise above an angry whisper.

"Dr. Sokolov, how can we continue to have a mutually beneficial therapeutic relationship if we don't first address the strong sexual feelings underlying our interactions? I can almost see the heat radiating from your nether regions."

I subtly motioned toward her vaginal area.

"Either you stop or I leave," she threatened.

"The city already paid for your hour here. We might as well enjoy it. Besides, this is important. As I was saying, your feelings of inadequacy crystallized around puberty, at which point you began fetishizing the disabled, because in your head you are an invalid yourself."

"Stop it, Ivan."

She was about as close to screaming as a whisper could come.

"Don't worry, Dr. Sokolov. This is a perfectly normal and understandable reaction. I have it all the time. We're not that different."

"We are *nothing* alike."

"Didn't you graduate from the Belarusian State University in Minsk? You could've treated tired oligarchs with midlife crises. Instead, you picked a peanut-paying job working for the City of Mazyr visiting kids like me. Have you asked yourself why?"

"My brother was sick like you."

She started to pack up her notebook and papers.

"How many times have you masturbated while thinking of me, Dr. Sokolov?"

"You're disgusting."

"I'm not the one with the fetish."

"I'm never working with you again."

"Probably for the best. It would never work with all this sexual tension."

That was my last appointment with Dr. Sokolov. Obviously, I was hooked. For the next six years, I used the *Diagnostic and Statistical Manual of Mental Disorders* (*DSM*) to convince Dr. Konstantinov that he had an incurable case of generalized anxiety disorder, Dr. Andreev that he suffered from repressed homosexual tendencies, Dr. Yakovlev that he had schizoaffective personality disorder, and Dr. Otken that she had Munchausen. The only therapist that I was unable to crack was Dr. Berkinov, but that's only because he was a psychopath. I know this because two years ago he was arrested by Mazyr authorities midsession for carving *matryoshka* dolls from the bones of corpses he exhumed from a cemetery in Minsk.

XIII

My Mother

Dear Reader, you will be the first to know. Not even Nurse Natalya or Polina knows. It's easier to tell you because I do not, and will never, know who you are. I have a mother, and we're quite close. In fact, I see her almost every day. It didn't happen overnight. At some point, I stopped blaming her for handing me off and then evaporating like spit in the Sahara. I acknowledged there were a gamut of possibilities that did not make her a demon. Maybe my mother was dying when I came out of her. Or even better, perhaps she died in childbirth. Perhaps she herself was a victim of the same political calamity that made Ivan Isaenko and knew she couldn't care for me the way that I deserved. Perhaps she left to search the world for a cure for what went wrong in me. It's hard to hate when any of these possibilities exist. So when the distaste for my phantom mother subsided, it was replaced by a genuine desire to know who she was, what she looked like, and what her hands felt like.

I had never actually asked anyone at the hospital about her before. A long time ago, I had invented her effigy out of a mixture of my assumptions and defenses so that I could properly resent her. At some point, it occurred to me that this wasn't fair, so I decided to ask Nurse Natalya about her while she sorted through bags of blood in a large refrigerator.

"Tell me about my mother."

She waited a moment to respond while continuing to shift around blood bags.

"Why are you asking me now after all these years?" she asked. "I thought by now you didn't want to know."

"I didn't. But now I do."

"Ivan, *darling,* I'm sorry, but no one knows anything about your mother."

"I don't believe you," I said.

Nurse Natalya's face involuntarily twisted into equal parts shock and disappointment.

"Believe what you want, Ivan," she said.

"Nothing? Nothing at all?" I asked.

"Nothing, Ivan."

"Then how did I get here?"

"You came in an ambulance one day. You had no papers and no mother."

"And no one thought that was strange?"

"Yes, of course, Ivan, but look around you. Everything is strange here."

"What about my name? How did I get my name?"

"The same way all the kids without names get named at the hospital—boys get *I* names, and girls get *K* names."

"And my last name?"

"The same way."

"I don't believe you."

"Then what can I do?"

This was a rhetorical question, so I didn't respond.

Despite my accusations, a part of me did believe her. Nurse Natalya, aside from being human, had never done anything to make me question her scruples. But another part of me worried that she thought that she might need to protect me from something. So I decided that the only logical solution would be to call every Isaenko in Belarus. My only problem was that I had never once used a phone before due to the fact that I did not have a connection with anyone in the outside world. Consequently, I initiated the following conversation with Nurse Natalya:

Me: Can I call you sometime?

Nurse Natalya: Ay, Ivan, call me? For what? We talk every day, face-to-face, like people are supposed to talk.

Me: You take it for granted, don't you?

(There is no substitute for a little ableism guilt.)

Nurse Natalya: What exactly do I take for granted, Ivan?

Me: Simple things, like talking to someone on the phone. You do it every day. I've never even dialed a number. To me, it's magic.

Nurse Natalya: I promise you it's not all that exciting.

Me: Just show me how to call you, and I will call you tonight. We will talk for a minute, and then we will hang up.

(A distrustful pause.)

Nurse Natalya: Fine.

I knew she would put up some token resistance. I also knew that in the end she would give in and take out the old

1952 model rotary phone from behind the front desk and show me how to dial a number. Moreover, she somehow managed to get Nurse Katya (who worked the evening shift that night) to act as an accomplice. At 9:00 in the P.M., a customarily humorless Katya came into my room and said:

"Don't you have a phone call to make, Ivan?"

So I wheeled myself out to the front desk and began turning Nurse Natalya's numbers into the rotary dial. When I was finished, it started to ring, and after one and a half rings, a voice that sounded only marginally like Nurse Natalya's came through the earpiece.

Voice: Hi, Ivan.
Me: Hello. Is this Natalya?
Voice: Who else would it be?
Me: How are you?
Voice: I'm fine. Quite tired, actually.
Me: Yeah, it was a long day.
Voice: How is everything over there tonight?
Me: Quiet. No one is howling tonight.
Voice: Well, you should probably get to bed.
Me: I know.
Voice: Good night, Ivan.
Me: Good night.

When I hung up the phone, I noticed the three-kilo phonebook sitting on a shelf below the counter. This helped resolve the question of where I was going to get the numbers for every Isaenko in Belarus. The next issue of what to be done about the night nurse was also quickly resolved when I remembered that Nurse Elena was on nights in three days, and she typically passed out in the Main Room by midnight, due to her lust for vodka.

So, 12:02 in the A.M., three nights later, I wheeled myself behind the front counter and pulled out the phonebook. Before I ever turned the rotary dial, I made a list of the name, address, and phone number of every Isaenko in Belarus, including a small space to write in any notes that might be relevant to my investigation. There were 869 Isaenkos listed, and for the next seven days, from 12:01 in the A.M. until 5:59 in the A.M., I called all of them.

After dialing the first number, I panicked because I didn't have any idea what I would say, and because I forgot it was the middle of the night. But before I could end the call, the voice of Ivanna Isaenko said, "You'd better be the prime minister or the Holy Ghost to be calling at this hour."

"No, it's Ivan," I responded.

Then I hung up.

This sequence of events happened three more times before I decided that I would need a script to establish some legitimacy. After a bit of trial and error, I found something that worked:

Me: Hello. May I speak with Mr. or Ms. Isaenko?
Mr./Ms. Isaenko: This is him/her.
Me: Oh, hello, Mr./Ms. Isaenko. It appears that I have some good news and some bad news. What would you like first?

Mr./Ms. Isaenko: The bad news, please.

Me: It seems your son Ivan has passed away at the Mazyr Hospital for Gravely Ill Children. The good news is that Ivan was a genius. Before he died, he developed several computer patents that are currently worth over three million rubles. He had expressed a desire to leave the money to his biological parents in the event that he should pass away.

This script was far more effective at initiating a serious dialogue. Here are the results of my 869 phone calls:

- 506 Isaenkos expressed sympathy but stated that they did not have a son named Ivan.
- 68 of those 506 Isaenkos stated that they wished Ivan was their son.
- 59 Isaenkos said I sounded drunk, but I assured them it was just my voice.
- 196 Isaenkos hung up.
- 212 Isaenkos said they weren't actually Isaenkos.
- 27 Isaenkos told me to fuck off.
- 45 Isaenkos' phones just rang and rang.
- 38 Isaenkos' phones were disconnected.
- 7 Isaenkos were dead.
- 13 Isaenkos had a son named Ivan but said that he was sleeping peacefully in bed.
- 8 Isaenkos had a son named Ivan who was alive and well with a wife and x children somewhere in the suburbs of Mazyr.

- 5 Isaenkos claimed they had a son at the Mazyr Hospital for Gravely Ill children, but upon deeper questioning admitted that they were lying because they needed money.
- 0 Isaenkos were actually related to me.

Additionally, seventeen Isaenkos were long-distance phone numbers, which, altogether, cost the hospital 4,700 rubles, apparently enough to get the attention of the Director, who first blamed Nurse Elena, who then did some investigating, which revealed that the common thread to the calls was my last name. Consequently, I was never again allowed near a telephone.

This experiment made my options clear—I would need to invent my mother. I needed to write her into existence if only in my own head. Her hair would be dark and not yet grayed. This was because I've always felt dark-haired women are stronger than light-haired women, and with the freedom to dream my mother as I desired, I could adorn her with all the characteristics I deemed strong in a woman.

She had a fierce Polissian accent because, if I'm to be honest, she sounded a bit like Nurse Natalya, only without her rasp.

She had crow's-feet that wrapped around her eyes, but not deep enough to make her old, just enough to season her face.

She smelled like lilacs.

She was strong yet soft at the same time.

When I first began to assemble her image, I noticed it was hard to remain objective. At first, the hair flowing from her head was perpetually blowing back in some imaginary wind, an obvious side effect of watching too much Russian television. Eventually, the long hair remained, but I reduced the special effects.

Her physical features created a sense of comfort and safety, but it was the personality I carved into her that helped me to feel loved and seen in a way that no real person has ever made me feel. She was warm and maternal. She could hold me through anything. But she could discipline me too. She could tell me, without hesitation, what thoughts were toxic and which would make me float on.

Most importantly, she knew *me*. I concede she had an unfair advantage—she could see and hear every single thought that bubbled up and out of my head. This meant that no one in the world could understand the complex mess going on between my two ears the way that she could.

An example. There was a time when I decided to take Nurse Natalya's advice and keep a journal. Only it rapidly became an anti-journal, a written attempt to document the life that I would be living had I been born a normal human being who never stepped into the halls of the Mazyr Hospital for Gravely Ill Children. I was a teenager living in Prague. I had just graduated from secondary school and was about to leave for university in Berlin. I invented the more traditional dilemmas of having to leave my high school sweetheart for the excitement of a new life in a new city. I carefully articulated all the anxieties that I would have had in this parallel universe. And I deeply enjoyed all the problems that showed up there (if people only knew how pleasant their problems could be).

Of course, I would need a confidant, someone whom I could approach for counsel, so it only seemed fitting that I should write my mother into this world. I filled pages that brought her to life, carving out all her details, building a vital living creature with the wisdom to see me off to Berlin with the appropriate tools to handle life and lost love.

The only problem was that she knew the both of us too well. She knew the me in my story, but she also knew the me who was writing it. Suddenly, there was a sick feeling in my stomach when I realized that two handwritten pages had been inadvertently filled with a tirade of tough love.

Ivan, she ranted to me in my parallel universe, *what are you doing? What if the nurses read this? They may already have, those nosy* starye ved'my.* Life is unbearable, but it has the benefit of being real.*

I accepted her advice and burned the book by baking it in the kitchen oven. Since then, she's always been with me, mostly in the heaviest or in the lightest moments of my life. And when I begin to wonder if there was any point to my being alive at all, she whispers into my ear all the celestial reasons why I'm full of shit. Unfortunately, I haven't seen her since Polina died.

---

*   Russian for "old hags."

XIV

The Early Days

Like me, Polina was a pathological-type loner. Throughout our photocopied days, we occasionally wove in and out of each other's moments, in the cafeteria, in the Main Room, through the hallways, a few meters from each other in front of the TV, but we never once spoke. She, at least, attempted to maintain the basic rules of social courtesy. For example, if our eyes accidentally crossed paths, she would smile and nod as if to acknowledge that I existed. Rather than reciprocate her etiquette, I dribbled some urine into my shorts and wheeled away.

When she wasn't in the stairwell, Polina lived gracefully. One day, I calculated that during 60 percent of the day, she had some fraction of a smile on her face. When she walked into the cafeteria in the morning to receive cold cabbage and stale bread, she had a quarter smile. When she lay in the hammock in the Main Room and watched a movie, she had half a smile. Even when she sat in her chemo chair while turning the pages of some British tabloid, she had an eighth of a smile. She clearly had something that I did not, something that pushed a smile through her lips under all circumstances, and I used every bit of my intellect to explain her away.

Explanation #1: Polina had lived the life of a beautiful, carefree child. Of course it is easier for her to smile than it is for me.

Explanation #2: Polina had parents. Even though she'd lost them, they had the chance to program a levity into her that I'd never had. Of course it is easier for her to smile than it is for me.

Explanation #3: Polina had just started living in hell. I've been here for seventeen years. Of course it is easier for her to smile than it is for me.

But soon I realized that for every explanation I came up with for why she could smile easily, I could think of another for why she should be miserable:

Anti-Explanation #1: Yes, Polina was a beautiful, care-free child, but she must be stunned by how easily it could all go away.

Anti-Explanation #2: Yes, Polina had parents, but now they were absurdly dead just when she needed them most.

Anti-Explanation #3: Yes, Polina had started living in hell, but I've had seventeen years to get used to it.

In the end, all my rationalizing failed to make me feel any better, which made me wonder why it was such a popular defense mechanism.

XV

Polina's Chemo Hair

It only took the poison three weeks to chisel the first cracks in her perfect brown mane, revealing flashes of pale-white scalp. It was, not coincidentally, the same day I saw the first crack in her graceful poise.

I'm guessing that she could feel my eyes from across the room absorbing every detail of her hair loss, because she spontaneously combed her frantic fingers through it, which resulted in a mounting ball of fur in her right hand. She immediately called for the nearest nurse, who unfortunately was Nurse Lyudmila. Polina showed her the ball of hair and whispered something into her ear. Nurse Lyudmila took the hair ball and walked away, which is when Polina's eyes released streams of liquid anguish down her face. I wanted to tell her that she should only share catastrophic health developments with Nurse Natalya, but I still couldn't move my mouth around her. I wanted to tell her it would be okay, but there were a thousand reasons I couldn't make those particular words happen. First, I sound stupid when I talk, but I'm not stupid, and I didn't want her to think I was. Second, I had never said anything to console a human being before and didn't know which words consoled. The third and biggest reason was that everything was most definitely *not* going to be okay, and I'm a horrendous liar. So for the next two hours, she read while wiping away tears before they had a chance to form, while I, for the next two hours, waited for Nurse Natalya and awkwardly stared at Polina while pretending I wasn't.

Eventually, Nurse Natalya arrived for her shift. Before she could get her coat off, I said:

"I dropped my pen behind the bed, and I can't reach it. Help me."

"I know you're a proud curmudgeon, Ivan, but does that mean you can't say please."

"Please," I said.

"I'm on my way."

A few minutes later, Nurse Natalya came into my room and started moving my bed. I told her to stop and that Polina was losing her hair and would need a wig.

"Ivan, since when have you been this concerned about an Interloper losing hair?" she asked.

"Polina is not an Interloper. Don't you understand my system by now? And why does it matter? She needs a wig."

"I'll have her pick one out today."

At any given time, the hospital has three to four wigs to choose from in the Green Room, which holds most of the hospital's linens and gowns, and also hair for cancer patients. The next day Polina's hair had thinned a bit more, but there was no wig on her head. The day after that, patches of her white scalp were obvious to anyone. Still no wig. The day after that, I could see that Polina had taken matters into her own hands and had given herself a short cut to minimize the obviousness of her hair loss, but it hardly made a difference. The day after that, Polina's hair was once again long, shiny, and luxurious, in spite of another day's worth of chemicals oozing along into her bloodstream. And for a moment, the grace and poise and confidence that made me feel so broken returned to her face again. She looked happy in the most fragile of ways. And somehow I was glad for her despite the familiar feeling of thick molasses in my blood.

XVI

My *Hui*

No record of Polina's life could be complete without first mentioning my *Hui*. I had my first erection at the age of ten. Since then, I have had an extremely complicated relationship with my *govyazhiy svistok*.* There are several reasons for our knotty love affair:

Reason #1: I had no idea what to do with it for the longest time. Suddenly it was there, without warning, and with no books to explain it away. In my isolation, I lacked any routine sources for information regarding my genitals. Most of the programming on the TV in the Main Room is filled with shows suitable for His Holiness Patriarch of Moskow and all Rus,† so there wasn't much chance of me figuring out what I was supposed to do with my pee pole from these programs. My only source of sexual information came out of what I could eavesdrop, from which I learned that the size of a *Hui*

---

*   Roughly translates from Russian as "beef whistle." The translators had no idea what to do with this one.
†   The name given to the figurehead of the Russian Orthodox Church.

is important, as is the frequency with which it is used. At the Mazyr Hospital for Gravely Ill Children, the nurses appeared to be split between those who wished to see their husbands' *Hui* more and those who wanted to see their husbands' *Hui* less. None of them appeared to be content with the amount in which they were currently experiencing their husbands' *Hui*. Nevertheless, even after these conversations I still was not able to determine what I should be doing with my own *Hui*.

My first instinct was to ask my mother the next time that she showed up in my head. When she finally arrived a few days later, we exchanged some small talk before I said:

"Mother, can I ask you something personal?"

"Of course. Anything, Ivan," she replied.

"Could you please tell me more about my *Hui*?"

"Oh, Ivan, in the name of Saint Peter above, is that a question for a *mother*?" she said before scurrying off in my mind's eye. This is when I realized the limitations of fabricating your own mother—she can only help you with the stuff you already know the answer to. This left me with two options: I could beg the God-fearing Nurse Natalya for a book, or I could approach the Director, who seemed to have no shortage of experience with his genitals. As much as I dreaded it in every cell of my incomplete being, I decided that asking him was my best gambit. My decision may also have had something to do with the fact that he was the only other male at the hospital who didn't live with a stream of drool flowing down his chin.

Finding a moment when the Director was not in a

wretched mood, or on the phone, or behind a closed door, or advancing inappropriately with one (or more) of the nurses was approximately impossible. I waited three insufferable weeks until conditions were right, at which point I wheeled myself up to his room and knocked on the door.

"Yes, Isaak, please come in," he said without lifting his eyes from the papers on his desk.

"It's Ivan."

"Of course. What can I help you with that the nurses can't?"

"Yes, sir. I've experienced swelling. Here," I said, pointing between my legs. Even at ten, I remember seeing how uncomfortable this made the Director.

"That's an erection, Ivan. It happens naturally to boys your age."

"What am I supposed to do with it?"

"Nothing, Ivan. Nothing. Don't touch it. There could be consequences."

"What consequences?" I asked.

"Well, possibly difficulties with vision. It has also been correlated with mental illness and psychosis. Addiction and dependency too. Not to mention you may lose the ability to achieve orgasm during ordinary sex."

"How do you know? Do you touch your *Hui?*" I asked.

"No, of course not. And that's not what you call it, Ivan. It's a ..."

I stopped listening at that point. I was not too young to see that the Director couldn't be trusted.

One week (and three erections) later, I gave in and went to

Nurse Natalya. I found her in the Main Room changing an IV attached to Dennis and asked:

"Could you meet me in my room when you're done?"

She looked back at me with her maternally concerned eyes and said, "Of course, Ivan. I'll be there in two minutes."

One minute later, she showed up in my room.

"What is it, Ivan?" she asked, approximately concerned. "Is everything okay?"

"No, everything is not okay," I said. "I've been having erections, and I don't know what to do with them."

She was silent for a few seconds and then made a face that said, *You're choosing to approach* me *on this topic, Ivan? I'm almost your mother, for the love of God in all of heaven. Isn't there anyone else you could ask around this place for a sex lesson? Oh, wait, there is no one else. I* am *the only one who can help you out. Well, Ivan, the words sure as hell won't be leaving my lips. That is a promise.*

After she thought all those things, this is what she said in real words:

"Well, Ivan, I can understand your concern. Let me get you a book."

The next day she returned with two books. One was called *руководство по сексу*[*] and the other *искусство мастурбации.*[†] They were carefully placed on my bed when I wasn't in my room, which was unusual protocol for Nurse

---

[*]   Presumably a Russian translation of the bestselling American book *The Guide to Getting It On* by Paul Joannides.

[†]   Presumably, a Russian translation of the 1971 book *The Art of Masturbation* by Preston Harriman.

Natalya (she usually wanted to share her opinion of the current shipment, but not this time).

Clearly, the exploration of these books led me to the how-tos of sexual intercourse (which I simply found frustrating because I would never have the opportunity to put my *Hui* inside of another person) and also masturbation. Which brings me to the second reason for the complicated relationship with my *Hui*: after exploring *The Art of Masturbation*, I was immediately convinced that my physical body was not at all prepared for the challenges of self-pleasure. While I conduct all my daily activities with my left hand, I'm fairly certain I would have been right-handed if I had been born with both hands. I come to this conclusion because everything I do with my left hand is clumsy and requires exhausting effort. And, from what I understood about masturbation through my research, it is not supposed to be exhausting.

That did not keep me from trying. It took me exactly one hour and thirty-seven minutes to burn through *искусство мастурбации*. One of the few things I do fast is read—this fact mixed with my unique motivation regarding the topic meant that I conquered the 216-page book in less time than it would take to sit through *Swan Lake*. I put the book down at exactly 11:18 in the A.M. I know this because I was haunted by the realization that there would be another ten hours and forty two minutes required to get me to 10:00 in the A.M., which is lights-out, or more specifically the time that I could be convinced that I would not be bothered by any nurse for the rest of the night so that I could engage in uninterrupted experimentation. As you can imagine, Reader, the prospect of getting caught in the act of masturbation was horrifying, partly due to the inevitable embarrassment and partly because of the leverage that the nurse would have over me.

Thus, the day passed by in excruciating increments of tiny time. I would wait as long as I could to check the clock, only to find that what felt like an hour was eleven minutes. I've often wondered if the countdown to everyone's first orgasm is fraught with so much anticipatory anxiety. Regardless, the comforting truth about time is that no matter how slow it seems to move, it still passes nevertheless, and, eventually, I found myself alone in my room with a clock that read 10:03 in the P.M.

The next predicament was coming up with the proper stimulation for my first experience. The *искусство мастурбации* talks at length about using pornographic images to assist in the masturbation process. With that said, Reader, I'm sure you would not be surprised to find out that there is a limited supply of pornographic material at the Mazyr Hospital for Gravely Ill Children (and by limited supply, I mean I've searched every cupboard, drawer, and office—including the Director's—in this building and have found nothing except a catalogue for a Finnish company that sells everything from recording equipment to beach apparel). Though it was not ideal, especially considering my desire to educate myself on the female form, I decided to use the images promoting the sale of summer bathing suits for my first attempt. Of course, they needed to remain undiscoverable, so I hid them inside of a small cut I made in the corner of my mattress. By the time I pulled them out, they were wrinkled and already starting to fade, but even in this condition, I could feel my *Hui* begin to move heavenward. This was my cue to pull down my shorts and begin to follow the techniques enumerated in the *искусство мастурбации,* which turned into frustration upon discovering that three fingers are entirely insufficient for proper self-pleasure. This added to the fact that I have the strength and coordination of an infant meant that my first attempt was a two-hour collection of false alarms. I don't need to go into detail about my specific movements (I'm sure you're well aware of how ridiculous it looks). I can only say that every time I reached the point at which it felt like something truly transcendent was about to occur, my hand could not quite arrive at the proper rhythm and intensity to finish. Eventually, my arm would simply stop working out of fatigue, and I would need to start all over again. So I gave up in a fit of self-loathing on that first night.

The next night, I was at it again. This time, however, I made a sacred promise to myself that I would get *there* no matter how long it took. Apparently, my previous two hours of practice had enough impact on my strength and coordination that after ten minutes a sensation built up at the base of my *Hui* that was so powerful that I released all eleven years of my accumulated *malofya** onto my sheets, my floor, and three of my walls. During the eight or nine seconds in which it was happening, I could only think about how familiar the feeling was, and before the whole explosion ended, I realized that I had felt the same sensation several times before in dreams. This time, however, the sensation was so overwhelming that I

---

*   Russian slang for "semen."

almost aborted the mission by the third second. Admittedly disappointed with my first orgasm, I fell asleep debating whether the whole experience was worth the time, energy, and strategic planning that I invested in it. But despite this sentiment, I found myself tugging away at myself all the same the next night, and then the night after that. According to my current count, I haven't missed a night in the past six years. My daily practice has the added benefit of increased coordination, and my left arm now has twice the muscle mass that it had a few years ago. Still, the conflict between my lust and my physical limitations continues to result in masturbatory sessions that can run anywhere from thirty minutes to six hours. Conveniently, there is no shortage of time at the Mazyr Hospital for Gravely Ill Children.

There is, however, a downside to my habit. Inevitably, some evidence is left behind after every date with my Finnish models. I had been attacking my *Hui* for a solid year when I opened my door to find all the sheets off my bed, revealing that my hospital mattress was coated in overlapping circular yellowish-brown stains, resembling naughty Venn diagrams.

There was also a note:

Dear Ivan,
It looks like we might need to find a new mattress for you.
    I see the book helped.
    I left some tissues in your closet.

Sincerely,
Natalya

Before I even finished the letter, Nurse Natalya and Nurse Katya barged in with a new mattress. I watched them remake my bed for three painful minutes. Then I said:

"It's because I'm bored."

"No explanation necessary," said Nurse Natalya.

To you, Reader, I can confess that boredom is not the only reason I'm hopelessly addicted to touching my *Hui*. There is a far more insidious reason. As the pressure builds just before I'm about to spray my wasted seedlings onto my bed, there is a tiny piece of a second in which I feel whole, complete, and unbreakable. As quickly as it comes, it fades away into a mixture of guilt and self-pity. But that tiny part of a second where everything is perfect somehow makes all the guilt worth it.

XVII

The Sarcophagus

The Mazyr Hospital for Gravely Ill Children is hiding something.

Not in its walls but in its name.

To my recollection, I've cried twice ever in my seventeen years. For the majority of my life, I've had a prodigious control over my emotions. This is because I'm Belarusian. We are known for having harder hearts than our Mother Russians, thicker skin, and heavier *mudya** (or at least so I'm told by

---

* Russian slang for "testicles."

Nurse Katya, who loves to rant about Belarusian stock, which I find strange considering she is of African descent). Simply put, tears are not in our wiring. And in the rare moments when a few do leak out, it's no doubt due to some temporary malfunction in our chemical and genetic hardware.

It was because of this genetic hardware that I did not have a nervous breakdown when I awoke into this life to find that I only had approximately one-half of a body. Instead, I took all the shock and all the disillusion in that moment and turned it into a cold, pungent piss that I could spray on any-one who got too close. And all the decisions that resulted were rooted purely in the instincts coded in my DNA. Not that any of it was a conscious choice. Nor did I have any en-vironmental influence to help mitigate the decision. This was the equilibrium of the first few years of my life.

And then in one earthquake, arising somewhere in the center of my chest, that all changed. It lasted approximately two and a half minutes and came without warning. In every book I've ever read, the protagonist's shifts in emotion come slowly. You can sense the change coming and building over chapters. You can feel the billows before the calm of the storm. Then the cloud bursts, and nothing is the same again. Not so for eleven-year-old Ivan. I was at the breakfast table putting spoonful after spoonful of cold plastic into my mouth, bounc-ing listlessly from thought to thought, much like I did every morning. And then, with no warning at all, I lurched and spit out my bite, and squirts of salt water leaped from one or more of my eyes. And in a moment, all the nurses feeding all the children dropped the spoons they were holding and turned to me, looking every bit as shocked as I'm sure I looked. I dropped my spoon too and then turned around and wheeled myself into a hallway and let the rest of it out. It took about twenty seconds for Nurse Natalya to arrive and throw her bat wings around me (that's what I call arms with droopy fat that dangles all the way up to your armpits). After twenty or so more seconds, she saw the storm wasn't about to end, so she pulled me tightly into the soft velvet of her enormous breasts while I purged myself of every trace of sadness I ever held but never knew I held. Then it was over. For a few minutes, Nurse Natalya continued to hold me. When I finally pulled away, I could see that she had been crying right along with me.

"It needed to happen" was all she said.

Then she wheeled me back to my room, where she picked my small body out of the wheelchair and put me into my bed.

"Should I be mad at God?" I asked.

"No. God didn't do this, Ivan."

"Then who?"

"You'll find, Ivan, that most of the evil in the world is done by men who are addicted to their own thoughts."

Nurse Natalya could tell I wasn't really satisfied with this answer, and, at the time, I never really understood what she meant. To be honest, I'm not even sure I understand now either. But it strikes me as one of those utterances that one will finally understand later in life in one sudden epiphany, so I carry it with me in the back of my head and wait for it.

In the meantime, I resolved to squash whatever mental germs led to those feelings.

It was never discussed further. I spent a long time wondering if her silence was an expression of her disappointment in me or her guilt for not knowing the right words to say in order to make everything all right. The answer came about six months later while wheeling myself into my room en route to bed. That night, instead of sleep, I spent hours flipping through the scrapbook I found sitting in the middle of the floor. There was no note to accompany it. No name, no nothing. No evidence at all as to who put it together or why it was sitting there next to my bed.

The first page had a single picture of your standard industrial building with smokestacks and steel guts and dense edifices nestled sloppily next to each other. The second page had a picture of that same complex of buildings with a crater in the middle of it. The third page had several pictures of children who looked ominously like the residents of the Mazyr Hospital for Gravely Ill Children. One boy had legs that were long and twisted, like a comic book character. There was a girl with bulging eyes and a fat tongue. There were pictures of kids with gigantic heads, which reminded me of Alex.

The articles began on the fourth page. Pages upon pages of articles. That night I couldn't bring myself to actually read the sentences. I could only scan and note the most commonly occurring words such as *Soviet, radiation, wildstock, core, communist, reactor, moral,* and *bankruptcy.* It occurred to me that Nurse Natalya couldn't find the right words, so she picked the right pictures and let a few international journalists and scientists pick the words for her.

I sat in my bed without moving for the next twenty-four hours.

When Soviet engineers were trying to figure out how to stem the massive waves of radiation flowing from Nuclear Reactor Number Four, they decided to create a massive concrete-and-steel enclosure to cut the radiation off from the rest of the world. They affectionately named this structure the sarcophagus. It didn't take me long to realize the symbolism. There isn't just one sarcophagus. There never was only one. This hospital is a sarcophagus too. And there are probably hundreds more sarcophagi out there filled with Maxes and Dennises and colonies of heart-hole children.

There is nothing innocuous about the Mazyr Hospital for Gravely Ill Children.

⤫

Currently the clock reads 11:50 in the P.M.
I've been writing for twenty-four hours.
It is the third day of December.
The year is 2005.

A moment ago, I wiggled my flask and found it to be about half-full, which is plenty for my body weight. Eight in ten mutants agree: extreme susceptibility to alcohol is one of the few perks of having only half a body. It may be the only perk.

Nurse Natalya came in a few minutes ago. She was not at all pleased to find my clean clothes sitting at the end of my bed where she left them, while I played aloof, scribbling words like a mental patient.

"You asked for two hours, Ivan. I gave you six," she said. "Change them now."

"Not with you in the room."

"You lost the right to privacy when you proved you can't change without me."

She barked with such love.

"Turn around," I said, and Nurse Natalya obeyed.

The removal of my clothes was slow and laborious, mostly because I was still shitty from the Stoli. I repeatedly missed the hole in my shirt where my arm was supposed to go. After one-point-five uncomfortable minutes, I asked for help.

"Since when can't you dress yourself?" Natalya asked.

"Since someone put a full flask on my table."

She turned around and threw my arm into the correct sleeve while my skin hung from my bones and my body laughed hysterically. Then she pulled my underwear up over my boy parts, and I laughed some more at the sight of that. I know she enjoyed seeing me laugh, even if I was deranged. Then Nurse Natalya put the majority of her nose into my mouth.

"You stink of it, Ivan," she reported.

"Sorry," I said disingenuously.

XVIII

Ivanism

When Nurse Natalya found books she thought might make me leave the hospital for more whimsical worlds, she mostly did so without any input on my part. She knew my perverse sensibilities well enough that I never needed to make a formal request. I was thirteen before I ever begged Nurse Natalya for a book. It was the Old Testament.

"I want the Bible," I told her.

She looked approving, but surprised, and then asked, "For a doorstop?"

"For my life," I said.

A few days later, a copy of the Slovo Zhizny* showed up on the table next to my bed. Unfortunately, it only took a week before I was using it as a sedative. To be fair, I tried. I tried as hard as any fifteen-year-old boy could try to make any cosmic sense out of a convoluted and poorly edited book. I was, after all, used to Tolstoy. But, in the end, it was the prophets who tied their own nooses. I already knew enough about plate tectonics and erosion rates to completely discount Genesis. Exodus had a certain sexy appeal in the same way that an epic saga flickering on the TV in the Main Room would. Unfortunately, I'm not a Jew, so I felt left out.

---

* The Russian equivalent of the English New International Version.

Leviticus was a list of archaic rules that will never be relevant to me here at the Mazyr Hospital for Gravely Ill Children. Furthermore, it seemed to suggest that the world is "very good" and only subject to evil through "sin and defilement," but I was a victim of evil well before I even had the opportunity to defile anything. Numbers tickled me until God decided to will his darlings to get lost in the wilderness and starve to death because they had doubts about their ability to win a war in Canaan—not the fatherly persona I was hoping for. I had high hopes for Deuteronomy, but after ten more pages of Moses ranting, I gave up.

So I tried to find God in Hinduism. Instead, I found several thousand of Him, each adorned with anywhere from eight to twenty arms. I only had one arm, so none of these could be my God. Then I looked for Him in the Greek and Roman myths, but those Gods were pettier than our nurses. Then I tried to find Him in Islam, until I heard that this God was the same ornery bastard from the Old Testament. Eventually, I put down all the books and said, "God, clearly I'm trying here. Could You just come talk to me? No books, I promise." I sat there for a while listening very hard, but I didn't hear anything. So I said, "Please, God, anything. Give me something, and I will be loyal to You for as long as I live." I listened hard with a scrunched and pensive face for thirty minutes. Still nothing. No booming voice. No burning bush. Not even a piece of paint falling off the wall.

Logic suggested that my next step be to find God with my intellect. So I crafted every mental argument I could dream up to prove His existence. Then, after consulting Saint Thomas

Aquinas, I discovered that I had accidentally re-created both the teleological and ontological arguments for the existence of God, which had previously been invented by Socrates and Anselm of Canterbury, respectively. Neither of these satisfied me. In the end, they were just words, and when I looked inside them, still no God.

Eventually, I drank so much of Nurse Elena's laundry room stash of Beluga* that I stopped thinking at all. When everything turned black, there was space for questions to start to bubble up. Questions like: Who makes someone in His image, then chops off his or her arm and several fingers? Who goes through the effort of creating something that will never be able to mate and therefore propagate its genes, which, ultimately, is the only purpose of life? And, of course, was God Himself drunk when He made me? I noticed I had no good answers to these questions, so I pulled out a blank piece of paper and wrote down only the things I knew for sure. When I was done, I had three principles, which I dub the Three Tenets of Ivanism:

1. There is no Creator, at least not in the way that we hope for.
2. There is no fate, no destiny, no prewritten laws that say how things are supposed to be.
3. The only order in the universe is the laws of physics—besides that, the universe is amoral and chaotic.

---

* Popular Russian brand of vodka.

There are two reasonable reactions to Ivanism. Reaction #1 goes something like: *Bravo, cheers, well done, Ivan! This is the only conclusion that makes any sense.* If this is your reaction, I'm only preaching to the choir. Reaction #2 sounds more like: *I refuse to believe this. Of course there is a God. If not, then who made everything? Besides, I need to believe in a God. I need something to give all of this meaning.* If this is your reaction, there's nothing I can say to change your mind.

Currently the clock reads 12:03 in the P.M.
I've been writing for more than thirty-six hours.
It is the fourth day of December.
The year is 2005.

Nurse Natalya just came in.

She says she had a dream.

Have you been up all night? she asks.

More or less.

Do you need anything?

Vodka.

Besides that.

I'm all right.

Can I read it?

No.

I couldn't sleep either. I had a dream about you.

About what?

You were a student at the university.

I saw you walking in the street,
so I stopped you.
You looked at me like you didn't know who I was.
Then you walked away.
I had legs?
Yes.
What do you think it meant?
I haven't decided yet.

XIX

Polina's Journal

If Polina had an addiction, it was writing in a small, seasoned notebook. Sometimes with a hand that was calm and precise, and sometimes on the cusp of violence. Sometimes she would look up and around in between sentences, and sometimes her face would be buried in the page for an hour at a time. Sometimes she would just hold it during TV hour while slowly stroking the cover with her left hand. Sometimes she would read old pages with a fraction of a smile on her cheeks, which activated her shallow dimples. Sometimes she would read old pages with eyes that held varying degrees of blue water.

I'm not ashamed to tell you, Reader, that I wanted to read every private and lascivious thought inside that book. Unfortunately, this was close to impossible because she brought it everywhere. She brought it to breakfast first thing in the morning. She brought it to her chemo session, where it turned salty from her cold sweats. She brought it into the bathroom, where the pages would slowly start to turn wavy from post-hand-wash moisture. She brought it to lunch and then to dinner, where it slowly became stained with unidentified animal grease.

There is not a lot of wisdom that comes with being a seventeen-year-old boy who has spent his entire life inside of an asylum for mutant children, but you do eventually develop a deep understanding of the benefits of patience. Since this was my only strength (as well as my only option) I waited for her to fumble. Every girl has a moment when she is helplessly lost to her own world at the expense of the contents of the real one.

The infamous fumble came after six weeks and three days of stoic waiting. After lunch on a Wednesday, a day when her features were particularly glum, she walked into the common bathroom with it and walked out without it. I waited a few minutes to give reality a chance to catch up with my eyes. I was four meters from the bathroom door, there wasn't a nurse to be seen, and the only others in the room were Dennis, who was rocking away like a grandfather clock, and the two ginger twins, who were absorbed in an intense game of chess, neither of which was an obvious threat. A few more fidgety moments passed before I realized that everything was as it seemed and the book was mine for the taking. So I wheeled myself over to the bathroom door and made my way inside after banging my chair multiple times into the metallic doorframe due to my accelerated heart rate and sweaty palm. Once inside, with the door closed firmly behind me, I found it sitting innocently enough on the floor beside the toilet. So I carefully placed my awkward ass on the porcelain seat and reached down with Old Lefty to pick up her book, which instantly began to vibrate along with my trembling hand.

My first instinct was to fan through the pages, back to front, in order to scan for any words that resembled my name. Then it occurred to me that it was entirely possible that after two months she did not know my name. So I turned to the last entry, which she had just written this morning (at that moment I had little interest in what she had to say before coming to the hospital) and started reading with a fever. Two sentences later, I learned two things: first, Polina had thrown up her last five consecutive meals; and two, I forgot to lock the door. I learned the latter because the door opened, and there was Polina looking at me looking back at her from my throne, holding her journal, which carried her most personal and private thoughts, while my *Hui* dangled over the porcelain bowl.

I knew I wouldn't be the first to open my mouth. Instead, I just sat there on the commode with my droopy face, hoping that at this particular moment it did not look too droopy, and waited for her to slap me, or call a nurse, or worse, call the Director, or even worse, say something so unbearably mean that I would spend the next year of my life reassembling the pieces of my broken psyche. Instead, she said:

"Why didn't you just ask for it?"

Which, of course, startled me because the particular look on her face made me feel that it was entirely possible that she was laying a trap.

"Can I read your journal?" I asked.

To which she replied:

"First, I need to know your name."

To which I droopily replied:

"I'm Ivan."

To which she said:

"I know."

To which I said:

"Then why did you ask?"

To which she said:

"Because that's how people do things. They know each other's names before stealing their diaries. Yes, you can take it. But you have to give it back at dinner."

To which I said nothing, but might have nodded.

To which she said:

"You broke the first rule of petty theft: if it looks too easy, it's not."

To which I said:

"Thanks for the acumen."

To which she said:

"I'm leaving now. Would you like me to lock the door?"

To which I nodded again. Then she locked the door and left, and I remained on the toilet and read steadily until dinner hour.

The first thing that I noticed was that she wrote in Russian, not Belarusian, and that both her handwriting and her grammar were impeccable, which, of course, knowing me as well as you do now, Reader, rattled my tail.

First, a disclaimer. Out of respect to her, I refuse to share anything from that book that she didn't later tell me out loud to my face. The things she released from her mouth out into the world are the things I believe she would be okay with me sharing with you. Here are those things:

I read that Polina was an orphan like me. But, unlike me, she had parents until about three months ago, when she lost them both at the same time when a bus they were in fell off a bridge into the Pripyat River because the driver was drunk and wanted to die and didn't care if other people died too. I read that she was also on that bus and was one of only two people who didn't drown. I read that they would not even have been on that bus if they were not returning from a consultation with a doctor in Odessa who specialized in experimental procedures to treat leukemia, which she had been diagnosed with a month earlier. I read that she blamed herself. I read that she wished one of the two surviving spots on the bus were not wasted on her, since she was going to die anyway. I read that she had a boyfriend named Sergei, who stopped talking to her after she told him about the leukemia. I read that she loved American rock from the decade of the '80s including bands that were named after geographic locations, like Asia, Europe, Boston, and Kansas. I read that this was a mild form of rebellion against her father, who conducted the Lviv Philharmonic Orchestra before falling into the river. I read that she was a perfect student, but she was also a bit of hooligan. I read that her *Dead Souls* caper was less of an outlier and more of a lifestyle. I read that from the ages of eight to fifteen she stole things, any things, not because she needed them but because her parents squeezed her into a "model seraphim, whose twin succubus still needed feeding." (Incidentally, the revelation of her sinister side only deepened the venereal tension I was experiencing.) I read that, like me, she loathed the Mazyr Hospital for Gravely Ill Children and thought of ways to escape. I read that her chemotherapy was the most lonesome two hours of her day. I read about the synergistic effects of solitude and nausea. I read that she missed her parents. I read that this place was filled with creeps, especially "the androgynous boy who could be anywhere between twelve and sixteen years of age who stares at me for too long and thinks I don't notice." I read that she used to love to dance ballet and received a standing ovation once for her solo in *Giselle*. I read that her first kiss happened when she was fourteen years old and that she didn't understand what all the hoopla was about, since "not only were there no fireworks, but it also tasted like cold mustard" (data that made me perk for obvious reasons). I read that she was scared to die and that she thought about it during all her minutes. I read that she was 555th on a list for a bone marrow donation, which is the equivalent of "never" in marrow donation parlance. I read that she hadn't dreamed since she'd been at the hospital, but she used to dream all the time before she got sick. I read that she was still a virgin and was glad that she didn't waste her virginity on that "pond scum Sergei." I read about all her celebrity crushes including Ilia Kulik, Anton Yelchin, and Vitas[*] (all of whom I now secretly, or not so secretly, despise). I read that she loved her mother but was scared of her father, but now that he was dead, she couldn't even remember why she was

---

[*] Stage name for Russian singer Vitaliy Vladasovich Grachov.

ever scared. I read that we had a lot of the same favorite thoughts. I read that she stopped believing in God too. I read that her favorite color was cornflower blue, as is mine, which, statistically speaking, is rather striking. I read that in other ways we couldn't be more different. I read that she loved figure skating, which I hate. I read that even though she stopped believing in God, she still occasionally pleaded with Him. I read that she didn't think she had a choice. I read that she refused to die here. And then there were no more words that I could read because I finished the last page, which made me flush with anxiety because now I was supposed to say something to her because that's what people do. Despite my primitive grasp of social etiquette, I understood that when someone hands you a diary, it is because there is a palpable desperation. I'm all too familiar with the storm that buzzed through Polina's body when she let the "creepy invalid who stares at me all day" sift through her most private thoughts while he sat on a toilet. After two lonely months of nausea and hair loss, she needed to be seen by someone. The only problem was I couldn't say anything to her because I had no idea what words to use.

If I were you, Reader, the question I would be dying to ask would be: *But, Ivan, this is what you wanted. You wanted her. You wanted anyone. You wanted a one-way ticket out of loneliness. You wanted a friend. You wanted real. What's the drama?* Valid question, Reader, so I will try to explain with three simple reasons.

Reason #1: When I speak to the nurses, doctors, psychologists, or anyone else I could possibly interact with on any given day, I'm a twenty-four-carat bona fide asshole. More importantly, I have institutional carte blanche. No matter what I say to the nurses, I know they will come back, if for no other reason than because they have to if they plan to stay employed in a hostile post-Soviet economy (I read the newspapers). Consequently, I have seventeen years of excellent practice at being a truly competent asshole, but I have exactly zero years of practice at being kind and interesting and spontaneous. Being an asshole is much easier, and, for me, for all the classic pseudopsychological reasons, it comes much more naturally. This is why I was terrified to open my mouth in front of her—I knew I could not be both myself and likable at the same time.

Reason #2: Over the years I have learned that men have a deeply programmed fear of talking to the opposite sex, which I believe is older than God. My best explanation for this phenomenon is that in the earliest tribal villages there were only about three potential mates in the whole known world to choose from and if you said the wrong thing when you approached one of them you became the sexless reject of the tribe and ruined your chances to fulfill your life's singular evolutionary purpose. The chumps (chimps) with the biggest nerves tended to be more disciplined with their approach, whereas the buffoons without a care attempted the mating ritual too soon or said something unflattering, as men are often prone to doing, and sunk their own ships. Thus, those with the nerves won and went on to make judiciously nervous babies, and now we are all descendants of those nervous babies.

Eventually, villages turned into cities, and it didn't matter anymore if you were a nervous baby or not because you could spew any gibberish at all to a million potential mates, and who cares if the *tyolka** spread the news because next door there were a hundred more *tyolka*s. But still, genes are the true gift that never stops giving. The irony now, Reader, is that I am back in the tribal village, only my village is the Mazyr Hospital for Gravely Ill Children, and we are a tribe of mutant kids, and there is only one possible mate. How does anyone avoid crumbling under these kinds of stakes? If I botch this particular game, I'm destined to an isolated existence where my seed is forever stuck inside of me. Talking to Polina was too high stakes regardless of all the social norms that suggested I acknowledge the fact that she laid her whole soul bare to me, a perfectly creepy stranger.

Nota bene: Of course, I never had any expectation that I would be spreading any seeds inside of Polina, both because my physical structure is a disaster and because Polina was knocking on death's door. Nevertheless, this was the battle raging unconsciously in my prehistorically programmed circuitry. Now to continue:

Reason #3: I look weird when I talk.

So with these concerns running through my head I was able to sit guiltlessly as I waited for dinner hour, at which time I would wheel myself down a few minutes early and leave the diary at her spot on the table and not say another word to Polina, perhaps for the rest of my life.

---

*   Derogatory term for a girl. Literally means "young cow."

The truth is that my mind is rarely that tranquil, and soon an alternative option started to materialize. As you can tell from the manifesto in your hands, I write much better than I can talk out loud to people. I decided that I could resolve all pending issues by writing her a message after her last entry. The only remaining issue was deciding the right words. I spent the next three hours staring at my ceiling dreaming up every topic of conversation (the sexual habits of bonobos, figure skating, Nurse Lyudmila's closet bulimia problem), every witty joke (Q: *What did Russians use to light their houses before they started using candles? A: Electricity*), and every illuminating question (*Why is every girl crazy about Vitas?*). In the end I settled on:

Polina, thanks for letting me read your journal.
—Ivan

Two minutes before I was about to leave, I realized that I had made a horrible mistake! I left no incentive for her to continue the conversation, no question, no query. So I quickly scribbled down in my messiest script the first curiosity that came to mind, which happened to be: *Please describe in complete and thorough detail the combination of events and circumstances leading up to the initiation of your criminal history.* Then, for good measure, I promptly added *Also, what do you think happens inside of a black hole?*

When Polina arrived at the dinner table to find her book meticulously placed at her spot, I could see the 25 percent smile on her face evolve into a 60 percent smile. I, of course, only observed this from the corner of my eye, as I avoided all eye contact with her. Polina, who was better versed in normal social behavior, was clearly looking for more. I could feel the heat of her eyes looking over at me between bites of food, scanning and searching for some glimmer of recognition that she was now visible for having revealed her shadow. When she saw that my plate was nearly empty and I still wasn't looking back, her 60 percent smile inverted to a scowl, which reminded me of the look on Nurse Lyudmila's face when she left the Director's office after midnight. It occurred to me that maybe Polina felt used like the hospital equivalent of the high school whore.

After forty-three minutes of my neglect, she stood up and marched off while hugging the journal over her breasts. The next time I saw Polina, she was sitting in the Main Room during TV hour with a chemo IV plugged into one arm, while the other was busy writing things into her journal at a determined pace. I parked myself a good distance from her and pretended to watch an episode of *Nu, Pogodi!** while actually soaking up every detail Polina let me absorb of her, no longer concerned about being the creepy invalid. And every detail of her body language told me that I had lost her, or whatever I had of her when she decided to let me see inside of her head.

---

*   An excerpt from a *Des Moines Times* review: "*Nu, Pogodi!* (Russian: *Hy, погоди!* [*Well, Just You Wait!*]) is a Soviet/Russian animated series produced by Soyuzmultfilm. The series was created in 1969 and became a popular cartoon of the Soviet Union. The latest episode was produced in 2006. The original film language is Russian, but very little speech is used (usually interjections or at most several sentences per episode)."

Then, while she was absorbed in whatever sentence or whatever thought was running through her head and down into her fingers, Polina vomited a supernova of color up out of her mouth and onto her clothes, chair, chemo plug, and the page she was frantically writing on, and it all eventually dripped slowly onto the linoleum floor and gathered into a pool of swirls and eddies. It was that particular variety of nausea that by the time you sense the irresistible urge to expel, it is already halfway into the world and all you can do is spend a moment in shock and embarrassment before your eyes tear up and you run out of the room to leave those who clean up vomit for a living to come and clean up vomit. In this case, however, Polina was plugged into a chemo bag, which meant that the only thing that she could do was sit tight in her own gastric juices.

I'm not lost to a modicum of chivalry, so when it struck me that her situation would become worse if any of the other nurses were to find her in a puddle of her own puke, I immediately called out for Nurse Natalya, who arrived at the scene in three short seconds and walked Polina and the chemo bag she was connected to away while muttering things like, "Oh, you poor baby," and "It's all right, darling." Somehow in all the pandemonium, Polina managed to remember to grab her diary, which was now coated in bright stomach acid.

I didn't see Polina again for three days, which I presumed was the minimum amount of time that it took to find the courage to show her face again. When she finally came back around, her first instinct was to sit back down on the dirty old couch in the Main Room, pull out her journal, rip out two pages, scribble through two more, stash the book under one of the couch cushions, and leave the room without ever even looking in my direction. It was clear that Polina was being what they call *passive-aggressive,* so I wheeled my way over to the couch to see what she had left me. Unfortunately, at the same moment, the ginger twins plopped their tiny ginger asses on the couch and started some nonsensical hand-clapping game. Since moving them would require an act of God, I was forced to wait and watch. Two hours and seventeen minutes later, they got bored and simultaneously pranced off, which is when I lifted the cushion, pulled out the diary, still pungent from Polina's stomach acids, and turned to the last page. This is what it said (I remember because I'm holding it right now):

Dear Ivan,

First, I would like to tell you that you are a terrible human. And in most ways I find you repulsive. And the only reason that I even let you read my diary is because you were my only option. But if this is how it works, then I will play along. You know too much about me, and I know nothing about you. So answer these questions if you want to continue talking (or whatever it is that we're doing).

(1) How long have you been here?

(2) Why are you here?

(3) How do you make this bearable?

Disrespectfully,
Polina

PS—To answer your first question, the first thing I ever stole was a cat named Anatoly. He was my best friend for seven hours until my father made me give him back.

PPS—Inside of a black hole there are mountains of chak-chak,* *which would last for an eternity, since a black hole contains all time.*

PPPS—Leave the book back under the couch cushion where you found it.

I wasted no time crafting an eloquent response and then tucked the book back inside the couch before lunch. This is what it said:

Dear Polina,
Thanks for your response. To answer your questions:
(1) I have always been here.
(2) I'm here because I've always been here. And because, like you, I don't have any parents.
(3) I turn everything into a game.
                                        Respectfully,
                                           Ivan

I returned an hour later, and it was already gone, meaning it was back in Polina's hands. Then I checked again anywhere

---

* A popular Russian dessert made from soft dough and raw eggs, molded into short delicate sticks that look like vermicelli or marbles, which are then deep-fried and placed in a pile before hot honey is poured over them, and then left to harden.

from twelve to eighteen more times that day, but the couch was empty. Then I remembered that once again I forgot to continue the conversation like a normal person and concluded that I had most likely ruined our budding rapport.

The next morning, I woke up an hour early and wheeled myself out to the Main Room and checked the couch again much like children check the Christmas tree at 3:00 in the A.M. on Christmas Eve in American movies. To my surprise, I found it there this time. It said:

I have a game. I used to play it with my father when we had to drive for a long time. Meet me in the Main Room during TV hour after dinner.
—Polina

Okay, Polina, I will was the first thought in my head. The second was *But this does not mean that I will make eye contact with you.* So I quickly scribbled into the diary:

Okay, Polina, I will. But this doesn't mean that I will make eye contact with you.

My first instinct was to look at the clock on the wall in the Main Room, which told me that it was 9:47 in the A.M., which meant that there were eight hours and thirteen minutes until dinner hour and nine hours and thirteen minutes until TV hour, which I knew meant eight hours and thirteen minutes of Kafkian dread.

But the comforting truth about time—and all the Buddhists agree—is that nothing lasts forever, and after eight hours of kamikaze thoughts and one-handed nail biting it was 7:00 in the P.M., and I found myself parked a safe eighteen inches from Polina while an episode of *Bednaya Nastya** played on the big TV. And while I kept my promise and refused to look her in the eye, I could tell from my peripheral vision that Polina had chosen not to arrive with her wig tonight. Her face was pale and gaunt and almost transparent like mine. She looked tired and a bit soulless, but she put it all behind a 45 percent smile. And somehow, in spite of her deterioration, she made my heart beat to the rhythm of "Sexual Healing," which is a song written by the late soul singer Marvin Gaye.

Polina wrote a few sentences down into her book and passed it over to me. It said:

I'm thinking of a person. It could be a him or a her. It could be fictional or real, dead or alive. You get to ask me twelve yes/no questions to guess who it is. You are supposed to get twenty questions, but my personal record for this game is twelve. If you guess my person in twelve questions, then you get to ask me any question in the world, and I have to answer honestly. If you don't guess it in twelve questions, then you have to say something to me. Do you agree to the terms of this contract?

---

* Translates as *Poor Nastya,* a popular Russian telenovela based on nineteenth-century imperial life.

I pulled my own pencil from my pocket and wrote back:

I agree to your terms. Is your person a woman?

Then I handed it back to her, at which point she quickly scribbled:

Yes, eleven.

And then she handed it back to me.

Is your person fictional?

Switch:

No, ten.

Switch:

Is she anyone that we have seen on the screen during TV hour?

Switch:

No, nine.

Switch:

Is she a character in a book?

Switch:

No, eight.

Switch:

A historical figure?

Switch:

Yes, seven.

Switch:

Biblical?

Switch:

Yes, six.

Switch:

On God's side?

Switch:

No, five.

Switch:

Was her flesh eaten by stray dogs at the time of her death?

Switch:

Yes, four.

Switch:

Jezebel.

Switch:

Polina laughed, which startled me because no one had ever laughed in response to something I had done, nor had I ever considered the possibility that I was capable of making a person laugh. Then she scribbled down a few words and handed the book back again.

I hate you, Ivan.

Switch:

Why?

Switch:

Because that was only nine questions.

Switch:

It was too easy. She's your alter ego.

Switch:

Ask your question.

She dropped the book back into my lap, and I sat for a few minutes dreaming up questions, and a thousand came to mind, all of which were the type of deep and existential questions that inevitably result in long nights on the linoleum floor (n.b.: I've never actually had a long night on a linoleum floor). Such questions included: *What do you think happens after you die? Have humans evolved to be monogamous? Why do bonobos have sex more than other primates? Is there a boundary to the universe? What is true happiness? What if a one-armed man robbed a bank; how would you handcuff him? If vampires can't see their reflection, why do they have such perfect hair? Is it possible to daydream at night? and, of course, Do you think it would be possible for you to see me in a sexual sort of way?*

In the end, I decided to ask her for more time. So I wrote:

Can I have the book for the night?

To which she responded:

If you don't mind my puke.

To which I responded:

*I have smelled a lot of puke at this hospital, and yours is
not the worst.*

To which she laughed (that was two) and responded:

Good night, creep.

Which I hoped was also a joke.

Then I wheeled myself back to my room, where my mother
was waiting up with a mouth that was clearly ready to explode with maternal-like things.

"So, how was your first date?"

"Dates involve words, Mother."

"I'm submitting a request for a grandchild."

"What is wrong with you?"

"What is wrong with *you*?"

"For one, I'm not built for procreation."

"Max Moyovich. Quadruple amputee from the Second
World War. His son is currently mayor of Yakutsk. You have
a whole arm on him."

"For two, she'll die before any zygote is the size of a ten-
ruble coin."

"Have you not seen the latest incubators?"

"Good night, Mother."

I spent the rest of the evening reading through classic literature in order to come up with a question for Polina. At
some point, it occurred to me that there might be nothing
left to ask. I knew the names and faces of each of the demons
that populated her world. She painted all their faces with

her words. It only seemed fair that I should offer the same courtesy.

The clock read 6:53 in the A.M. when I finished writing *The Retroactive Diary of Ivan Isaenko*. I was as honest as I'd ever been. As I could ever let myself be. It was the unabridged history brimming with all my crippling phobias, my morbid games, and a dictionary for my exclusive lexicon. There were other things I couldn't bring myself to share. For example, my obsessive masturbation habits.

As soon as I put my pen down, I fell asleep and had a dream that Polina and I were walking down a street that looked nothing like somewhere in Eastern Europe. The road was as long as I could see, the sky was gray, the streets were foggy, and the scene was almost entirely black and white except for trees that lined the road, each one of them blooming with little purple flowers that were being shed all over my black-and-white road, which looked like little pieces of purple candy.

I turned to Polina and asked:

"What are these trees?"

"Jacarandas," she said.

Something about her voice made me realize that I was dreaming, but somehow I didn't wake up. Instead, I wondered how I knew the name for something in my dream that I didn't know the name of in real life. I was, however, able to let this paradox go and choose to enjoy the dream for as long as it would play out. We continued to walk without saying anything to each other until it became apparent that under one of the trees clarifying itself on the horizon there was a body lying limp and lifeless over the strewn purple candies.

Eventually the ripped jeans and T-shirt could be ascertained, and a few steps later it was clear that it was the Polina who walked into the hospital two months ago. I leaned down and shook her body, but it was uninhabited. Then I turned to my left, and the Polina that I had been walking with was gone. Like a balloon, the scene popped, and I found myself in my bed with *The Retroactive Diary of Ivan Isaenko* bobbing on my torso to the rhythm of my escalating breath. I leaped quickly into my morning rituals of urination and dress and proceeded to breakfast hour. But this morning, Polina would not be reading my diary. This would be the morning that in spite of waking up in Abaddon every day, in spite of the debilitating isolation I weather and my daily broken heart, in spite of the unbroken stream of thoughts hustling like loyal little slaves to erect some meaning out of my existence, in spite of all this and everything else, I'd never really hurt before.

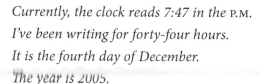

Currently, the clock reads 7:47 in the P.M.
I've been writing for forty-four hours.
It is the fourth day of December.
The year is 2005.

Natalya knocked again.
I told her to come in.
It's the day after tomorrow.
(Silence.)

I will pick you up at nine.
I'm not going.
I disagree.

∞

X X

The Case for Diacetylmorphine

I wasn't completely honest when I said that I had correctly guessed every three-monther since I invented the game. I was wrong once, and not long ago. I was wrong because denial is the voluptuous mistress of puppy love. By the time I made it to my spot at the breakfast table, on a Wednesday morning of a particularly cold November, everyone had already started eating, including Polina, whom I audaciously avoided with my eyes. The plan was to rush through my cold plastic food as per usual, only this time I would leave my book with Polina and wheel away like a two-legged puma.

Wednesdays are also med days. If there are meds to be delivered, it happens during breakfast hour on a Wednesday. On this particular Wednesday, I had forgotten it was a Wednesday for all the obvious reasons. So when I saw Nurse Katya approach the table with her big box of plastic Baggies tucked in her big brown arms, I instinctively made my guesses for the week. As usual, the ginger twins, Alex, Dennis, and the heart-hole children all had normal six-month bags. I also correctly called Anton, the ten-year-old autistic progerian, who received a three-month bag. But on this day, for the first time ever, I was wrong. On this Wednesday in the month of November, Nurse Katya dropped a bag in front of Polina that was about half the size of her usual med day bag.

I was surprised to find out just how many thoughts could arrive in the width of a second if the circumstances are right. Thoughts like thought Number One: *Well, less of a thought and more of a complete body experience of devastation.* Thought Number Two: *Polina had not been here long enough nor did she have (yet) a sufficiently morbid enough sense of curiosity to know about the two classes of patients at the hospital. Nor is there an adequate system of communication here which would have helped Polina to understand the meaning of her reduced-sized bag of pills. This meant that Polina had no idea that she had somewhere between one day and three months left to live. It also meant that the only two people who did know were me and Nurse Katya and whatever higher powers decided that Polina was about to die.* Thought Number Three: *Everyone deserves to know when they are going to die.* Thought Number Four: *Thought Number Three is all wrong.* If not for the fear, death is just a word, and if I never tell her she doesn't have to be afraid. Thought Number Five, *Thought Number Four is all wrong. Knowing when one is going to die helps one to make informed decisions about how one would live one's last days.* Thought Number Six: *Somebody needs to tell her.*

Thought Number Seven: *It is me or Nurse Katya. I can't even look her in the eye, so it must be Nurse Katya.* Thought Number Eight: *I need to talk to Nurse Katya.*

All these thoughts arrived in this sequence in about the time it took for my bite of food to drop from my lips. I had hoped that Polina would not notice this, but Nurse Katya would. Unfortunately, it was the other way around; I could feel the heat of Polina's clearly disgusted eyes baking my skin while Nurse Katya aloofly continued to pass out her pills. I decided it might be easier to get her attention by taking a dull butter knife to the nub that would have been my inner thigh and doing my best to get a nontrivial stream of blood flowing. This resulted in a suitable commotion of crying among the heart-holes, an unbearable eruption of "*Shoko*" by Alex, and some Olympic-style rocking by Dennis, which was, of course, enough to get Nurse Katya to drop her box of meds and scream, "Christ, Ivan! In the name of Saint Thomas Aquinas!"

Now, the sight of blood makes me pass out, even if it's my own, so by the time I saw her run over to me, the cabbage on my plate turned blurry, and my face fell flat into my partially chewed bite. When I woke up I was in the White Room. The first thing I saw was Nurse Katya's big brown arms slapping my droopy cheeks back and forth.

"I'm awake, I'm awake," I said.

To which she responded by slapping me twice more, harder. I tasted a bit of blood, which almost made me pass out again.

"Why in the hell would you do that?" she asked.

"Were you worried about me?" I asked.

"Not in the least. But now the hospital is in a frenzy, and I have a pint of blood to mop up. And don't you even think I'm about to change that," she said, motioning to the blood-soaked gauze that was taped over my nub.

"I can handle it," I said.

"What the hell is wrong with you?"

"I need a favor."

"Yes, I need a favor too. I need someone to mop the blood off the floor."

"I'll do it if you do me a favor back."

"There's more chance of getting struck by lightning, child."

"You wouldn't be helping me. You need to tell Polina she's dying."

"She knows she's dying," she said while pouring water into the mop bucket.

"I need you to tell her that she's dying in less than three months."

"How do I know when she's dying?"

"You know she's a three-monther."

"Ivan, what in the hell is a three-monther?"

"The kids who get the small bags."

"Not my job, Ivan."

"Then whose job is it?"

"Not mine."

"Is it anyone's job?"

"Nope."

"So you're saying it's no one's job to tell people when they are going to die in a place where people die all the time?"

"Yes, that is what I'm saying," she said, and she left the White Room with her bucket and mop.

I gave myself sixty seconds to bring myself together. Sixty, fifty-nine, fifty-eight . . .

By fifty, forty-nine . . . I fell out of my chair.

By forty-three, forty-two . . . water was trying to work its way out of my eyes.

By fifteen, fourteen . . . I had successfully sucked most of the water back into my eyes.

By one . . . I was back in my chair.

By zero, I was frantically wheeling myself to Nurse Natalya, who was also the only person left who could fix this. I started with the Blue Room (laundry room), then the Red Room, then the Yellow Room, but she was nowhere. I went to the front desk, where I found Miss Kristina chewing on an already overchewed pen.

"Where's Natalya?" I asked.

"She's not here today," she said.

"Where is she?"

"Niece's baptism or something."

"You need to call her."

"Ivan, I c—"

"Yes, you can. I will dial the number."

"She is at the Mass."

"Don't you know that baptisms don't happen at 8:00 in the A.M.? Actually, no you wouldn't because you're an idiot."

"That was mean."

"That was true."

"There is a reason I won't let you call. Would you like to know the reason?"

"Not really."

"I'm not supposed to ever let you use the phone again since the time that you made a hundred long-distance phone calls in one night."

"For one, that was three years ago; for two, someone is going to die."

She looked down at my bloody gauze in alarm.

"Is it you?" she asked.

"Yes, and I need Natalya."

"I think we should just call one of the other nurses over here. Everyone else—"

"I can't talk to them."

She responded with a face that said, *I understand exactly what you mean . . .*

She put the phone up to my ear and asked, "Do you need her number?"

To which I said:

"No, I remember."

To which she said:

"Hurry."

It took about twenty-seven seconds for my clumsy index finger to spin through all the numbers. It was 8:00 in the A.M., so I hoped she was awake, and if she was awake that she wasn't praying. As I had already learned, hope, like prayer, almost never works. Only being a pest works. The phone rang through seventeen times, and no one picked up. So I hung up the phone and started all over again, which was met with various protests from Miss Kris, which I adroitly fended off. Then, after eight more rings:

"Ivan?"

To which I was startled but responded:

"How did you know it was me?"

"I'll be there in ten minutes."

Then she hung up.

Nine minutes later, she plowed through the double front doors, in a heavy black coat, and no nurse's uniform. In seventeen years, I don't know if I had ever seen her without her scrubs. Her chubby little figure immediately charged over to me, took the handlebars on my chair, and wheeled me off to a quiet stairwell on the third floor. Then she threw her arms around me and started to sob.

"Ivan, my baby, I know about your *Dear Diary* game," she confessed through her tears. Her crying motivated me to cry.

Then I said:

"Sorry for interrupting baptism day."

To which she replied:

"Oh, stop it!"

Then we cried some more, and when we finished, she dried us both off and wheeled me back to my room, which is when I asked:

"Can you tell her?"

"Who else?" she asked, which I knew was a rhetorical question, so I didn't respond.

She left, and I decided to hide in my room for the rest of

the day while I alternatingly read various medical books and attempted unsuccessfully to masturbate.

The next morning, we were all back at the breakfast table, precisely the same characters in precisely the same configuration, but this time, Polina and I both knew she was dying. All I could think to do was send her a forced smile from across the breakfast table (or at least as much of a smile as my droopy cheeks could muster). I was shocked by how easy it was to get a smile back considering the circumstances. I concede it was a courtesy smile, no doubt about it. It was a smile that said, "I'm weak, tired, and dying, and you are a freak, but, despite these facts, social courtesy dictates that I reciprocate your kind sentiment." And maybe, just maybe, she was also charmed by it on some level.

I decided at that moment that breakfast would become my training ground. I would use a system of smiles and glances to slowly melt the ice and desensitize myself to her Goddessness. Every morning I would wait for her to be ushered to her spot at the breakfast table, while I exercised my cheek muscles with a series of techniques that I developed to improve my smile. Every morning, when she finally arrived, I would patiently wait for her eyes to randomly move in my direction, and when they did, I would pitch my best beam. And every morning, she would reflect it back to me.

Eventually, I wouldn't have to wait for her eyes to randomly meet mine. She would come to expect my smile, relish it maybe, and consequently when she took her place at the table, her first impulse would be to look over to me and receive it. Soon I would be glancing over at her several times during each meal, partly to deepen my desensitization regimen and partly to fish for any reason to tell myself that she would see some inexplicable beauty in me.

I had hoped for at least three more years to complete the systematic desensitization required to achieve the comfort and confidence required to verbalize utterances to Polina. But, as the universe would have it, we would not even get three more months. In reality, we would only have three more weeks, which, of course, reminds me of Maxwell Maltz's 1960 book, *Psycho-Cybernetics,* which explains that it takes exactly twenty-one days to establish a new habit.

PART TWO

The Count Down

Hazing and Initiation

The next morning, I prepared all my facial muscles for breakfast. I knew she would instinctually turn to me, if for no other reason than there was no one else to turn to. And she did. But I couldn't. I knew the second I lost my focus, the pseudo-smile would snap back to the other face that I was actually feeling. This was a contingency I had not planned for.

Of course, Nurse Natalya witnessed all this, as she was particularly curious about my next play. So, in response to my coldness, she took it upon herself that at the onset of TV hour she would, without my consent, and for the first time ever, wheel me right up next to Polina's wheelchair so close together that our elbows touched, skin-to-skin, closer than ever, and leave me there to drown in whatever storm erupted.

Reader, please understand this: this was the first time I ever had non-nurse epidermal contact with anyone at all, let alone Polina. I was completely unprepared, and consequently my pee pole jumped to full attention, twitched to the rhythm of my escalating pulse, and pushed the fabric of my shorts taut,

Now, it may be difficult for you to imagine a mutant with one arm to harbor any trace of self-consciousness. But please believe me when I tell you that this was my most horrifying twenty-two seconds on record. I instinctively used my one flailing arm to conceal the protrusion in any way possible, but this only brought more attention to the situation. As artfully as possible, I tucked my *Hui* between the nubs that would have been my legs and clenched them together to keep it hidden. I waited several painful moments for the fallout to die down. I was red and sopping with sweat. But this didn't keep Polina from speaking.

"Natalya told me."

I just sat silently and sweat some more.

"Ivan, are you okay?"

"I like your hair, Polina."

"It's a wig, Ivan."

The next hour was an incandescent blur. A hazy smear of conversation that I do not remember but only know resulted in a phase transition in my life and Polina's. From that moment on, we talked through most TV hours and met after lights-out for shenanigans and banter and anything else that might make us feel less lonely. We began by discussing the weather and eventually moved on to our pet peeves and then to our preferred methods of paying rent if we had another chance. Nurse Natalya, of course, was thrilled by our brewing courtship and did everything possible to cultivate it. She raided the homes of her relatives for old Russian games. Then she would secretly wheel us out to the Main Room after lights-out and let us play unchaperoned. Looking back through diminishing vodka eyes, these nights seem so perfectly surreal. Reader, in that place, at that time, Polina wasn't dying, and I wasn't a mutant. We shed our bodies and met in another place.

DAY 20

The Day We Contributed to Max's Rearing

I spent the night after the day that I found out that Polina was going to die considering everything that I would like to do with her before she would be committed to the Red Room. Because I believed we had three months together, the initial list was rather long and included such activities as playing hide-and-seek, sampling Central American coffees (most notably Guatemalan), beholding the Siberian auroras, playing the famed American game truth-or-dare (which often leads to erotic play), composing a song together using the guitar and the piano, visiting Paris and in particular the Eiffel Tower, cooking saag paneer for Nurse Natalya, swimming with dolphins, visiting Nabokov's grave, making out under a waterfall, riding an elephant, having sex on a water bed, making a snowball taller than both of us, inventing a new color that's never been seen before, surfing waves in the Maldives, climbing mountains in Central Africa, feeding a giraffe, getting our palms read by a convincing charlatan, visiting a real bona fide carnival freak show, sleeping on a beach overnight (without a tent), singing karaoke in Chinatown or Little Korea, or any other Asian-town, having sex in an elevator, skiing (both on snow and on water), riding a cable car in San Francisco, having multiple children and naming them after where they were conceived (like Madagascar,

Middlesex, or Malcolm), having sex on a rooftop (preferably under some form of precipitation), eating lobster in Baja, California, and dressing up in priest-and-nun garb before driving to the beach to make out.

When the list was finally finished, I put down my pen and looked at the clock. It was 4:00 in the A.M. I put my head down and daydreamed for another hour until I seamlessly slipped into sleep. Life was black until Nurse Natalya knocked considerately on my door.

"Ivan, are you up?"

"I am now."

"Can I come in?"

"I suppose."

She stepped inside and closed the door behind her. Then she slowly walked to my bed and sat down where my legs would have been if I had them. Her head and mouth looked like they were overflowing with things to say.

"Are you in love?"

"Sometimes you ask all the wrong questions."

She smiled, and I forced an insincere one back.

"Go ahead and ask then," she said.

"Ask what?"

"If you don't like my questions, then ask one."

"What happened when you told her?"

"She blubbered like a baby."

"Is there anything I can do?"

"There's always something you can do."

And then we didn't need to say anything else. She stood up, adjusted her scrubs, and exited, while I peed and slithered into my clothing. Two minutes later, I had some pungent cabbage in front of my face and no Polina across the table. I rushed through my food and hunted down Nurse Natalya, who was cleaning a toilet.

"Where is she?"

"They doubled her chemo. They're hoping for a miracle," she said as she scrubbed dried hairs from the base of the toilet. This meant that Polina was too sick to eat. Also, that Nurse Natalya did not believe in this type of miracle. Also, after seventeen years at the asylum, I still don't know who "they" are, as there are almost never any doctors here.

I considered retreating back to my room to masturbate and fall asleep until dinner, except it occurred to me that her fugue might give me time to plan a rendezvous. So I pulled out my list, which was already stained with Vaseline and cabbage juice, and read through my plans for the next three months. Given the severity of Polina's current chemico-gastro-upheaval, I decided to abandon this particular list and start smaller. I wheeled myself into the Main Room, where thirteen hypnotized patients were watching TV with gaping mouths, and the gingers were tangled up in a yoga move I like to call *lesbiyanki v sumerkakh.** I parked myself next to our mutant bookshelf and scanned for my favorite book by Theodore Geisel, which happens to be *Slon Khorton Vysizhivaet Iaitso.*† It was old and ragged after approximately fifty-seven years of illiterate-mutant abuse. Still, I tucked it

---

* "Lesbians at dusk."

† The Russian translation of the Dr. Seuss book *Horton Hatches the Egg.*

under my ass and finished out TV hour like all the other misfits.

I waited through the morning and returned to the cafeteria for lunch, hoping she would have worked up some hunger by then. She had not. Then into the Main Room for post-lunch TV hour. Still, no Polina. Then again for dinner, *Slon Khorton Vysizhivaet Iaitso* still tucked beneath my rear side. Then to the Main Room for the post-dinner TV hour, where I sat through fifty wretched minutes of *Chetyre tankista i sobaka*, after which Polina, looking like the world's most exquisite zombie, finally showed her face. My lips prepared to make words, which she must have noticed, because she preemptively said:

"I'm fine."

In response, my lips began to gather themselves again, to which she repeated:

"Yes, Ivan, I'll be okay."

To which I sat confused for a moment, and slightly deflated, and then said:

"How did you know that I was going to ask if you were okay? Maybe I was going to ask you about quicksand and why they call it that if you sink slowly. And why didn't you stop me before this sentence that I'm saying right now?"

"After my parents died, people have asked if I'm okay more times than all the other times people have ever asked that question in the entire lifetime of the universe. Faces look a certain way just before that question."

This didn't occur to me because people rarely ask me if I'm okay.

"Have you met Max?" I asked.

"I've only met you. And hardly."

As she spoke, I noticed how much thinner her face had become, and how much paler her skin was, and how she had gone back to being bald, which I interpreted as a step back in our rapport building, or maybe a step forward because it signaled a certain comfort, or maybe it meant none of these things at all. Then I turned my head to the TV because I felt like I was looking at her for too long, but was also entirely not sure about what I wanted to say next. *Nu, Pogodi!* was on the black-and-white TV.

"Do you like cartoons?" I asked.

"They're okay," she said.

Her words were short and curt and distracted, which made me think that she was fighting back the contents of her stomach. I wasn't worried because there couldn't have been much in there.

"I want to show you something," I said.

"Later, I hope."

Because I felt like it was the right thing to do, I didn't say anything to Polina for the rest of *Nu, Pogodi!* or for the remaining time it took for Nurse Elena to clear out the mutants and return them to their rooms for lights-out. I didn't say anything again until Nurse Elena told us to go to sleep. That's when I told Polina to follow me, and I rotated myself in the direction of the elevators, which I activated. Then I clicked the button for the third floor, which was the floor of the Yellow Room. Polina was lagging, so I held the door open for her by repeatedly hitting the button with the two arrows facing away from each other, which was the most masculine thing I had ever done for someone until that moment, which inflated me like a sage grouse.

"Where are we going?"

"A surprise."

And besides those words, the elevator ride was silent. When the doors opened, I held the button and motioned for Polina to go first, then I followed. Then I led her down the long, dark, post-lights-out hallway, into the Yellow Room, which was also dark except for small flickering lights, which, I remember, reminded me of small nocturnal critters hiding in an African savannah.

Polina said, "I've never been up here," with the faintest trace of thrill, leading me to believe that she felt approximately alive. Then she turned on the lights herself, as if she'd been here a million times. Without saying anything, I wheeled my way over to Max's manger, and Polina followed. I reached over the low barriers and pinched his toes, which was the signal I developed to let him know that it was me. His eyes moved to mine in his endearingly rigid and panic-struck way. Then I looked over at Polina, right in her own eyes, which I never did, and noticed that they were filling up.

"What's wrong with him?" she asked.

I said, "I think it's called arthrogryposis multiplex congenita."

Which, of course, actually came out something like "arfogypsos mootopex cogeta," because I'm not good at English and because my facial muscles were never meant to speak medical jargon.

"But how do you know?" Polina asked.

"I asked Nurse Katya, who takes care of him, but she didn't know. Then I asked Nurse Natalya, and she didn't know either, but she brought me his file, which only said 'congenital deformation,' which just means that he was born with something messed up with him. Then I asked her what was messed up, and she said that she already said that she didn't know. So she gave me her books from nursing school to figure it out."

"Can he talk?"

"No."

Polina reached her arm into the cradle and touched Max's face, then traced her fingers over the full length of his sickle-like shape, and then back to his tiny clenched fingers, which she held between her thumb and index finger.

"Sometimes I read to him," I said.

I removed the book from my posterior.

"'Sighed Mayzie, a lazy bird hatching an egg: "I'm tired and I'm bored. . . ."'"

I felt uncomfortable reading in front of Polina, because it highlighted my droopy voice. This prompted me to look up over the words as I read.

"'"And I've kinks in my leg from sitting, just sitting here day after day.

"'"It's work! How I hate it! I'd much rather play . . ."

And I could see Polina was just crooning to Max with a sequence of oohs that I could not connect to any particular song but was probably the melody to something written in the '80s, which made me feel relieved because I'm sure she could barely hear me read:

" ' "I'd take a vacation, fly off for a rest,

" ' "if I could find someone to stay on my nest!" ' "

And she sang and petted the panic-stricken child, like the cherub I'd projected onto her when she'd first walked into this hospital.

" 'Then Horton, the Elephant, passed by her tree.

" ' "Hello!" called the lazy bird, smiling her best,

" ' "You've nothing to do and I do need a rest.

" ' "Would you like to sit on the egg in my nest?" ' "

I understood Polina's fixation, which connected us for a few seconds. For her, this was a momentary time warp to a future she knew she'd never have. A chance to touch, for even a moment, her entire purpose for living at all.

" ' "Me on your egg? Why, that doesn't make sense . . .

" ' "Your egg is so small, ma'am, and I'm so immense!" ' "

The Oedipal tones of an impending lost motherhood.

And as soon as this thought occurred to me, I saw one shiny streak drip down Polina's porcelain cheek, which momentarily magnified her beauty mark as it passed.

Then she turned to me and said, "I want to read now."

I handed her the book, and Polina started reading in her exaggerated maternal tones. She slipped right into a Seussian rhythm, like she was born for this sort of thing, which felt momentarily unfair given the circumstances.

And I just sat back and quietly watched as she got lost in the pages and forgot that I was in the room, which didn't bother me.

That night, we both fell asleep next to Max, until the beeps of his heart monitor woke me up. I couldn't bring myself to wake her up, so I quietly wheeled myself back to my room and let her sleep next to the baby.

Game Night

I awoke the next morning in a state of "holy shit!" and also to the metallic rapping of Nurse Natalya knocking at my door. "Ten minutes left for breakfast hour, Ivan," she said, resonating through the metal like a robot version of herself.

"All right, all right," I said.

"Three times in one week, Ivan?"

"All right, all right," I said.

"Can I come in? I have something for you," she said.

My mind has been Pavlovianly conditioned to salivate when Nurse Natalya comes to my room with any somethings. Typically, the somethings are books, but I had a feeling, given the circumstances, that this particular something might be something even better.

"Yes, please."

Nurse Natalya entered with a large plastic white bag and tossed it onto my bed.

"This is all I have, Ivan. I haven't used them in years."

I opened the bag and started pulling out box after box, each one an edition of a game, most of which I had never heard of, with odd names like *Underwood*, *The Hat*, *Pantomime*, *The Victory Day*, *Backgammon*, and *Great Hooduu*.

"Look at this," she said. "This is Monopoly. I bought it when I visited New York. Twenty years ago, we would have been detained by the Committee for State Security* for owning this capitalist smut," she said.

"So I've been rotting in this dreary hospital for eighteen years, and all the while you've been hoarding these games?"

"And who were you going to play with, Ivan?"

"You, for one."

"Stop being so dramatic. You were too buried in your books to play games with an old lady. You stopped playing chess with me ten years ago."

"Only because you're wretched at it."

"My point."

"I get to keep these?"

"Long-term borrow."

"And the ginger twins don't get to play with them?" I asked.

Nurse Natalya scoffed and waved her hand dismissively.

I started sorting out the boxes on my bed into various categories according to the details listed on the side of the box and almost forgot that Nurse Natalya was still in the room until she started booming on about only five minutes left for breakfast hour, to which I asked:

"Is she there?"

"No, and she won't be anymore. Not in the morning, anyway—6:00 A.M. dose."

---

* The English translation for the Russian agency otherwise known as the KGB.

"I will be fine without breakfast today," I said.

I found a colorfully stained napkin and a nearly dead pen next to my bed. Then I scribbled some words in my atrocious handwriting. Then I wheeled myself to Polina's room and slipped the napkin under her door.

I waited patiently throughout the day, extraordinarily aware of every ticktock of every clock in every room in the hospital (despite the limited funding and technology at this hospital, there were a frustrating number of clocks). I took a few bites at lunch hour and a few more during dinner hour. I made an appearance in the Main Room for various TV hours, wandered the halls like a ghost unsure of its destination, and made several trips to the community bathroom, all of which were veiled (and failed) attempts to locate Polina, which I largely expected, given the fact that she was likely huddled over the toilet in her room with fluids coming out of both ends of her body.

On this particular day, Nurse Natalya was in charge of distributing food during dinner hour. As she pulled small pieces of unidentified meats from what looked too much like a bucket, I stopped her.

"Have you seen her today?" I asked.

"I heard her howling into a toilet," she said, and she returned to rationing out boiled meat.

Hearing this incited the voice inside my head to begin to mentally prepare me for the possibility that everything would not go as planned. I had become extremely familiar with this automated defense system over the years. It said things such as *You know you'd rather be in your room masturbating,*

Ivan, or *Girls are unapologetically uninteresting,* or *She's going to die in a minute anyway.*

As the voice finished making a rather compelling case for remaining unfazed, I returned to my room, where I pulled three books out from under my bed: *The Pathological Basis of Disease* by Gustav Stein (Russian translation by Kierkegaard Polov), *The Molecular Biology of Cancer* by Mark Roman (Russian translation by Sergei Ilikov), and *Genetics: Analysis and Principles* by Robert Brooker (Ukrainian translation by Vladimir Medvedev). These were the only books Nurse Natalya never sold from her nursing school days, and in a place where self-diagnosis is an essential means of survival, they were vital to my personal library.

I decided to spend the remainder of the night prior to rendezvous hour reading up on why chemotherapy causes people to experience bouts of vomiting and explosive stool. According to Roman (page 342), cancer cells reproduce like Australian bunnies, and the chemicals in a chemo cocktail kill rapidly reproducing cells. Unfortunately, the cells that line human stomachs and intestines also fit into this category and become collateral damage.

At 8:50 in the P.M., I put the book down, got into my chair, collected chess, *Pantomime,* and a deck of cards (variety is the spice of life, according to my mother) and rolled down to the Main Room, which was empty of nurses and mutants but illuminated by an oil lamp and about twelve candles, clearly lit by Nurse Natalya, who actually had no intention of doing this as a kindness but rather as a charming joke designed to make my nubs squirm. I panicked and began blowing out every candle, which is difficult due to my limited lung capacity. When I got to the oil lamp, I made the strategic decision to leave it on, since the alternative (hospital lighting) made me slightly nauseous, much like blood, sloppy eating, and the Red Room. Then I writhed out of my chair, grabbed the first box from my bag, which happened to be chess, and started placing the plastic pieces onto the board, but quickly decided against this after my mother appeared and told me that Polina probably wouldn't want to think that hard after vomiting consistently for the better part of her day. So I threw all the plastic pieces back into the bag and pulled out *Pantomime* before realizing that I didn't actually know how to play, which inspired me to speed-read through the instructions at high velocity before my mother appeared again and said, "T-minus fifty seconds, Ivan. You can't learn this game in fifty seconds. Just play it safe with the cards," at which point I frantically rummaged through the bag, pulled out the deck of cards, and began dealing them into two *Durak* piles.

After the last card was put into its pile, I thought exactly two thoughts. The first thought was *How pitiful if in thirty minutes from now I find myself sitting out here alone doused in oil lamp lighting, with cards dealt and no Polina?* The second thought was *How can a game of cards ever compete with a slow leukemic demise, which left her weak, tired, irritable, and in a constant state of anti-vomit concentration?* The joint effort of both of these thoughts caused me to abort. I quickly messed up the piles and started putting the cards away, which was just in time for Polina to wheel herself into the room asserting (somewhat joyfully):

"I haven't played cards since I've been here."

Which resulted in the involuntary reflex of pretending to be dealing the cards rather than putting them away.

"*Durak*?" she asked.

"Yes."

"How do I know you're not cheating?"

"You don't."

"You know it's bad karma to let a dying girl win?"

"I would never."

As I said this, I placed our last card, and as I placed our last card, I looked up at Polina for the first time that night. Even in the forgiving light of Nurse Natalya's oil lamp, I could see the bruises slowly climbing up Polina's arms and onto her face.

"Stop staring and pick up your cards."

I did.

"Attack," she said.

I played my first card with my hand while inside my head I was fumbling around for conversation given this particular set of circumstances (i.e., Polina is getting sicker and sicker, so sick in fact that she can't show her face but for a few minutes at night, so sick that she can't keep down a few bites of cabbage, so sick that she . . .). And then out of the silence:

"Play your card, Ivan."

"Is it hard to get up in the morning?" I asked.

"That's your best card?" she asked, which I'm almost sure

was rhetorical, because then she threw her cards down and destroyed our piles.

"This is how it works: we don't talk about it."

I nodded through the oil light and shadows.

"I'm dealing this time," she said.

Polina slowly collected her body up and out of her wheelchair and started picking up the cards, which by now were strewn across the cold linoleum and diffused to almost every corner of the Main Room. I writhed around the floor wormlike as best I could to collect a few myself and handed them back to her. Then she sat back down across from me and started dealing the cards, during which time we were both quiet because I could feel the residue of her anger. This lasted well into the first hand of the game. Polina was first to break the silence.

"I thought about you today," she said.

And for the tiniest part of a second I was flooded with a wave of euphoria until she continued:

"Intellectually, I understand why you should be so odd. I would be strange if I were trapped in this hellhole for a year, let alone however long you've been here. But you are levels of strange I've never met, and I've met strange. Mostly prostitutes and derelicts in Moscow."

She said all this without taking her eyes off her cards.

"Not sure I have anything to compare me to," I said.

"Well, you're weird. Devastatingly weird. With no appreciation for social rules of any kind. Which makes you both weird and an idiot," she said.

Luckily for Polina, I was enjoying the abuse.

"You're being a prick to me because you're dying," I said.

"Fuck you, Ivan," she said.

"Really?" I asked.

"Never," she said.

"Furthermore, you're being a prick to me because I'm safe to be a prick to and there's no one else here that you can safely be a prick with at the moment. So, actually, I find it endearing. Prick away."

"Does it makes you feel big to know things?"

"It makes me feel even bigger to know I'm right."

"You're wrong."

"I've lived it already."

"Lived what?"

"Lived being a prick to anyone who is willing to smile at me. So go ahead. Get it out."

"Okay. Besides being a social idiot, I think you're disgusting to look at. But what's worse is that you will never have an authentic relationship because it will always be out of pity."

"Too bad there's no one left to pity *you*."

As soon as the words left my mouth, I knew I'd broken all the rules and immediately tried to suck them back in. This was not how this game worked. I wasn't supposed to hit back; I was supposed to absorb and imbibe until there was nothing left but trust.

Polina set her cards back down, quietly, coldly, indifferently, and wheeled herself away.

"I'm sorry," I said.

But, of course, it didn't matter.

The Nothing Day

On the eighteenth day, I ate breakfast, watched three episodes of *Nu, Pogodi!* (none of which I actually remember), masturbated twice (possibly three times), organized my three pairs of socks, read eighty-eight pages of *Les Misérables,* spent two hours catatonic, another two sleeping, read seventeen pages of *Love in the Time of Cholera* (imagining that I was Florentino Ariza), helped Nurse Natalya fold laundry (mentioned the candles), practiced holding my breath for over three minutes, practiced a card trick I read about in a book of magic from 1933, and considered how the *DSM* might diagnose Van Gogh if he lived today. At no point on the eighteenth day did I see Polina. According to Nurse Natalya, she was busy getting her first blood transfusion and then some more chemotherapy.

Stars and Stairwells

I woke up on day seventeen at about 6:58 in the A.M., checked my body parts, and slithered across the cold linoleum floor to empty my pee bag. Only this time on my squirm to the toilet, I found four pieces of paper scattered around my door.

I read each one and then rearranged them into their most probable order. The first one read, *You awake?*, the second one said, *Forgive me?*, the third, *I'm still here . . .* , and the fourth, *Fourth floor, stairwell, lights-out, tomorrow.*

As every day is exactly the same, there is really no point in sharing the details leading up to the moment, probably 10:01 in the P.M., when I pushed through the non-cripple-friendly double steel door leading into the fourth-floor stairwell, which was, incidentally, the top floor of the hospital, to find Polina sitting on the highest step without her chair and doodling in her journal. Behind her there was a red steel ladder leading up to a red door, which opened up to the roof. There also happened to be a long white bedsheet dangling from the opening.

"I'm done with the chair, so don't ask," she said while bouncing up and stuffing her journal into the ass section of her sweatpants. "Did you know this existed?" she asked.

"Yes," I said.

And I did. If I were to issue my best guess, I'd say I spent approximately five hundred hours sitting underneath this door pondering the engineering required for me to make it up the ladder and through the hole with one arm and no legs.

"Have you been up there recently?" she asked.

"Have you looked at me recently?" I replied.

"Yes, I have actually. Which is why I made you a mechanism."

"A mechanism?"

"Yes, a mechanism."

"All I see is a bedsheet."

"A bedsheet and a pulley," she said.

Which is when I realized it was in fact a bedsheet plus a wheelchair wheel, which she was using as a pulley-like device (and also explained the absence of her wheelchair).

"You only need to hold on," she said.

"Hold on with what?" I asked.

"With your hand."

Then we both synchronistically looked down at my three fingers.

"That won't be a problem," she said, and then she produced a roll of state-approved medical gauze.

"Where did you find that?"

"Behind Miss Kristina's desk."

Inspiration and zealot-like fervor: *DSM*'s diagnostic criteria for a manic state.

A manic state: *DSM* diagnostic criterion for bipolar disorder.

Then my mother appeared just behind Polina to say: *Try not to judge. Death brings out the manic in the best of us.*

"You're going to tie me to this sheet?" I asked for further clarification.

"I'm going to tie you, *and* you're going to hold on with all your fingers."

"No," I said.

"Come here," she said, and I obeyed, rolling out of my chair, onto the ground, and writhing my way over to the sheet dangling from the roof.

"Hold this to your chest," she said, pressing the white linen to my T-shirt, which I did, and when I did, she started wrapping my body to the sheet, possibly twenty or thirty revolutions worth, at which point I said, "I think that's enough." Then she added two more for good measure.

"Hold on," she said, which I did, eventually, but my nubs left the ground before she finished the directive. My first thought was that it looked entirely too easy for her to pull down handful after handful of sheet, which made me feel approximately emasculated. But I let it go after I remembered my second thought, which was that Polina recently had to endure vomiting all over herself in my presence just a few days ago. So I attempted some relaxation techniques I'd read about in a book on managing stress and let my head fall back while watching the night sky get steadily closer through the hole in the roof. This was the first time I'd ever seen the sky at night, and I was, to be candid, surprised that stars twinkle just like the songs say.

By the time I finished thinking this last thought, I found myself in the precarious position of being eye to eye with the ceiling door with no more sheet above me.

"I can hold you for now, Ivan," Polina said. "But you're going to need to get your ass on the roof."

"But I only have one—"

"Blah, blah, blah. And I've had enough chemotherapy to kill Rasputin, which means you'd better pull yourself up, or I'm going to drop you like a dead baby."

My best guess would be four minutes. That's how long my one extremity fumbled around the opening in the roof in order to establish the leverage required to hoist myself the rest of the way up, while Polina held the sheet steady as she sweat, quivered, and verbally abused me from below. There were several moments when my head already decided to give up. But then my mother would show up for a moment to tell me stories of pregnant women lifting cars up off their trapped children, which inspired me to summon the pissed-off pregnant mother inside of me, who I truly believe lives in all of us.

I was probably on the roof for thirteen seconds before I realized that I was on the roof. It took hearing Polina's voice to pull me back into reality.

"How is it up there?"

Instead of answering, I decided to take the sky in for the first time and also peel the thirty revolutions of gauze from my torso.

"Ivan, say something."

I heard her feet climbing the metal rungs of the ladder.

"I'm okay."

"Good," she said as her shiny bald head popped out of the opening. She took a moment to drink in the night sky with me before continuing:

"I grew up in Lviv, where there is too much light in the city to see the stars at night. Thank sweet baby Jesus of Bethlehem for piece-of-shit Mazyr."

I was too stuck on the stars to respond.

"*Blin!** My little Ivan, you've never seen the night sky before, have you?"

"Yes, I have."

---

* Literally translated as "Pancake!" but the connotation is "Shit!"

"But only through your window."

"That is accurate."

"No one would take you?"

"No."

"Not even Natalya?"

"She would. She asked once. She actually asked more than once."

"And?"

"And I said no."

"Why?"

"I don't know."

"Ivan, of course you know!"

And I did. We both knew that I knew.

"You're afraid," she said.

"Of what?"

"Of everything."

"It makes no sense to be afraid of anything, let alone everything."

"It doesn't mean you aren't."

To which I didn't respond, because I didn't know what to say, which led Polina to break the uncomfortable silence:

"Well, I graciously accept the award for taking your virgin flower."

I spit out a reflexive laugh, which caused Polina to spit one out too. Then we sat quietly, without saying anything to each other for the next twenty minutes, which was nice, though Polina eventually talked again.

"My mother and father were so different. My mother refused to believe in anything she couldn't see, and my father dreamed all the time. The sky reminds me of him. He was addicted to astrology. He explained every quirk and idiosyncrasy in everyone we met with the stars. He said that when he was a boy, he and his family spent a summer in Tallinn, because Chechnya was not safe. One night, he took a walk and met a Gypsy selling okra and cucumbers. She made a deal with him. She said, 'If I tell you three things that will happen to you in the next three days and they all come true, will you come back here on the fourth day?' And he agreed."

"What were the three things?"

"On the first day, she said, it would rain tarantulas from the sky, but aside from being a bit foul, he had nothing to worry about, since tarantula bites are not dangerous in themselves, and weather has a soul of its own. On the second day, she said, he would hear a droning hum for most of the morning, but, again, not to be afraid of it because it was there to repair his unconscious. And on the third day, everything would appear normal until he found himself, mysteriously, in a completely different place, disoriented, with no explanation of how he got there, but still he shouldn't be afraid because it meant that he transcended time and space."

"All of them came true?"

"No, none of them."

"Then why are you telling me the story?"

"Because I left out the best part."

"What's the best part?"

"He went back on the fourth day to berate the Gypsy, but when he got there, the Gypsy was laughing so hard she couldn't breathe, screaming, 'Oh, Russian boys!' between gasps of air. My father said it took her so long to calm down that he lost his patience and tried to leave, but she lured him back with some baklava."

"And?"

"And he stayed. And they talked every day."

"I don't believe in astrology."

"I don't either. But I do believe in stars. Astrology is concept. Stars are just stars."

I wasn't sure what she meant, but I didn't want to seem like an idiot by asking her to clarify, so I nodded and went back to looking at the sky.

"I was born on April 5," she said.

"Aries."

"What do you know about Aries?"

"Really?"

"Yes."

"Nothing."

"Aries want to be the center of the universe. Someone like you would say that's because I'm an only child. And that may be true. But that's not the only way I make the perfect Aries. I'm loud, and I'm in love with life. Or at least I used to be before I got sick. It's hard to love life anymore."

Her eyes moved from me back to the stars.

"When were you born, Ivan?" she asked.

"I don't know."

"You don't know when you were born?"

"No."

Polina was silent for a few seconds, and I remember her eyes looked calm and gentle like she was trying to be careful with me, which, incidentally, was not very Aries of her. Then in her most high-pitched, academic, nasally voice, she said:

"Ivan, could you tell me more about that?" which sounded entirely too much like Dr. Boulatnikov, our current resident psychologist. And with those words, Polina accidentally pushed the button inside my brain that was responsible for releasing all the laughter that was ever held inside but never allowed out. It started with innocent enough burps. And then a river of thick saliva started running down my chin and pooled onto my lap, which made me laugh harder, which instigated Polina to laugh too, which brought the feedback loop to the next level, which made me lose control of my proprioception, which made me roll all over the cold cement of the rooftop. I lost the ability to breathe. I was gasping for air, tears streaming down my face, begging for Polina to make it stop, somewhat aware that I was in the process of laughing out all the absurdity, and all the isolation, and all my grievances against the universe in one spastic, uncontrollable fit. And eventually, Polina was scared.

"Ivan!" she yelled while cradling my tiny spasming body. "It wasn't *that* funny."

I tried to say words back to her, but I was too busy trying to breathe.

"Ivan, what? What are you trying to say? Calm the fuck down," she said while slapping my cheeks repeatedly. Her face looked stuck between panic and not falling back into the pit of laughter I was stuck in. Still, she had the presence of mind to hold my head off the concrete and wipe the tears off my face.

Eventually I could say, "I never laughed like that before."

"Not once?"

"I practiced in the mirror, but never for real."

"Never?"

"It needed to happen."

As I looked up at her, it occurred to me that this was the moment when, if we were trapped inside of a TV set, we would have kissed, which is when, not coincidentally, she gently let my head back down to the concrete and slid a few inches back.

"Glad you didn't break your head," she said. "I'm too sick and tired to clean the blood."

To which I answered:

"I can answer your question."

"What question?"

"Why I don't know my birthday."

"I'm listening."

"I wrote it down. I can read it to you. Or you can read it."

"What?"

"Everything from my nonexistent birthday until three days ago."

"You wrote it for me?"

"It felt like the right thing to do after I stole your diary. I could keep you company while you get poisoned tomorrow."

"Is it depressing?"

"My story?"

"Yes."

"Of course."

"I'm not sure I can handle depressing while I'm being poisoned."

"Actually, it's a fairy tale, and I'm the boy version of Cinderella."

"You would need a foot to be Cinderella, Ivan."

Touché, Polina.

"That was mean, which means you owe me."

"No, I don't."

Those were her last words. I accepted her reticence, and she accepted my silence. Then we stared at the Milky Way until the urge to urinate forced me back inside.

Currently, the clock reads 2:58 in the A.M.
I've been writing for fifty-one hours.
It is the fifth day of December.
The year is 2005.

I slept for a few minutes.
It would have been longer if not for the
vodka having evaporated from my blood.
I shook the flask and heard a few drops rattling.
I drank all three of them and decided I needed more.
I knew the location of Elena's
hidden stash.
From the laundry chute,
I obtained an entire bottle, minus a few swigs.

The Retroactive Biography
of Ivan Isaenko

Click, check, repeat.

My internal alarm trumpeted. I checked my missing legs. I rolled off the bed. I slithered to the bathroom. I ignored the cold floor. I pissed myself dry. I slithered back. I mountaineered into my bed. I spread out a pair of shorts and a T-shirt. I wormed my way into both of them. I Tarzaned into my chair. I wheeled down to the cafeteria. I assumed my position. I checked Polina's empty seat. I let pungent cabbage juice drip from my chin. I quit after three bites, which is when Nurse Elena strolled by half-inebriated and said to me, "The sick girl wanted Natalya, but Natalya's not here. She gave me this."

Then she dropped a piece of paper, and it careened down half into my cabbage juice.

"Sick girl has a name," I said.

To which Elena did not respond.

So I said, "Polina."

To which she still did not respond, which forced me to whisper *bitch* under my breath while I read the piece of paper. It said, *Poison on high. Where are you?*

I crammed the note into my shorts, and the wheels on my chair started moving by themselves. They rolled themselves back to my room, where I pried out my retroactive diary from under the edge of my mattress and then crammed it under my ass. Then my wheels turned themselves around and started rolling down to the Orange Room, which is where people receive chemotherapy.

As I had expected, Polina was the lone chemo patient in the room, since all the leuks, lymphs, and brainers had died in the last year. She was sitting in her poison chair, sketching in her diary, with yellow morning sunlight splashing her from different directions, ricocheting off the orange walls, mixing with the peach of her skin and the purples of her bruising, and curving around the new curves made out of her newly exposed bones. She looked like an expressionist painting, possibly brushed by someone suitably insane like Munch or Marc or Kirchner.

I decided to stay quiet and roll in slowly and wait till she noticed me so that I could enjoy the candid view for as long as I could. This was easy, since the room was a veritable labyrinth of old, defunct, obsolete, or irrelevant medical equipment that easily concealed my meandering wheelchair. And as I rolled like a wheel-bound ninja, it occurred to me that Polina, as bald and bony as she was, made this room about as tolerable as it was capable of getting. And as I was lost in these thoughts, I collided with some gray machine or another, and Polina's startled head swung over to me and she reflexively yelled, "Please!" To which I agreed. Then I continued to weave myself through the equipment until my chair was next to hers. She was facing the outside window, where the sun was particularly new.

"You look okay," I said.

"I don't feel okay."

"What do you feel?"

"Like a mouse in a mousetrap just before it dies."

She smiled like she knew she was being dramatic and then looked down at the notebook I'd just removed from under the seat of my pants.

"Is that it?" she asked.

"Yes."

"Let's get on with it."

"I thought it was too depressing."

"I'm bored," she said.

"You must be," I said.

"Let me see it."

I handed the notebook over to her.

"You wrote all this?" she asked.

"Yes."

"In three days?"

"In one night."

She stopped talking for a few seconds and just fanned through the pages of what I'm sure appeared to be the handwriting of a young epileptic child living through a nonstop seizure.

"I was going to give it to you, but then you became a three-monther," I said.

"This is a first."

"What?"

"No one has ever written me a book."

"Obviously."

"Start."

She handed the book back, and I turned to the first page. The words started falling out of my mouth with the slow, extremely deliberate, and overly academic delivery that the loose muscles in my face could accommodate. I read to her about the anonymous doorstop drop-off and how that meant that I've never been anywhere else. I read that I never met my parents but that I do have a mother who is a Tinker Bell–like apparition that pops into my life primarily when I'm contemplating suicide or about to commit a social blunder. I read about how every nurse, Nurse Natalya included, is far too squirmy and twitchy when I bring up my origins for there not to be more to the story. I read to her about waking up to the universe with a slap in the face and colorful language coming from a woman with a fuzzy mole on her upper lip. I read to her about how so much of my life isn't real because it's spent asleep, but really awake, but not really awake. I read her the fifty faces I wear, which I'm sure really only look like one. I read about the full encyclopedia of my defense mechanisms, ranging from denial to dissociation to displacement (not to mention repression, rationalization, and regression). I read every flavor of self-harm that goes through my head. I read through my various options for escape and how I haven't the testicles for any of them. I read through the secret lives I've written for the Ivan I would be under any other set of circumstances. I read her the tenets of Ivanism. I read about how mad I am that He put such a big life into such a small, broken box. I read about being trapped with people just like me in every way except for the fact that they will never understand a thought that goes through my head. I read to her about my mistrust of karma. I read to her about my fourteen useless shrinks. I read about how none of it makes any sense, yet the little brain stuffed in all our heads needs things to make sense even though nothing makes sense. I read to her about her and about how when she arrived, things made a little more sense, and as soon as some sense was made for the first time, suddenly things stopped making sense because she became a three-monther. Sometimes I stuck to the script. Sometimes I stopped in between sentences to elaborate in order to accommodate the new level of rapport we had developed. Sometimes I paused to swallow a storm that was welling up my throat, which I blamed on a rare type of asthma. And not for one second of the whole confession did I dare look at her face for fear that I might shit my pants. I waited for the last sentence to be over before finally looking up, which, according to the clock on the Orange Room wall, came eighty-seven minutes after I started reading. And when I did look up at her face, I found that her cheeks were red, moist, and puffy despite her emaciated state.

"I would kill you myself if you even thought . . . ," she said slowly, on the cusp of a murmur, choking on some sympathies she clearly wasn't expecting.

"I would never."

"But you said—"

"I don't have the balls."

She was just close enough to touch my hand, which she did. Then she slowly moved her fingers around in little circles. This lasted for about seven seconds, until she said:

"From what I understand, you have quite active balls."

To which I said:

"Not really."

To which she said:

"I overheard them talking about your bedsheets."

To which I said:

"You're lying."

To which she said:

"How else would I know that the nurses have to replace them twice as often as every other patient's?"

And just as the repartee began to crescendo into its most playful state to date, her face changed into something frozen, as if one of her internal organs had exploded or she'd received a prophetic message that rapture would commence in T-minus five seconds and she wasn't yet quite right with the Big Guy.

"You should go," she said.

"But—"

"But you should go."

I wheeled out of the Orange Room.

I didn't see Polina anymore on the sixteenth day.

DAY 15

Polina's Magic School Bus

(Three days until lab results)

Stem cells live inside bones. Stem cells can turn into either a myeloid stem cell or a lymphoid stem cell. If a stem cell turns into a myeloid stem cell, it will eventually turn into a myeloid blast. Myeloid blasts can become either a red blood cell, which carries oxygen to the brain, or platelets, which make it so that we don't bleed to death when we get a paper cut. If a stem cell turns into a lymphoid stem cell, it becomes a white blood cell, which fights infections (and anything else that's not supposed to be in blood). When old white blood cells die, stem cells make new lymphoid stem cells, which turn into new white blood cells to take their place. I know this because that's how it works according to *The Basic Science of Oncology,* by Ian Tannock and Richard Hill, published in 1987 by the McGraw-Hill Companies.

I made Nurse Natalya find it for me on the fifteenth day. Not this book in particular but any book like it. She said she found it in Mikhail's personal library and that he would never miss it, because in twenty-three years of working at the Mazyr Hospital for Gravely Ill Children, she never once saw him touch a book. I made her find it after I rolled up to the Orange Room shortly after breakfast to find Polina in the midst of some combination of coughing and dry heaving while Nurse Natalya was catching the contents of her expulsion, which included a Pollock-esque mixture of mucus and blood. At some point, Nurse Natalya made the mistake of noticing me, which made Polina turn in suit, which inspired her to say, "Not now, Ivan. Go away."

Polina makes bad white blood cells. Her white blood cells are immortal and vampiric. They overpopulate her blood and clog up all her good blood cells, which slowly die. Polina needs new stem cells that don't make bad white blood cells. Then Polina would be okay.

Like most things in the universe, it's not that simple. First, Polina has to use chemotherapy to kill every white blood cell in her body because the poison can't tell the difference between the good guys and the bad guys. This approximately makes her an all-you-can-eat buffet for infections. Second, Polina's new white blood cells can only come from another person, and every person has antigens. Antigens tell the white blood cells which cells belong to the body and which do not. In other words, they tell the white blood cells who are the good guys and who are the bad guys. If a leukemia kid gets new bone marrow that doesn't match his old bone marrow, the old white blood cells will think that the new white blood cells are bad guys. Within days, all the white blood cells kill each other, and she's back to being an all-you-can-eat buffet. Polina needs stems cells that have her antigens. This is not easy. It's not easy because we live in Chernobyl-town, Belarus, the blood disease capital of the world, where bone marrow transplants are more common than dental office visits.

On the fifteenth day, I approached Nurse Natalya while she was disinfecting a windowsill.

"How long is the list now?" I asked.

Nurse Natalya stopped wiping away germs from the hard-to-reach area underneath the lip of the sill and put down her towel. This meant that I was about to hear something that I didn't want to hear.

"Thirty-three months," she said.

"But she only has three months, and that's only if she's lucky," I noted.

"The ones at the top of the list are the ones who have three days. Or the children of government ministers," she said.

According to Tannock and Hill, you get half of your antigens from your mom and half from your dad. Consequently, there is a 25 percent chance of finding a match in a sibling. According to Polina's journal, she was an only child. This left the rest of the Belarusian donor community, which was small and included a wide range of misfits, most of which already have their own colorful genetic fingerprints. The chance of finding a match in someone who is not a sibling is about 3 percent.

"What do I need to do to get tested?" I asked.

"No, Ivan."

"Why not?"

"It's not a good idea."

"Hypothetically."

"I would need your blood. And some cheek cells."

"That's easy. Test me."

"You're not the gambling type."

"Today I am."

"It would take a Saint Christopher–type miracle."

"Could she catch anything from me?"

"Like what?"

"Like what's wrong with me."

"Probably not."

"Then test me."

Nurse Natalya looked over my face, breathed out all the air in her lungs, and made a calculation. She calculated that there was no amount of arguing in this particular situation that would convince me to quit. When she was done calculating, her body surrendered, and she wheeled me into one of the supply rooms on the second floor, where she pulled out a needle and easily inserted it into a vein, possibly without even looking, mostly because my skin is like peach-colored plastic. Then she jammed a piece of cotton in my mouth, violently swabbed the inside of my cheek, and put everything in a plastic bag, which she then put into a brown envelope.

"The lab will take three days," she said. "Or three weeks. It all depends."

"On what?"

"On the moon."

"She can't wait that long."

"I can't change the laws of physics or laboratory wait times, Ivan."

Then she knelt down to me so that our faces were close together.

"I know how you are."

"How am I?"

"You're rationally irrational."

"What does that mean?"

"It means you get hopeful even when there's no hope."

I chose to ignore this comment.

"How was she when you left?"

"Coughing. Badly. With a forty-degree fever."

"Pneumonia?"

"Yes. Probably."

Symptom #7 on my diagnostic criteria for a leukemia three-monther. Her white blood cells are too beaten up to stand up to a pimple, let alone a type-A flu virus. See above.

"Wasn't she vaccinated?"

"It's November, Ivan. There are no vaccinations."

Which was true. They typically ran out the first week of October—well before winter.

"Don't tell her anything," I said.

"About what?" she asked.

"About testing me."

"You don't want her to know?"

"No."

"Why?"

"Reasons."

I know I didn't have to tell her because I knew she would read the reasons right out of my brain, only to smile once, hug me twice, and then wheel me back out to the Main Room for evening TV hour, which I hated because it made me feel helpless, but I know it made her feel helpful, so I let her. As soon as she dropped me off and her chubby little frame was out of sight, I rolled my way to the drinking fountains, which really was just so that I could pass the Orange Room and see what was happening inside. Polina was asleep in her chair with the bag of drugs dangling above her in its last throes. There was a luminous river of saliva flowing from her lips to her collarbone, which was now chiseled like a Greco-Roman sculpture. Then I forgot all about the drinking fountain and went back to the Main Room to finish watching an episode of *Nu, Pogodi!* while actually not watching any of it.

DAY 14

The Janis Joplin Day

(Two days until lab results)

The next morning, most of the patients living at the Mazyr Hospital for Gravely Ill Children and I were woken by the sounds of Polina coughing out several of her thoracic organs from her room in the girls' wing clear across the hospital.

I dressed early and stole some dextromethorphan from one of the supply closets, as well as some individually wrapped honey packets from the cafeteria, wheeled myself to Polina's room, and slid them under the door. For a moment, the coughing stopped. Then the configuration of shadows spilling from under Polina's door danced a bit.

"Take the medicine first, then the honey," I whispered.

"Thanks," she whispered back. "Water, please?"

"I can't pass that under the door. Use your spit."

"I'm out of spit."

I heard her swallowing, then coughing, then wrestling with the packet of honey.

"You didn't even ask what it is," I whispered.

"It doesn't matter," she whispered back. "It can't make me worse."

"Okay, I'm going now," I said.

"Wait. Don't go."

"Okay."

"Let's talk today."

"Okay."

"But not right now. Later. Because I don't feel good."

"I'm vaccinated, so yes."

"Okay. Now you can go."

I turned my chair around and then:

"Ivan, wait!"

"What?"

"Can you do me a favor?"

"Yes."

"There is a record in the second drawer down in the cabinet behind the front desk. Can you get that and slide it under my door too?"

"But you don't have a record player."

"Yes, I do."

"You do?"

"I do."

"Natalya?"

"Yes."

"Okay."

"Wait, Ivan."

"Yes?"

"Thank you."

"Okay."

I wheeled my way over to the front desk and pushed my way inside the area I was never supposed to go since the Incident, and then to the cabinet where I dutifully opened the second drawer down and found an old ten-inch record mixed in with about two hundred sheets of medical records and accounting. I dropped it into my lap, rolled back to Polina's room, and slipped it under her door.

I heard her whisper:

"What would I do without you?"

This question, I realized, was rhetorical, so I simply said:

"You would get it yourself."

To which Polina laughed acutely, like a belch.

As I rolled back to my room, in the midst of the unique morning light wrestling its way through the barred windows on the Main Room, it occurred to me that the day was November 8, which meant it was the second week of November, which meant that Nurse Natalya no longer worked nights, which meant that Nurse Lyudmila, the only nurse who really instilled a sociopath-like fear in me, was working, which meant that if we were caught together after lights-out, we risked quarantine or worse, which seemed like a ridiculous thing for one dead person and another almost dead person to have to worry about, but a valid concern nevertheless. After breakfast hour, I found Nurse Natalya sterilizing some previously used syringes and made her aware of my dilemma.

"What can be done?" I asked.

"Nothing."

"Nothing!"

"Nothing."

"Can't you tell her that you approved it?"

"Do you like having me be your nurse?"

Another rhetorical question, so I stayed silent.

"Then I can't," she said. "You and I both know that Mikhail is pathological about his rules. I only broke them because I could. If Lyudmila wanted, I could be at another hospital. We both know that too."

"But you've worked here ten more years than her."

"But she's fucking Mikhail."

Which was the first time Nurse Natalya admitted that fact in words. Also, Nurse Natalya rarely uses such colorful language.

"Just don't get caught," she said, and the conversation was over.

I decided to time my ride to Polina's room at 11:30 in the P.M., which was typically the time that Mikhail's family was sleeping deeply enough for him to slip out of his house unnoticed, return to his office, and get lascivious with Nurse Lyudmila. Typically, the wheelchair ride to Polina's room takes about ninety seconds. Tonight, it took six minutes and eight seconds, due to the ninja-like stealth that I employed while making the trip undetected. There were momentary lapses where the natural excitement of the moment had me rolling at speeds that created an audible hiss, but when this happened, my mother appeared and said, "They probably can't hear you over Lyudmila's hideous wailing, but you should still be careful, Ivan." To which I nodded and lowered my velocity to inaudible levels and held steady all the way to Polina's door.

I was about to knock, but the door opened up before my knuckle ever had a chance to hit the wood, revealing a wigless Polina.

"Come in. You're late. I almost went to sleep."

"It's because Lyudmila is working."

"So?"

"So, she hates me. And probably you too. She hates everybody, except for Mikhail, who she fucks, and most probably she is fucking him right now."

"You know about that?"

"Of course I know. You know about that?"

"They don't even try to hide it."

"True."

"I'm going to play some music."

This is when I noticed that Polina had a pile of records spread over her bed, which she was sifting through.

"Playing music is exactly what we should not be doing at this particular moment if we don't want to be quarantined."

"I will play it low," she said. "And like you said, she's fucking Mikhail."

At which point, Mother arrived to say, "I'm all for setting the right mood on this date, but you need to be the voice of reason in this situation."

"Very low," I said.

That was the first time I didn't listen to my mother.

Eventually, Polina settled on a record, placed it delicately on the turntable, and set the needle. Someone started singing, but I couldn't tell if it was a boy or a girl.

"Is this Floyd Pink?" I asked because it was the only name of a singer that I could recall in my head at that particular moment.

To which Polina seized, rolling off her bed, heaving in a manner that was consistent with both a grand mal seizure and a full-bodied cackle. I couldn't decide which until she started talking.

"Ivan, what is *wrong* with you?"

"Why would you ask that?"

"For a thousand reasons."

"For example?"

"Well, first, it's Pink Floyd."

She overemphasized the order of the words, which felt condescending.

"Second," she said, "this is Janis Joplin, who couldn't be more different from Pink Floyd. Third, I feel like you are a baby boy who was raised by wolves and for whom I bear the sole responsibility of providing a basic musical education."

I think Polina expected me to smile, and when I didn't, I think that she realized that I had, in fact, grown up with wolves, and maybe that had been an approximately traumatizing event.

"Janis Joplin died from choking on her own vomit," she said, presumably to change the subject.

"Natalya got all these records for you?"

"Yes. I love records the way you love books."

"But not the one in Miss Kristina's desk. Natalya didn't give that one to you?"

"No, you got that one for me."

"Then how did you know it would be there?"

"You already know how I knew."

"Because you're a *tat*?"*

---

* Russian slang for a common thief.

"I prefer *vor v zakonye*."*

"I thought you quit."

"I did after walking in on my mother flagellating herself in front of a statue of Saint Francis because she thought it was her fault."

"Was it her fault?"

"Freud would suggest my father. But you should be all caught up on that topic after your own pilfering stunt."

"Why the relapse?"

"I'm not sure it qualifies as a relapse. When I die, they will come clean out my room and find the stash, and then everyone gets everything back."

Polina pondered for a moment, then continued:

"Also, it's fun."

Freud would also call this rationalization, though I had to admit it was persuasive.

"What's in your stash so far?" I asked.

"Just the record, which technically *you* stole. And this, which I found in Mikhail's top drawer."

She tossed me a condom, which I immediately threw to some corner of the room.

"And *Dead Souls*."

"You can have that too."

Polina produced my copy of *Dead Souls* from beneath her mattress and pitched it at me.

"*Merci*," I said.

---

* A much more prestigious position in Russian criminal parlance, equivalent to a mob boss.

"There is another perk to my filching."

"What?"

"I know what's inside of every drawer, corner, crack, shelf, cupboard, locker, and closet in this hospital."

"For example?"

"There's a small marijuana plant hidden inside of the utility closet. I think Nurse Elena is a closet botanist. Literally. There is a colorful assortment of blindfolds and nipple clamps inside Mikhail's desk, third drawer down from the top on the left. There are at least three keys hidden under three different rugs, though I'm not sure what (if any) locks they open, though if I start to feel better, I intend to try them on every lock I can find."

"Could be fun."

"There is one bottle of vodka taped to the inside of the laundry chute, and there are two more hidden behind the wall of cabbage cans in the food closet. There are about six unscratched lottery tickets hidden behind the cheap Van Gogh in the Main Room and a framed picture of a family hidden beneath the toy crate, which I believe features the ginger twins as infants."

"They have a family?"

"*Had* a family. Should I keep going?"

"Sure."

"There are about fifty chocolate bars hidden inside of Alex's bottom drawer, presumably put there by Nurse Natalya because Alex loves chocolate bars like you love books and I love records. There are a bunch of old pictures of Dennis and his mom when Dennis was a baby, underneath his pillowcase, presumably put there by Nurse Natalya, because Dennis loves his mom like Alex loves chocolate and you love books. There are also about twenty signed baseballs inside your top drawer. But I haven't figured those out. Where did you get them?"

"When were you in my room?"

"When you were in your bed."

"Sleeping?"

"What else?"

"I would have woken up."

"But you didn't."

I felt excited in my pelvic region knowing that Polina was in my room while I slept, despite the fact that I should have felt invaded.

"I think the music is too loud," I said.

Polina responded by turning the music up by approximately one to two clicks on her turntable.

"You're going to ruin this."

Take it, take another little piece of . . . [*]

"Enja, the heart-hole girl, has a note in her bottom drawer from her mother, which says that when she comes home, she will be Little Miss Mazyr. Vlad has a toy car with the initials of his great-grandfather on it. Natalya keeps a cuff link of her dead husband in the side pocket of her uniform at all times.

---

[*]   In Ivan's original writing, he attempted to phonetically spell the English lyrics associated with this song, which ultimately made the lyrics indecipherable. We replaced his well-meant attempt with the actual song lyrics after deciding that it would be true to the intention of the passage.

I know this because I can pick pockets too. I gave it back, though."

"It's entirely possible you will die alone if you don't turn down the Janet Joplin."

"You're being dramatic."

Her pale face was being danced on by the shadows of my one flailing hand. Something about the dancing light made her jaw and her cheekbones and her temples cut right through her skin, and for the first time, I realized that Polina had probably dropped below the thirty-kilo threshold, which was diagnostic criterion #117 for a leukemia three-monther.

"Let's talk some more about Mikhail," she said.

"Only if you turn down the music."

"The list of his buxom whores runs deep, if you didn't know."

She paused, presumably to wait for me to react, and I took her bait out of uncontrollable curiosity, while slowly wheeling myself to the record player.

"How deep?"

"He has pictures that go all the way back to sepia," she said.

"Sepia?"

"The orange pictures from the '70s."

"I'm not surprised."

I was close enough to the record player to reach out and turn it down, but Polina jumped across the room and slapped my hand, which, to me, was like severing my testicles.

"Relax your tense little face, Ivan," she said. "We don't have anything to worry about. I'm sure Lyudmila is currently riding Mikhail on that fake leather couch. Or possibly on the desk? Which—sidebar—disgusts me, since I've touched all his drawers."

"Then maybe you shouldn't be going through his drawers."

"What sort of filthy shit is she whispering in his ear right now?"

I was thoroughly uncomfortable with the content of Polina's verbiage, and yet I still answered.

"I don't know."

"Mickey, Mickey, Mick, Mick. Mmmmmm. Do you think he ever accidentally calls her by his wife's name? Or, even worse, confuses her with another nurse from his slutty past?"

I was becoming disgusted with Polina, and also this was a rhetorical question, so I stayed silent. Furthermore, it was clear that Polina was entertaining her dying self. It had nothing to do with me.

"Don't you love this song? Find me someone else who sings every word like she's crying," Polina said.

"It's good."

"Fifty-three pictures of fourteen nurses. That's how many I found. I could never be that slutty. Not even now with nothing to lose."

It was exactly when Polina said "slutty" that two other things happened simultaneously (which really just means I'm not sure which came first). The first thing is that it occurred to me that I had been unconsciously clenching my nubs ever since I left my room twenty-three minutes earlier. The second thing is that the metallic doorknob rattled and, just as quickly, swung wide open revealing a figure in a white uniform who happened to be the person who was supposed to be fucking the Director at that particular moment. Six or seven unbearable seconds passed before any of us said a word. This is because it was obvious that Nurse Lyudmila had three things on her mind that were competing for airtime. The first, and most obvious, sounded something like: *Back to your room, Ivan, and wait for the consequences to be revealed in the morning once the afterglow of the Director's recent orgasm has worn off.* The second, and slightly less obvious, sounded like: *Ivan, what is a comatose reject such as yourself doing in a sexy dead girl's room after lights-out?* And the third appeared to be directed at Polina, and surely said: *That desperate, hon?* But I acknowledge I could have invented thoughts two and three. Finally, it was Polina, empowered by her recent manic trip, who decided to speak first:

"Nurse Lyudmila, your left stocking is inside out."

To which Lyudmila, apparently unable to choose from any of the bitchy retorts running through her head, didn't say a word and instead grabbed the handles of my chair and pulled me out of the room after several collisions with various pieces of furniture and doorframes.

Reader, I fought her with a respectable mutant chivalry. As she aggressively maneuvered me across the linoleum path that separated my room from Polina's, I grabbed the rim of my left wheel and made a brake pad out of my palm. I may have also made retaliatory comments like *Stop infecting my only chair with your slut germs* and *You know you're going to bitch hell, right?* In response, Lyudmila continued to be speechless (except for her face, which said a gamut of hateful speech) and responded by ramming the wheels of my chair through the friction of my palm, resulting in the topmost layer of my skin being left on the wheel, rendering it impossible for me to resist anymore. This was approximately when Polina's frail little figure emerged in front of us and then sat down in the doorframe leading into the boys' wing. Her pale, wigless head reflected the limited light in the hallway, which made her look like a slightly imposing but beautiful monster.

"Move," Lyudmila said.

"I'll be in the ground in a month," she said. "Are you really going to hurt me just to spite an invalid?"

To which Lyudmila let go of the handles of my chair, walked over to Polina, and backhanded her across the face, which resulted in her thin, angular body collapsing into a pile of skin and bones in the doorframe. Nurse Lyudmila dragged the pile of limbs out of the way, which I used as an opportunity to ram her shins repeatedly with my chair, while cursing obscenities that I've since blacked out. Lyudmila easily regained control of the situation and forcibly wheeled me into the boys' wing, while I looked back at Polina and watched the purple bruise spread over her tiny unconscious face.

When we arrived at my door, Nurse Lyudmila offered me one last generous shove into my room, which I attempted to resist at the expense of my already bloody hand. The wheelchair stopped, but my body didn't, and I lurched through the air onto the linoleum. And before I could slither my way back out the door, she slammed it tight and locked it from the outside, which is a privilege every nurse has but almost never uses. From that point on, all I could hear were the clicks and clacks of her nurse shoes fading as she walked down the hall, and my vocal cords producing things like:

Otkroi dver', tvar'![*]

Zhirnaya blyad', otkroi.[†]

Pizdets.[‡]

Then I stopped hearing the clicks or the clacks, and I took the opportunity to cry. I cried until I was thoroughly numb and there was no more emotional energy to be found anywhere in my physical structure. When I finished, I wiped my puffy cheeks, leaving behind a thin film of bloody residue throughout my face because I had already forgotten about how the skin had been rubbed off my palm. Then I checked the doorknob to see if anything had magically changed but found that I was still locked in my room. I was acutely aware that that tiny bit of energy was the last that I had in me, and it occurred to me that people cry because it is blissful when it's over. My eyes couldn't hold themselves open anymore, nor did they desire to, and my bony back slid down the surface of my door as I fell asleep on the cold linoleum.

---

[*]   Open the door, bitch!

[†]   Fat whore, open!

[‡]   This is fucked up.

The Day I Conversed with the Director

(One day until lab results)

I awoke when I heard something that had the sibilance of a whisper yet was too abrupt to be a whisper. Instinctually, I whispered back at it:

"Polina?"

But there was no response.

So, instead, I thoroughly scanned my room and realized that the sound was most likely produced when two Polaroid photographs were slipped under my door while I slept. Both of these photographs depicted Nurse Lyudmila in slightly differing but equally naked and whore-like poses. Furthermore, both of these photographs were set on the desk inside of the Director's office. My first instinct was to mentally ridicule the unkempt and voluminous nature of Nurse Lyudmila's genital hair. My second instinct was to make photocopies.

Spasibo, Polina.

The antique digital clock on the table next to my bed read 5:30 in the A.M., which was well before breakfast hour and, more importantly, sufficiently prior to the time that Miss Kristina arrives at the front desk. *Anarchy hour.* (Shortly after becoming conscious of myself as a person, I began calling the hour between 5:00 A.M. and 6:00 A.M. anarchy hour due to a peculiar hole in hospital scheduling in which no nurse was present at the hospital.) Therefore, 5:39 meant twenty-one minutes to make multiple facsimiles of these nauseating photographs before the other nurses were scheduled.

Then I remembered that I was locked inside of my room like a caged animal. As per usual, my first instinct was to check the knob on my door, once again, just to see if anything had magically changed. This time something had changed, because *click, turn, creak* . . .

Danke, Polina.

I hid the photographs in the groin region of my shorts before quickly moving them under my leg nubs after reflecting on the proximity of Nurse Lyudmila to my *Hui*. Then I wheeled myself behind Miss Kristina's desk to the antiquated copy machine. I had never made a photocopy before, but I had spent long hours inspecting the machine prior to this day figuring out how I might make a copy if the need ever arose. Actually, the machine only has one button—a green one— so I laid the photos down on the glass and pressed it. Sure enough, a line of light passed up and down the paper, and within a second, a grainy, slightly indecipherable image fell out of the other side. In my professional opinion, I do believe that it bore a sufficient enough resemblance to Nurse Lyudmila to serve as an adequate backup if the need for blackmail arose. So I pressed the green button again. And then again. And then two more times.

I took one of the copies and slid it under Polina's door. "Sorry, no time to talk," I said, and I proceeded to the next destination, which was the utility closet, where I hid a second copy under a bottle of bleach, which I had noticed a while back had been there unopened since the late '90s. I hid a third copy in Alex's room, where I maneuvered myself around his colossal sleeping head to a tear in his mattress, which I knew about, since Alex's mattress was once my mattress. The final copy I tucked inside my shorts, again far clear of my *Hui,* and then I wheeled myself back to my room to wait for the inevitable summons by the Director.

I was expecting an early bud-nipping conversation, say 7:30 in the A.M., square in the middle of breakfast hour as per the rules of psychological warfare. Instead, I waited, quite impatiently, for over four hours, until at 10:38 Nurse Natalya knocked on my door. I was already waiting in my chair with all the wrinkles rubbed out of my T-shirt.

Nurse Natalya abruptly opened my door, hardly waiting for me to invite her in, and took up the space in my room like she owned it.

"What in the name of Saint Michael happened last night?" she said.

"What makes you think anything happened last night?"

"Well, first, the Director wants to talk to you, and he never wants to talk to you. Second, there's blood all up and down your face."

Nurse Natalya charged over to me while licking her thumbs, which she used to unsuccessfully rub the streaks of blood off my face.

"I can clean myself," I said.

Actually, I wanted to leave it on so that Mikhail could see the sadistic whore he exchanged fluids with.

"Clearly, you can't, Ivan, because it's everywhere. And stop avoiding the question. What happened last night? And why does Mikhail want to see you?"

"It doesn't concern you."

"If it happened to you, then it concerns me."

"I'm taking care of it."

I tried to wheel my way out, but when my palm touched the surface of the rubber wheel, I winced, and Nurse Natalya caught me because she catches everything. A new brand of consternation spread across her face like fire across dry spruce.

"Did she hurt you? Out of all the times to be a shit, this is not the time to be one."

"I told you I'm taking care of it."

"And are you taking care of the bruise on Polina's face?"

"Yes."

"How did it happen?"

"You should ask her."

"I did."

"And what did she tell you?"

"That she sleepwalked and fell on her face."

A likely side effect of an exhaustive chemotherapy regime. *Shrewd, Polina.*

"Tragic," I said.

"There are a thousand reasons why you need to tell me if Lyudmila did this."

Judging by the fervor in Nurse Natalya's voice, it occurred to me that ordinary words would not be enough to convince her to step back. In these types of situations, we do much better with telepathy. So instead of responding with words, I just looked at her with a face that said, *This is not me being ornery and difficult; this is me trying to protect you*. It took at least half a minute of me launching this message directly into her face with a variety of droopy but concentrated faces before she understood. I know this because she stopped wiping the blood off my face and said:

"Mikhail would like to talk to you now. If you care to let me know how your meeting goes, I will be in the Red Room dusting off heart monitors for most of the day."

"I will," I said, knowing quite lucidly that neither of us actually expected me to reveal the details of the meeting.

I turned around and started wheeling myself to the Director's office, swallowing every instinct to react to the postsurgical flames spewing out of my hand so that I could leave without setting off any more of Nurse Natalya's maternal radar.

There was a fraction of a quiver in my hand when I knocked on Mikhail's closed door, and the Polaroids of a naked Nurse Lyudmila seemed to be burning a hole straight through my ass checks. I was, however, quickly distracted by the sounds of the Director in the midst of a fairly animated phone conversation, which he abruptly ended. On his way to the door, my mother appeared and reminded me that I was about to speak to the Most Mediocre Man in the World.

"Come in," he said.

In the context of the situation, the time it took for my chair to make it to the opposite side of his desk, which, incidentally, seemed to me to be worth more than the rest of the contents of the asylum all put together, felt excruciatingly long. And by the time I finally arrived opposite him, he said, "Actually, let's talk over here," raising his arm to the corner of his office, which was furnished with a long brown (fake) leather couch and a matching recliner. Psychological warfare. I was not too naïve to realize that he was taking advantage of the vulnerability of my condition by asking me to leave my wheelchair for the much less mobile brown recliner.

"Please sit down," he said, pointing to the recliner.

"I'm already sitting," I responded.

"I mean you should sit comfortably," he said.

"My chair suits me fine," I said.

"I suppose it does," he said.

The Director paused for a minute, which allowed ample time for his words to settle into my bones.

"So, Ivan, how are you?" he asked.

"I'm fine. Can we get on with it?" I asked.

I had inadvertently rehearsed this conversation a few hundred times in my head since midnight, and not one iteration went like this.

"Get on with what, Ivan?" he asked.

"It. I'm ready to talk," I said.

"We are talking. Have you read any good books lately? Natalya says you like books."

"Every day."

"Every day what?"

"Every day I read a good book."

"For example?"

"For example, *Doctor Zhivago*."

"Oh, Pasternak? Never been a fan. What else?"

"*One Day in the Life of Ivan Denisovich.*"

"Much better. I fell in love with Solzhenitsyn when I was your age too."

"What is the purpose of this?" I asked.

"The purpose of what?"

"All this chatter."

"Just making conversation."

"We both know we're not here to have that kind of conversation."

"Why not, Ivan?"

"Because if we were, we would have had this conversation a long time ago."

The Director furrowed his brow as if he were considering my words and then nodded approvingly.

"Are you happy, Ivan?" he asked.

"Am I happy?"

"Yes, are you happy?"

"That's a dumb question."

"No, it's not, Ivan.

"It *is* a dumb question."

"Why?"

"Because of course I'm not happy."

By the time I finished that statement, it occurred to me that I was yelling it.

"Is that the first time you've told anyone you're not happy? The nurses here often talk about how you don't look happy, but they say you never tell them."

"Isn't it obvious enough?"

"Perhaps. But unhappy people usually try to do something about it. Or at least let other people know."

"What difference would it make? And who could be happy here?" I asked.

I realized that the surface of my words was inadvertently being covered with tiny microscopic razors as I spoke, and my insides were smoldering.

"It could make a difference. If it's the place that is making you unhappy, there are two things that we can do. First, we could change the place. Or, second, we could remove you from the place."

"This place never changes."

"Then we should remove you from the place?"

I wasn't sure if the question was rhetorical, so I didn't respond.

The Director continued:

"Have you ever asked to leave this place?"

After an eight-month-pregnant pause, I answered:

"No."

"I see. Well, if the place makes you unhappy, then why not tell someone?"

"I don't know."

"You don't know?"

"You heard me."

"Perhaps when you have an answer we can talk again."

"Perhaps."

"Is there anything else you would like to talk about, Ivan?"

"No."

"Ivan, what's in your shorts?"

"My *Hui*."

"Besides your *Hui*."

"What makes you think there is anything in my shorts?"

"Because you keep looking at them."

"There's nothing in my shorts."

The Director paused and sifted through the contents of his balding head.

"So we're done here then?"

"Yes."

"There is the door."

I turned obediently and began wheeling away, unsure of why I'd lost my nerve and ashamed of the lost blackmail opportunities.

Then the Director spoke again:

"Ivan, one more thing."

I stopped and turned toward him.

"So long as everything stays in your shorts, the two of you will be left alone.

Even in the blur of the moment, I knew there was nothing I wanted more. So I said:

"Okay."

At which point the Director sent me a smirk from across

the room. And with that single twist of his lips, everything changed. It was as if I were meeting the man for the first time. Like there was a beast living behind the skin and it finally decided to step into the light. Reader, it is impossible to transmit to you the contents of that smile. I can only say that it was as close to the grin of a fallen angel as I'd ever seen. It spoke so many things:

It said, "You may control the details, but I control your life."

It said, "I have more concern for the well-being of most species of roach than for you."

It said, "As long as you're here, I'm the personal dictator of your one-man nation."

It said other things too, but you probably get the point.

That was when I realized that my mother was wrong: the Director, Mikhail Kruk, was the Most Mediocre *Demon* in the World.

I promptly removed myself from the vicinity of that smile. My first instinct as I wheeled myself away was to dispose of Nurse Lyudmila's naked photograph in the nearest bathroom trash bin, which I did. My second instinct, conveniently, since I was already inside the bathroom, was to vomit every recollection of that meeting into the toilet, which I also did.

A Day of Sleep

(Zero days until lab results)

After my conversation with the Director, I returned to my room, shed my clothes, masturbated, fell asleep, and did not wake up until 7:50 in the A.M. the next morning, which was almost twenty-one hours of sleep. And even then I only woke up because Nurse Natalya was beating at my door like a distraught gorilla.

"Ivan, are you conscious? Ten minutes left in breakfast hour. You missed lunch *and* dinner yesterday. What about our deal?"

After missing twelve consecutive meals one week in the winter of 1999, we made a deal that I would never go twenty-four hours without eating.

"Ivan! Are you in there? Why is the door locked?"

"Come in," I said.

Through the metal door I could hear the jangle of Nurse Natalya's keys fumbling their way into the slit, followed by an abrupt turn of the doorknob. She walked in with a bowl of cabbage juice and a croissant.

"I'll bring it to you this time. But this is the last time," she said.

"A croissant?" I asked.

"I bought it downtown," she said.

"Just tell me," I said.

"Tell you what?"

"I know what it means when you buy me anything from downtown."

"You're not a match."

"Okay."

"There's more."

"More bad?"

"Yes."

"Please don't let me stop you."

"We ran her tests."

"And?"

"And she's not responding to the chemo."

This was Nurse Natalya's way of telling me that in all likelihood Polina was going to die before she found a match, which wasn't actually a surprise considering leukemia kids never find a match. Then my eyes crossed a bit, and I left the room for a few moments as various methods of escape began to flicker through my head like an '80s-style slideshow. I came back when Nurse Natalya said:

"Don't go there, Ivan."

"Too late, I'm there."

There was no reason for me to want to hurt myself. Nothing had changed. I was nestled in the exact same set of circumstances that I was in nine days ago when the smaller-than-usual bag of pills was dropped half into Polina's cabbage. And yet everything had changed, because there is nothing more bittersweet than when things can't be undone.

"Does she know?" I asked.

"Yes. To both."

"To both?"

"She also knows that you were tested."

"Please tell me that isn't true."

Nurse Natalya knelt next to my bed and put her face right up to mine.

"Don't," I said.

"Ivan, she asked if you were an option before *you* even asked."

Which meant Polina was not repellent to the possibility of having some of me inside of her if it meant saving her life.

"I would still like you to leave."

"Yes, Ivan."

She put down the croissant on the table next to my bed.

"One more thing," she said before walking out. "The nurses received a memo that Lyudmila will not have duty for the next week. Elena will be working her nights."

Then she closed the door behind her.

I took a bite of the croissant and then let it drop back out of my mouth after a few chews because the Director appeared in my room, sitting in the corner, telling me that surely I was unhappy now, and if so, shouldn't I leave? Then it occurred to me that the only way I would be able to make him leave instead would be to hurl the back of my head against the wall behind me, which I did several times until the splotch of blood made me squeamish enough to collapse and squirm to sleep.

⚬∞⚬

Currently, the clock reads 10:58 in the A.M.
I've been writing for fifty-nine hours.
It is the fifth day of December.
The year is 2005.

Nurse Natalya knocked a few minutes ago.
How's my baby Bulgakov?
I didn't answer her.
Because I was on the verge of asking her.
But the words got stuck in my throat
or somewhere lower.
Maybe I was a sip shy.
I'll be back later.
She closed the door.

⋘⋙

DAYS 11 AND 10

Crying with Nabokov

This time I woke up when the red digital matchsticks arranged themselves to say 1:54 in the A.M. I know this because just before I read it, I heard a slow, gentle, arrhythmic, and noncommittal knock at my door, followed by a slow, gentle, arrhythmic, and noncommittal whisper.

"Are you awake?"

The dread, the anxiety, the existential crisis, the arguable psychosis: it all evaporated with just those whispers, which resulted in a newfound respect for this particular drug (love? infatuation? addiction? enslavement?). I also felt personally humbled by my private ridiculing of the characters inside my novels and those who flickered across the TV and the icons from history who did asinine things in the name of romance.

To all the Romeos and all the Juliets—I absolve you.

"Polina?"

"Where have you been?"

"Asleep."

"Can I come in?" she asked.

"Yes."

Polina walked in, and it occurred to me that it was the first time I'd seen her since the Incident. A fraction of a moon bleeding in through my barred windows provided the only light of the room. It was an unforgiving light that emphasized every shadow caused by her ever-shrinking and sharpening face. She was, however, wearing a small red hat in place of her wig, which I found to be an alarmingly good look for her, despite her emaciated state.

"What happened with Mikhail?"

I wasn't at all prepared for this question or a perfectly truthful response. At the same time, lying to her was approximately impossible.

"I had to look into his cold, dark soul," I said with 60 percent of a smile to ensure that she knew that I was at least 60 percent playing.

"Seriously, did he threaten you like a big, fat buffoon? And then did you drop those pictures on his desk and pop his big, fat balloon?"

"I didn't need to."

"What?"

"He just wanted to talk."

"About?"

"Really?"

"Really."

"About nothing."

"Nothing?"

"Nothing of substance. Mostly small talk."

Polina thought while she looked at my pupils. Then she said, "Did you tell him Lyudmila hit me?"

"He knew."

"Did he mention it?"

"No."

"Then how do you know he knew?"

"Because he said it without words. It will never happen again."

"How do you know?"

"Because I said it too."

"In words?"

"No, I said it the same way he—"

Before I could even finish this sentence, I could see that there was a tremor in Polina's hand, which began to palpitate like a drug-induced metronome. Then the quaking spread from her hands into her arms, then throughout her entire body. And when it got to her face, it spread into her eyes, where the shaking turned to liquid and heavy streams started to flow across her face at biologically questionable volumes.

"I'm sorry," she said, but the last half of "sorry" was only air, so she said it again. And then she fell to the ground and started to heave and lurch like a fish, and the quaking mixed with sounds, such as tiny rhythmic howls and the staccato of her nose trying to snort all her liquids back into her body.

"It's okay," I reassured her, though I knew it wasn't, primarily because the quaking was contagious, and I noticed my own hand begin to waver.

"This is my fault," she said.

"It is your fault," I said. "But who cares."

"I'm sorry," she said. And she repeated it over and over with her head in her own hands.

I'm sorry. So sorry. So sorry. Sorry. I'm sorry. So. Sor—. Sorr—. Sorry.

She was breaking up before my eyes.

"Come here," I said.

She didn't move.

"Come here," I said, forcefully, like a man.

She brought her knees beneath her and crawled over to the edge of my bed. Then I cradled her tiny head and wiped the tears off her face with my thumb because that's also what I had seen in movies and also because the quaking had spread to my own eyes.

"I'm done. I'm over," she said.

"Not quite."

"Quite."

In my professional opinion, that was when all the barriers and all the defense mechanisms fell to the floor like battle-pocked plates of armor, because the storm turned to hysteria, and she struggled to take breaths in between sobs.

I wanted to tell her that she wasn't dying, but she was.

I wanted to tell her that we're all dying, but that was annoying.

I wanted to tell her that it would get better, but it was about to get worse.

So I just said, "I know." And repeated it at intervals that felt appropriate, while rocking her body at the pace of my own clunky rhythm. And she repeated, *I'm dying, dying, dying, dy-ing, I'm going to give up the ghost.* And then the refrain turned to whispers, and eventually the whispers faded into air, as did the quaking, and Polina's tiny pale face was asleep in my arm.

I waited for as long as it took for my brain to catch up with the moment so that it could fully realize the absurdity and improbability of itself. The corresponding endorphins must have been enough to lull me into a sedated opiatic state, because I have no more memories of that night until approximately 4:32 in the A.M. when I half awoke to find Polina fully in my bed, with my partial body cradled around her, my one arm draped around her body, and blankets spread over the both of us, without any recollection of how we arrived in that configuration.

I lifted my body high enough to see her sweet, undulating face, which was now prone and open and void of any resistance, almost as if she fast-tracked through the Kübler-Ross model of grief, from denial to acceptance after nearly suffocating to death on her tears.

I shifted the blankets and checked my legs.

I thought about waking her. I thought about telling her that she should go before someone found us here together. But I decided to let us sleep. And after a few minutes of trying, I realized that my eyes wouldn't close, so I just held her and let her sleep and got acquainted with the rhythm of her breathing.

At some point, the sun cracked the horizon wide open, resulting in Polina shifting through the sheets, and rolling away from the sun—which meant toward me—causing her to jump six inches vertically when she found us in bed with our noses glancing.

I scanned my head for the appropriate thing to say in this particular situation, but everything that came up was faintly self-deprecating, or suggestive, or defensive, or awkward. So instead, I waited for her brain to collect the memories of the last eight hours and recall on her own why she was in bed, braided up with a circus freak. In her eyes, I could watch the filmstrip of recollections pass by until she accepted the story line and said, "Hi."

To which I said, "Hi."

To which she said, "Remember how when I first came to this hospital you just stared like a bug and wouldn't talk?"

To which I said, "Fuck you."

To which she attempted to put her pillow into my mouth.

She closed her eyes and looked like she was heading back to sleep, which I took as a promising sign of comfort, though I did not know why I still unconsciously and habitually searched for signs of comfort considering that Polina would be dead in a few days.

With her eyes still closed, Polina interrupted my stream of thought.

"I'm done," she said.

I assumed she meant with her life again, but I thought it was worth clarifying.

"With what?" I asked.

"With the poison."

Which seemed reasonable to me. Three months and seven days, ten hours a day, a gleaming bald head, vomit and diarrhea all day, and nothing to show for it in the way of depleted bone marrow. From a utilitarian perspective, it made more sense to quit than to live the last days of her life in formidable misery. Still, something inside urged me to play devil's advocate or at least pretend I didn't know as much as I did.

"Are you sure?" I asked.

"They told me it wouldn't make a difference anymore," she said.

"Who told you?"

"Some doctor from the city who comes in to tell me how much I'm dying, and his student."

She was referring to Dr. Stanislav Kariyev, the city oncologist.

"Dr. Kariyev?"

"Yes. He told me it would only kill me faster at this point."

Polina coughed several times, which made the veins extending from her temples to her neck bulge through her cellophane skin as they wove in and out of the red splotches that were flourishing across her face like poinsettia. (Dr. Kariyev called these spots *petechiae* when referring to other leukemia kids.) I also noticed a smell drifting out of her skin, not quite sweet and not quite sour; not subtle but not pungent.

"Then I agree with you."

I suspected that I should say this confidently, so I did.

"You know what this means?"

"What?"

Once again I expected her to remind me of her upcoming death.

"It means we can see each other during the day, and I'm not at risk of shitting myself in your presence. We can start checking things off your list."

"My list?"

"The one that you made with everything you wanted to do before they buried me."

I must have looked surprised, because she said:

"Don't look so surprised. I obviously saw that while you were sleeping too."

To which I replied:

"So were you leaning toward making out in priest/nun attire or having sex on the roof?"

To which she laughed courteously, so I added:

"I think the roof is closer and, therefore, the more realistic option."

Still face-to-face and somewhat pretzelized in the bed,

Polina laughed, and a burst of moist air, which smelled sweet like warm jam, flew into my face. Then she pinched her lips together, and her eyes rolled into her imagination.

"We should read the best book ever written," she said.

"You have one foot in the ground, and you want to spend your time analyzing classic Russian literature?" I asked.

"I suppose we could ski the Alps like I always wanted," she said.

Touché, Polina.

"Your pick."

"My last book needs to be Nabokov," she said.

"*Invitation to a Beheading?*"

"Too depressing."

"*Laughter in the Dark?*"

"*Lolita.*"

"*Lolita* is less depressing?"

"*Lolita* is sexual. And dark. But not depressing."

"*Lolita* is acceptable."

"Of course it is. It's my last book."

"I propose we read it straight through. No sleep until the last page."

"Do you turn *everything* into a game?" she asked.

"Everything."

"Ivan?"

"Yes?"

"How do you even start a book you know is going to be your last?"

"You lie and say it's not."

"Lying is impossible at the moment. Dying is like truth serum."

I writhed out of my bed and wormed my way into the pseudocloseted region of my room, where I had not two but three different copies of *Lolita*. I knew this because it was my favorite book from 1998 to 1999, and I lied and told Natalya I'd lost it twice, only to make sure I had extra copies in case of some apocalyptic event. I rummaged through a miniature avalanche, which spread over my floor, until I found one, and then two, *Lolitas*; the latter I tossed to Polina. She looked at the book from every angle and caressed all six surfaces.

"When do we start?" she asked.

"After breakfast, or Natalya will worry."

"You love her," she said declaratively.

"You can close your eyes again. I will make sure we wake up in time."

She looked at me with unimaginably blue eyes for a few more seconds, and then she let them fall closed, where they stayed hidden until breakfast hour.

We sipped cabbage juice like normal. In the middle, Nurse Natalya approached her with a clipboard and a pen, and whispered a few somethings into her ear, at which point Polina scribbled her name down. Natalya's eyes couldn't help jerking over to me a few times in the process, which provided an opportunity to catch her attention during one of them, at which point she walked back over to me and whispered a few somethings in my ear as well.

"Why are you whispering?" I asked. "No one knows, and no one cares."

I said: "One, two . . ."

"No, when the clock says eight," she said. It was 7:59 so . . .

Fair enough, Polina.

When the red matchsticks shifted, we both entered a trancelike state of absorption, where the only thing that evolved was our physical configuration, which morphed from parallel (with a holy ghost between us), to perpendicular (with her legs draped over my trunk), to antiparallel (with her feet in my face).

The only interruptions came when Nurse Natalya would knock twice, open the door, and drop off two pieces of baklava, or two boiled pierogi, or two pastillas, all nonstandard menu cuisine. She spoke to us only once: "Are you sure you wouldn't rather be in the Main Room with the gingers?"

Translation: "There is only so long I can make excuses for your disappearances."

We both slowly rotated our heads from our books, to each other, then to her and shook them categorically *no.*

"I see," she said, then left.

Other interruptions came in the form of our favorite lines bursting out of our mouths like Tourette's tics.

Polina (33 minutes in): *Human life is but a series of footnotes to a vast obscure unfinished masterpiece . . .*
Ivan's response: *And the rest is rust and stardust.*

> **Ivan (339 minutes in):** *I need you, the reader, to imagine us, for we don't really exist if you don't.*
>
> **Polina's response:** *Imagine being stuck inside of a story?*
>
> **Polina (608 minutes in):** *He broke my heart. You merely broke my life.*
>
> **Ivan's response:** *Do not be angry with the rain; it simply does not know how to fall upwards.*

We were interrupted again much later on, somewhere around the eighteenth hour, by Polina herself. Spontaneously, she stopped reading and set the book over her chest, which was now flat and taut enough to serve as an adequate surface. Her eyes locked onto the ceiling as if she were looking through to the clouds on the other side. Potential diagnoses included absence seizure, Ivan-like coma, or rapturous daydreaming.

"Polina?"

"Is any of this happening?"

I wondered if this was a rhetorical question in disguise so I said:

"I think so."

"It doesn't feel real."

"What?"

"Any of it."

"The book?"

"This book, all books, my thoughts, all my dreams, the dreams of my parents. It doesn't feel like it should be over."

"It doesn't feel real because it's not over."

It was almost too obvious to me. To her too, because her

eyes came back to life and rolled over to me, while her body remained still.

"Don't die before you're dead. And if you do, let it be the good kind," I said.

"What's the good kind?"

"When the only part that dies is who you were supposed to be."

"Ah, the good kind."

"Yes."

"Good kind, good kind, good kind." Her words became weaker and more whimsical with every iteration as her eyes wobbled on the edge of some invisible fulcrum until gravity had its way, and they fell shut. Polina slept, and I was the first to finish *Lolita*.

DAY 9

Blood Brothers

I awoke to the simultaneously welcoming and shrill voice of Polina, along with the feeling of her shaking my body like I was a bath towel.

"You shit," she said.

"What?"

"You weren't supposed to let me sleep."

"That was not a stipulation of our parley."

"I expected more from you. Also, I'm heading to my room.

I haven't changed my clothes in three days. Plus my cheeks are salty."

Polina *had* developed a smell that was sweet like a soiled baby, only with a hint of death. I quickly gathered the two remaining pastillas from our literary marathon along with all associated crumbs and said, "Take these." I knew that at this stage the thought of food in general turned her stomach inside out, and nothing less than sugar would overwhelm the disgust response. She thanked me and left. I, however, was obligated to show up at the breakfast table due to previous contractual commitments I had made with Nurse Natalya.

Most of the mutants were assembled in their seats by the time I arrived, and just like always, I took my seat unnoticed. But somehow, everyone, the entire ensemble, the scene, and the setting all looked different. Pinker maybe, or more innocent (maybe pink is the color of innocence) or less caustic, or a fraction less dreadful. I've inquired to the authority inside if something in the breakfast-hour routine had truly changed (possibilities include a new brand of lightbulb, some trimmed trees outside the barred windows, or some mass hygiene initiative for the less-abled patients). I only know that for a few seconds while I sipped a tolerable bowl of cabbage juice, I felt as though I was coexisting and not merely tolerating the other bodies at the Mazyr Hospital for Gravely Ill Children.

After my fill of cabbage juice, I wheeled my way around the asylum with no agenda but to count the number of objects that seemed different. When I'd had enough of this, I returned to my bedroom to read a few pages, but I only made it through a noun and two adverbs before Nurse Natalya burst into room without knocking, holding a stack of linens.

"What is it?" I asked.

"I need to change your sheets," she said.

"No, you don't need to change my sheets. It's not a Tuesday, and it's not the third week of the month."

Nurse Natalya dropped the linen and sat her plump ass on the edge of my bed.

"We have a favor to ask of you," she said.

"No promises."

"I think you will want to do this favor."

"Okay."

"She needs transfusions. They might give her a few days."

"Are you looking for permission?"

"We're looking for help."

"With the transfusion?"

"With your blood."

"You want me to give her my blood?"

"She is AB negative, and the banks are dry."

Which, I'm regularly told, has been the case since Ronald Reagan. Furthermore, AB negative is the rarest blood type in the universe. I, however, am O negative, which means my blood mixes with the entire human race. I know this because the city of Mazyr (under the auspices of Mikhail Kruk) has approached me every month for eleven years to donate blood, and I've categorically refused. This is because no individual human life in the abstract has ever been important enough to face my pathological fear of blood.

"Yes," I said.

"I thought so," she said.

And with that, Nurse Natalya dove inside her stack of linens. Tucked inside were an empty pint bag, a syringe, and a few feet of tubing. She dropped the linens and instantly stabbed the needle into my vein, before there was any chance for me to (A) change my mind, or (B) have any psychophysical reaction that would hijack the process.

Clever, Natalya.

Blood that touches the atmosphere has always been worse than blood that runs through a plastic tube. This offered me just enough space to approximately enjoy the way the blood spiraled and spurted up through the translucent tubing and pooled into the plastic bag, while my nubs trembled and my forehead obtained a glossy sheen.

"Just ten seconds, Ivan," she said. "That's all it takes."

This was true, except that time lives in the mind, and seconds stop being seconds when your heart is on fire.

"Eight . . . seven . . . six . . . ," she said, as entire masturbatory episodes flashed through my head.

"There's nothing wrong with it?" I asked, just to clarify.

"Your blood?"

"Yes."

"It can't be worse than hers," she answered with a demonic smile. "Three . . . two . . . one . . . and we're done. You kind soul."

"She won't know?"

"Only if she asks. Belarusian law."

"In the Red Room?"

"Where else? But I'm sure you don't want to watch."

She closed the door with her bag of blood in tow as I turned to the clock and waited for the minute to be up and then one more before wheeling my way over to the edge of the Red Room. I leaned in as unnoticeably as possible. Nurse Natalya, Nurse Katya, and a doctor from the city, whom I had seen several times before but whose name I never knew, were all surrounding Polina. I watched as Katya made a pincushion out of Polina's forearm by repeatedly missing her vein. When she finally found the vein, I watched several heartbeats worth of hot blood spurt (which also was not supposed to happen) while Polina winced and moaned.

"No worries. It's bad blood anyhow, kid," Katya said.

Just shy of the fourth spurt, Natalya managed to connect the tube coming out of Polina's arm into the plump purplish bag dangling from the mobile IV stand. A few seconds later, I watched the level in that bag begin to drop as my blood mixed with Polina's.

I rolled back into the Main Room, found a tennis ball inside the toy box, and started bouncing it off the wall repeatedly while the universe around me fell away. Then I dropped the ball and fell into a coma, recognizing I was due one. Unfortunately, it was short-lived, because seven minutes later, I opened my eyes to find Nurse Natalya shaking me awake.

"She's asleep. We'll have to monitor her in the Red Room for most of the day. We need to make sure she doesn't have a reaction to the blood," she said.

"Why are you telling me?"

"I figured you would want to know."

"I do and I don't."

"You do."

"What if she reacts?"

"We suppress her immune system."

"It's already weak."

"I know."

"She will die."

"Yes," she said. "She will. Either today or tomorrow or next week. Or in a hundred years."

She turned around and started walking away, and as she did she said, "I will help with the pieces."

I went back to comaland but realized that my standard feigned comas were haunted by ghosts and ghouls when bad things were happening. It occurred to me that I should make my coma legitimate. So I wheeled myself into the Red Room, kissed Polina's sweaty forehead, pulled a syringe of morphine out from the morphine drawer, rolled beside her, and injected the needle into my vein.

DAY 8

The Organic Wonderland (and Other Conversations)

I awoke on the eighth day in my bed to Polina combing the shaggy hair off my sweaty forehead with her fingers. Her eyes were yellow, and the skin on her face was starting to crack. I could also feel her fever radiating through the molecules between her face and mine. But in spite of all the decay, her irises continued to be heartbreakingly blue.

"Don't go away like that again," she said.

"Where did I go?"

"Apparently into a morphine syringe."

"I did?"

"They said you could've died. It's the dose they use to sedate Dennis, and three of you fit into him."

"I was just trying to pass the time."

"You almost beat me to death."

That's when the door swung open revealing a frenzied Nurse Natalya. She walked over to my face, propped my eyelids open with her fingers, shined a bright penlight into my retina, let the lids snap back closed, slapped me in the face, and then exited the room.

"How do you feel?" I asked.

"A bit better. Thanks to you."

"They told you?"

"I overheard that too."

"When?"

"When I was asleep. Or waking up. Or some combination. We're blood brothers, I suppose."

Then Polina pulled on a fistful of my hair and asked:

"Does this hurt?"

To which I said:

"What the fuck? Why are you pulling my hair?"

To which she replied:

"Because you need to wake up. You just took morphine."

To which I said:

"I'm awake. And now prematurely balding."

Then Polina said:

"Let's go outside."

"And do what?"

"Just sit. Talk. Listen to things."

"Really?"

"These walls are making me ill."

"We can't go outside."

"Really, have you asked?"

"Since I was old enough to talk."

"Let's ask Natalya."

Polina stood up carefully because leukemia makes balance a coveted commodity and walked out of the room, ignoring two or three protests on my part. I wormed into my clothes and made it halfway into my chair before she returned with Nurse Natalya.

"Ask her," she said.

"No," I said.

"Ask me what?" Natalya asked.

"Ivan, I'm going to be in the dirt in a few days, so grow some *mudyá* and ask her."

"Polina would like to know if we can go outside," I asked.

"Well, obviously you can, Ivan, but you won't," she said. Then she turned to Polina and said:

"I've been trying to get him outside since before he knew words."

Before I could protest, Polina shoved me the rest of the way into my chair, and I was suddenly halfway down the hall. Elena and Lyudmila and Kristina ("Hi, Polina; Hi, Ivan") all watched with varying degrees of gape as I crossed the threshold of the big brown double doors for the second time since I arrived at the asylum.

There was a small concrete ramp that led down to a courtyard with scattered flowers of differing varieties and colors and a modest fountain bath that had not been used in the twentieth or twenty-first century. The sky was Belarusian gray with thick patches of drunk clouds.

"Stay as long as you like, or don't come back at all," Natalya said, and she walked away. Once her body disappeared back through the doors, I said nothing. And Polina didn't either. And almost as if it were planned, droplets started to pelt our heads and skin as we sat silently and, at least on my part, awkwardly, as my muscles and tendons worked together to shrivel my skin. Polina reached with her glossy pink tongue, which looked strikingly healthy compared to the rest of her decaying body, to catch the acid rain.

"That can kill you," I said.

She only looked back at me like, *Stop being a curmudgeon.* Then the frequency of the droplets increased, and our clothes started to soak.

"Let's get back in before you get sicker," I said.

She gulped a mouthful, gargled it in her throat, and spit it out like a Roman fountain.

When her mouth was empty, she asked, "What is it?"

"What is what?" I asked.

"Why are you crawling out of your skin?"

"I'm not."

Polina stopped collecting water in her mouth and looked at me for a few seconds. Then she wiped away the beads of rain accumulating on her bald head.

"Never mind. I already know."

"What?"

Polina continued to play with the water falling from the sky.

"Look at you. You're shaking, Ivan," she said.

"It's cold."

"It's your heart beating through your skin."

"I'm fine."

"Want to know my theory?"

"Sure."

"When you're inside, everything is comfortably broken. When you're out here, everything is alive. But you feel better around broken things."

By now, every cell in my body was shaking. But I was stuck in my head, which meant that my eyes were stuck on a single bead of rain sliding down a single blade of grass.

"Why are you still here, Ivan?"

"Here in this life, or here in this hospital?"

"The hospital. Actually, either . . ."

Then, before I could answer, she performed an unexpected kindness. She stood up and held either side of my quaking face in her hands, and she kissed my lips. And instead of pulling away quickly, as if out of charity, she kept her face close to mine and looked at me with her intolerably blue eyes until I stopped. Then her fragile little body weakly pushed me through the grass underneath an oak tree, which was largely impervious to the rain. Then we sat without talking for the rest of the afternoon and watched things happen.

We were back in the hospital before dusk, and by the time the sun set completely, Polina's fever rose to forty degrees. Nurse Natalya was running around flailing her arms, gathering acetaminophen, and publicly berating herself for letting us sit in the rain.

"She'll be taking an ice bath tonight, Ivan," she said.

They wheeled her delirious body into the White Room, which has a large stained tub and almost nothing else. I followed because it was easy to stay cloaked in the chaos of the moment. I watched them pull off her clothes, one cotton article at a time, until all that was left was her purple-and-white body, which looked like it had been starved and tortured in a Kazakh prison. The cancer had become like a time machine, eating her curves away until she arrived back at her prepubescent state. Katya and Natalya lifted her up, while her semi-lucid head dangled like a pendulum off her torso. Lyudmila started the cold water running and then poured a bucket of ice into the cold soup. When her body hit the water, Polina screamed, and her arms punched the air while she hollered a variety of obscenities. The nurses did their best to hold her body down, until she stopped screaming and just twitched in the water while her eyes focused loosely on some hallucinated event on the ceiling.

Polina was brought into the Red Room, where she slept, and I went back to the lab to give up another pint of blood. Nurse

Natalya took the needle out of my arm and put my blood in a refrigerator. Then I wheeled myself to the Red Room and wiped the fever sweat from Polina's head, determined to be present for any last heartbeats.

DAY 7

дзень я закахаўся*

I woke up on the seventh day to find that I had been using the metal rail of Polina's bed as a pillow all night and that her fingers were laced with mine. Given that I did not have the confidence to initiate this degree of intimate contact on my own, I deduced that our fingers somehow found each other while we were sleeping.

A few seconds later, Nurse Elena, vodka vapors abounding, came in and slipped a thermometer under Polina's tongue as she slept. Polina stirred gently, whimpered slightly, but didn't wake. Then Nurse Elena pulled the thermometer from her mouth and swung it up close to her eyes.

"What does it say?" I asked.

"Thirty-nine."

"So, she's better."

"Somewhat."

Then Nurse Elena left, and a few seconds later I followed her.

"What's next?" I asked.

---

* Belarusian for "The day I fell in love."

"Another transfusion."

"And then?"

"Then nothing."

I wheeled back to the Red Room, put our fingers back into the configuration they were in when I woke up, and waited for something to happen. I waited for her breath to change, or for her body to shift, or her eyebrows to scrunch, or for her eyes to flutter below her eyelids, which would tell me she was dreaming. At some point during the waiting, I must have fallen asleep too, because there was a break in my consciousness followed by waking to the sensation of suffocation, which was Polina pinching my nose. I gasped for air, and she laughed a mischievous but evidently dying laugh.

"That wasn't funny."

"Then why am I laughing?"

I noticed our interlaced fingers again and quickly reconfigured them to something less intimate.

"I had a weird dream," she said.

"Forty degrees will do that."

"Don't you want to hear about it?"

"I do."

"Everyone was there. And by everyone, I mean *everyone*. The entire world. All seven billion people or however many there are now. All in one big, empty field with long grass and nothing else."

"How did you know it was everyone?"

"I just knew. You know how in dreams you just know?"

"Sometimes."

"You were there, and my parents, and everyone I knew was close by. The people I didn't know were on the outside."

"I was there?"

"Yes."

"What did I look like?"

"Like you."

"Anything else?"

"My mother was crying. And everyone else—the whole world—just turned to me. Even the trees. And the weird part was that they didn't have faces. And everything was perfectly quiet. Except for Sputnik, who was barking like it was the end of the world."

"Maybe it was."

"Maybe."

I tried to feel her forehead, halfheartedly because I did not actually know what an inappropriate temperature felt like but wanted to appear like a competent caregiver.

"Still there, huh?" she asked.

"Not like yesterday."

"Ivan, you can put your hand back."

"On your head?"

"On my hand."

I followed her orders.

"What is this!" she asked.

"What is what?"

"This?"

She lifted our interlaced hands for a few seconds and then let them fall back to the bed.

"It's nothing."

"It's strange."

"You don't want to die alone."

"Nothing more?"

"Anything 'more' is your brain making meaning—"

"And the brain needs meaning . . . I know. You're so unbearably you, Ivan."

"But I'm right."

"Maybe."

"If we weren't in this hospital and you saw me in a restaurant, you would be just beautiful enough to be disgusted by me and just soulful enough to pity me."

"You don't make me wet, Ivan, if that's what you're asking."

"I'm not asking anything."

"If we were in any other two bodies, in any other place, at any other time, I would still feel like we first met as two quarks a few seconds after the big bang."

"You expect me to take you seriously after that?"

"Gravely serious."

"I think you need some blood. I should tell them you're awake."

I wheeled out of the Red Room and informed the nurses that Polina was ready for more blood. Then I went back to my room, picked up a book, unaware of what book it was, and started reading, hoping my eyes would get heavy enough to sleep. Fifty pages later, I was still wide awake. So I skipped the morphine, went right for one of Elena's caches, and sipped the burn until I choked. I almost made it back to my room before I passed out.

I awoke hours later in my bed with a respectable amount of vomit on my chest. My first thought was, *Is it mine?* My second thought was, *Of course it is.* My third thought was that it was the first day of Nurse Natalya on the night shift, which meant that I could take care of it now and face fire and brimstone, or I could take care of it tonight and live in a full body cast of my own vomit in the meantime. I decided to embrace the vomit and clean up later. In the meantime, I mitigated the circumstances by cleaning as much as I could with standard tap water, a change of clothes, and hiding the dirties in the far reaches of the netherworld beneath my bed.

Next, I wheeled past the Red Room to check on the current state of Polina's transfusion. I was not surprised to find her in a deep trance with all the necessary tubing still attached. *What do I do with myself?* I wondered. To be truthful, I wanted to disappear. And more than just into my head, while my body remained in plain view of the rest of the hospital. I wanted to disappear in the way of Houdini or Hoffa.

I remembered a branch next to Dennis's window when we were in the courtyard on the eighth day, which, if it were a Rorschach test, would have reminded me of a handicap ramp sloping to the rooftop, and at that particular moment, the rooftop seemed like a great place to disappear to. Moreover, the clang and clatter of plates coming from the cafeteria meant that in three minutes Dennis would be in the Main

Room rocking away to an episode of something. Which meant nurses arranging mutants for TV hour, others packing up the kitchen. Which meant the stars were aligning. So I ditched my chair in my room, slithered two doors down to Dennis's room, broke in (basically, I turned the doorknob), slithered to his window, opened it, squeezed my body through the black bars, maneuvered my way onto the handicap branch, nearly fell two stories to my death, spent about twelve minutes learning to crawl on a branch using only three points of contact (my arm and two leg nubs), nearly fell to my death thrice more, arrived at the corner of the rooftop terrace only to realize that at this point the branch was a bit farther away from the building than I had originally calculated (myopia), decided that if I had come this far I would play the odds, and rolled my body off the branch with as much (virtually none) momentum as I could, and (just barely) made impact with the unforgiving concrete roof, resulting in at least three bloody scrapes distributed over various nubs and my elbow.

After that, I didn't want to move anymore, so instead I just lay there and watched the blue fade from the sky at an unnoticeably slow drip until nothing was left but black and the hydrogen fingerprints of stars. In the interim, I, like Polina, noticed how nothing felt real. I noticed how the last few months could be erased like chalk, leaving only a blurry residue of the original words, which of course serve as the bones that imagination uses to fill the space with meat and striated muscular details, and I wouldn't question the fact that it was all suddenly gone, that the flesh was eaten off the bone, and the bones would soon be buried deep beneath the layers of silt and dirt, and new civilizations would be built on that dirt, and new beings would populate its cities, and live in its architecture, and new loves would grow, while old ones that once felt so important would be forgotten, and

∽

clearly I'm drunk.

my apologies, Reader.

∽

After about an hour of blue, thirty minutes of dusk, and two hours of black my thoughts were interrupted by her voice.

"How'd you get up here without bedsheets and duct tape?" said Polina's bald silhouette as it peeked out of the hole in the roof.

"I used the handicap ramp over there. How did you know I'd be up here?"

"I didn't, but it seemed like the only option after I checked your room, the Main Room, all the stairwells and colored rooms, the bathroom, and behind all the couches."

"How are you feeling?"

"Like I have new blood."

"Like a modern-day vampire."

"Already occurred to me."

Polina moved a little bit closer, so I started shivering.

"Are you cold?" she asked.

"Not really."

Polina leaned toward my neck, opened her mouth, and blew moist, hot air onto my skin. I shivered some more.

"Ivan?" she asked.

"Yes," I said.

"Take your shorts off."

"That won't help with my shivering."

"I asked you to pull down your shorts."

When Polina said this, my *Hui* filled completely.

"I can't."

"Of course you can."

"No, I can't."

"Why can't you?"

"Because my *Hui* is hard."

"I want to see it."

"I don't want you to see it."

"You want me to touch it?"

"No."

I meant yes. Fortunately, Polina pulled my shorts off anyway while I feigned resistance. My twitching *Hui* pointed to the moon, which was full and big and bright. I was too conscious of its size and appearance, as well as her face, which was an unsettling mixture of sex and sickness.

"Can I touch it?" she asked, but the question was rhetorical because she wrapped her palm and fingers around it before I had a chance to answer.

"It's nice."

"It's not."

"I like it."

Polina began to slide her palm up and down the length of my *Hui*. Then she stopped to lick her palm in one long, thick lap and wrapped it back around, slowly sliding up and down, then twisting subtly. My head was clear and silent, except for the faint weight of my self-awareness and the occasional recognition that someone who was not me was touching my *Hui*.

"I'm going to do something now, okay?"

"What?"

"I'll show you."

Polina opened her mouth and consumed my whole *Hui*, right to my flesh, and sucked on it with her lips and tongue. I didn't withdraw from it, but I said, "No, not this way."

Polina pulled her mouth away long enough to say, "What way?" and then started licking the entirety of my *Hui*.

"Let me lick you first."

"No, Ivan." Then back to sucking she went.

"Why not?"

"Because I'm sick."

"So am I."

"No, you're not. Enjoy this."

"Would you enjoy it if I were doing it to you?"

"I would."

"Then let me."

"No. This is for you."

Polina decided to abandon words and instead began to attack my *Hui* with her mouth and wet palm with devout piety. She momentarily paused to describe how I tasted.

And with almost every oscillation of her hand, her technique seemed to sharpen as if she knew exactly what my particular *Hui* needed to burst in her mouth. That's when an ugly thought came into my head, microscopically and wordlessly at first, but altogether uninvited: *Has she done this before?* And a flush of some as-of-yet-unnamed emotion, which felt like a stew of insecurity-jealousy-anxiety spread from my chest down into my *Hui* strong enough to make me worried that the whole apparatus would come down right in her mouth, but as per usual, reproductive biology won over fight-flight, and the thought dissolved in her saliva as my *Hui* became progressively harder, threatening, against her tongue, to erupt.

She stopped for a minute to say, "*Ya hochu chtoby ti konchil.*"*

And before I had a choice in the matter I did, I gave it all, filling her mouth I'm sure, but entirely unaware because I was too busy noticing how a mixture of vulnerability and kinship results in orgasms that leave nothing the same ever again, irrevocable, a complete earthquake, screaming, *If this person goes away, I will die.* No one ever told me that would happen, which was inconvenient because Polina was going away.

Polina swallowed graciously and looked at me with a sultry smile most likely induced by the tremors in my thigh nubs and the gape in my mouth. She gently pushed my torso back down to the concrete, which was colder now than I

---

*   "I want you to come."

remembered, and rested her head on my chest, through which she could feel my heart beating tortured little beats.

"Are you okay?" she asked.

"I'm fine."

"Did you like it?"

"Yes."

"Why are you so quiet?"

"You should get back inside. We know what happens when you're out here too long."

"Just five more minutes."

"Three."

"Fine. Three."

"Natalya is working tonight. I can stay with you."

"Okay."

"Touch my head."

"Okay."

"Pet it?"

"Okay.

"Thank you."

After five, not three, minutes, we both descended the handicap branch to Dennis's window. Inside, Dennis was asleep, and Polina adjusted his blankets so that they covered all his uncovered spots. Then she walked, and I slithered, back into my room and into my bed, where I fell asleep to the things Polina was saying.

The Little Green Folders

I don't think we deviated from our morphology once. Apparently, the less publicized side effect of a catastrophic orgasm is hibernation. I only know that I lifted my head to find my body in precisely the position it was when I collapsed on the bed last night, with Polina's arm wrapped around me from behind, and the early rays of morning sunlight starting to fill the room. If not for the death hanging in the air like smoke, it would have been a perfect way to wake up.

Polina sensed the motion.

"Hi, Ivan."

She coughed some and then winced like a rodent.

"How do you feel?" I asked.

"Like *Khalva* and *Kozinaki.*"*

"Gifted liar."

"I had a crazy dream last night."

"Another one?"

"Yes."

"What happened in this one?"

"I dreamed that I sucked on your *Hui.*"

"What a nightmare."

"I know."

Polina aimed for my eye but kissed my nose, which was

---

* Two popular Slavic nut-and-syrup-based desserts.

followed by a smile, followed by the playful creases in her face becoming deep and solemn. And with those new wrinkles, somehow the air in the room congealed. Enough for me, with all my limited understanding of social cues and inter-personal intelligence, to know that something bad was about to happen.

"What is it?"

"What is what?"

"Something bad is about to happen."

"It's been about to happen for a long a time. One more day won't hurt."

Which is exactly when I discovered that I don't do well with any form of uncertainty. So I said:

"I don't do well with any form of uncertainty."

"Can't it wait another day?"

"No."

"Then I need to show you something."

"Okay."

"But it's not here."

"Okay."

"I'll be back."

"Okay."

And she left, closing the door behind her, shuffling like a sprite, while I waited on the edge of a knife in my bed. In my ensuing dread, I started to count and made it to sixty-seven before the doorknob turned and Polina reentered with three army-green folders, which were quite familiar to me because they were the same folders that every patient at the Mazyr Hospital for Gravely Ill Children gets on his or her first day at the asylum. She sat down on the cold linoleum next to my face.

"You're like me, Ivan. A curious punk, right?"

"I guess."

"Is there a patient in this hospital whose file you haven't read?"

"No, I've read them all."

"Of course you have. Max, Alex, Dennis, the gingers. Even the ones who have come and gone before we even got here. Before *you* got here. They're all too interesting, and we get bored, right?"

"Right."

"Where have you found every file you've ever read?"

"In the cabinet behind Miss Kristina's desk."

I said the words as if they were formalities rushed through on the way to the point.

"And who filled in all the blanks in every one of those files?"

"Miss Kris."

"Right."

"Can we skip the questions I already know the answers to?"

"You know the difference between you and me?"

"You're a burglar? And you're attractive when you have hair."

"Yes, but I'm also much more patient than you."

"Maybe."

"You've never opened the safe in Mikhail's office."

"It's locked."

"Yes, but you would never think to sit in front of it on the nights he's not fucking Lyudmila and try every combination, would you?"

"I would think about it."

"But you would never do it."

"Probably not."

"I would."

"And you did."

"I did."

"And you found those."

"Yes."

"And?"

"Look at the handwriting."

Polina pulled a random page from the top folder and put it in my hand.

"Does it look familiar?" she asked.

"No."

"So, it's not the same handwriting that's on every file in the hospital?"

"No."

From the bottom of her stack, Polina pulled out another piece of paper.

"This is a letter Mikhail wrote to the city treasurer requesting more funds for the hospital, but he never sent it because I stole it."

Polina gave it to me. It was clearly the same handwriting as in the green file I was holding, which confirmed that Mikhail Kruk filled out those files *instead* for an as-of-yet-unknown reason, which I was sure she was about to share. I nodded to confirm as much.

"So whose files are those?"

"The oldest one is for a patient named Albina. She had leukemia just like me. Didn't make it to her eighth birthday. She died before you were born."

"Okay, next?"

"Next is Dimitri."

"I remember Dimitri."

"Do you remember what was wrong with him?"

"Nothing was wrong with him."

"Almost true. He had a connective tissue disorder like you. But his was apparently called Dupuytren's contracture, which, according to his file, means he had little pits in his hands that no one could even see unless they were up close."

"So?"

"So, why was he here?"

"Maybe that's why he left."

"Maybe. But he left when he was fifteen. It's hard to explain a fifteen-year prison sentence for a few weird tendons."

"And the last one?"

"The last one is yours, Ivan."

"Not possible. I already have a file."

"You have two files."

Polina handed me Ivan File #2. I opened the cover and started flipping through the pages.

"This is the same exact file. These are just copies."

"It is the same. Except for Mikhail's handwriting and one more thing."

"What?"

"This one has your date of birth. It says you were born on June 10, 1987. You're a Gemini, in case you were wondering."

Specks of black started to fill my eyes, and the right angles of my room, which I had long taken for granted, started to bend and bulge.

"There's another difference," she said.

"I see it," I said.

To inform you, Reader, on Ivan File #1 the word "unknown" was written on the lines reserved for the names of my mother and father. In Ivan File #2, there were names very clearly once written but now blacked out with a thick marker.

"What are you thinking?" Polina asked.

I had been too deep inside my own head, dreaming up every possible explanation for this new intelligence, to notice that I was shaking wildly and that the paper I was holding was being crushed into a ball. I couldn't see the name beneath the ink on the line that said "Father" but there was only one explanation for these files, penned by Mikhail, to be defaced with a marker and then locked away. The devil wouldn't protect a soul, unless it was his own. I wished I were an idiot like the others. I wished it because even if I tried to turn my head the other way and stick mud in my ears and claw out my eyes, under the surface, the calculations would continue uninterrupted, and I would come to the conclusion that this ended only one way and that Polina already had it figured out: I was an unintended fuck child. I was the bastard spawn of the Most Mediocre Man in the World and a large-breasted nurse. I was unwanted in the purest of ways, an accident of the universe, bad news, a typo, and my whole life I've been kept from the world because I'm shame encoded in bastard DNA.

Despite the monsoon ripping through my head and then chest, I had enough presence of mind to look up. Polina was spewing tears down her face, as if I had said each of those thoughts out loud. Maybe I did.

"Maybe this isn't bad, Ivan. You might have a family. You have a brother. Maybe a mother."

"Does Natalya know?"

"How would I know?"

"He could have erased us. Why didn't he erase us?"

"I haven't figured that out yet."

"Or even better, never let me out of her *pizda*."

"I don't know. He's not okay, mentally speaking."

Before she finished that sentence, a colossus of a thought appeared in my brain, big and bright, but too quick to hold down and pummel, a true mindfuck typed up all pretty on a shiny banner carried across by miniature imps, cackling and jeering.

"How long have you had this?" I asked.

"Two months, maybe."

"Before we started talking."

"Yes."

"Please tell me what's in my head is wrong."

"What?"

"This is why you talked to me."

"No, Ivan," she blubbered harder.

"You did. I was a pet puzzle."

"No."

"You were bored."

"*No.*"

"Admit it."

"At first. But then you became a person to me."

"*You* were always a person."

"You would have done the same."

"To the gingers, sure."

"I'm so sorry."

"Leave."

"Don't do this."

"Go."

"I'm dying, Ivan. Any minute. I don't want to die alone."

Promptly, all gauges turned cold.

Some insignificant voice told me I could be wrong, but it didn't matter. The finite number of days lost their weight, because I lost the line between what was real and what was not as it pertained to Polina. And I suppose a part of me wanted to join forces with the leukemia and punish her for that.

"Good-bye," I said.

DAY 5

Conversion Disorder

"What happened?"

I didn't answer.

"Ivan, what little life she has left is being sucked out of her."

I didn't answer.

"If you're happy killing her, I don't mind. It's on you."

This was the first conversation of the fifth day. Technically, it was not really a conversation because only Nurse Katya was participating.

I had had an almost identical conversation with Nurse Natalya about twelve hours earlier, shortly after she arrived for her night shift. That conversation sounded like this:

"What happened?"

I didn't answer.

"Ivan, what little life she has left is being sucked out of her."

I didn't answer.

"It's going to kill her, and you will live the rest of your life in a hole because you won't forgive yourself."

Nurse Natalya's response was a bit more poignant. That said, responding to conversational advances was complicated for two reasons.

Reason #1: I couldn't move my body. I tried, though. I sent orders to my mouth, and others to my hand, some to my neck, but the nerves didn't respond. Freud would argue that there are very reasonable explanations for this phenomenon. Every human is a collection of conscious and unconscious thoughts, which all contribute some share of vitality to a human organism. These are typically thoughts about meaning, passion, and purpose; thoughts about why you were picked by the universe, and what your role should be in the cosmic dance. Polina unwittingly stole every single one of these thoughts when she handed me that green folder. In one valiant ballet, she detonated the ground I wheeled on, which had previously been built from my love and trust for Natalya and the plausible deniability of my absurd creation story.

Reason #2: There were new questions running through my head. Too many questions. Unbearable questions. For example:

1. Who knew I was Mikhail's bastard kid? Mikhail's affairs were the worst-kept secret of the Mazyr Hospital for Gravely Ill Children. Did this mean I was the best kept?
2. Did this explain the unconscious hostility that every health care professional in this institution directed toward me since I was old enough to fake a coma?
3. Did this explain Nurse Natalya's unconscious sympathy? My Natalya, the only creature I trusted, did she lie to four-year-old Ivan, and then ten-year-old Ivan, and every-other-year-old me?

No, no, Katya. It's not on me. My body won't move. Even now, days later, as I scribble through these pages, all I can move is my wrist, which is the minimum requirement to hold a pen or unscrew a flask. Tragically, even masturbation is off-limits.

To be fair to Polina, she tried to fix what she broke. Leave it to the dying to know that stubbornness has no place in death. I recall as the hands of the clocks spun around the perimeter of the day, there were plenty of knocks at my door. At least a few of these belonged to Polina, because the knocks were in her own language. I know this because the rhythm and cadence of remorse has its own dialect.

The other knocks belonged to nurses who burst in and lifted my eyelids only to have them snap back closed, each one accusing me of being a stubborn asshole, except for Natalya, who was wise enough to lure me with the most indecent pornographic images available in southern Belarus, only to find me still unresponsive. And as the big hand on the clock dragged the little one with it, they subjected me to an anthology of tests, needles in my median cubital, stethoscopes on my heart, hammers on my reflexes, lights in my eyes, pointy things in my ears, only to have everything come back negative for everything and Nurse Elena come in to yell at me, again in a different language, but by this time I could read her lips, which appeared to say, *It's all in your head,* to which I responded, *It's all in my life,* but I'm sure it actually came out, *Baaaa ba baa bi baa,* which was still a stunning development because it was my first response to anything in eighteen hours, but still without a reasonable diagnosis they brought in the big guns, the Director, Mikhail himself, to offer his assessment, only to bask in confusion when he found a boy, supposedly comatose but actually not at all, gnashing at his face with small, pointy teeth, clawing his eyes, spitting into his mouth, slapping his cheeks, pulling at his (remaining) hairs, screaming what would appear to be obscenities if only they were in the language of Mother Russia, which obliged him to order a cocktail of sedatives to be shot into my arm and then the rest was black squid ink.

That was the fifth day, the day I regret most. I had no way to know there would only be four more days. Or that only one of those days would be bearable.

∽

Currently, the clock reads 5:45 in the P.M.
I've been writing for sixty-six hours.
It is the fifth day of December.
The year is 2005.

I can feel the end
of this.

∽

DAY 4

Good-Bye, Yellow Brick Road

I awoke in the middle of the next day, departed.

Emotionally at least, I was blank like paper.

My first thought of the day was that I had thrown away a day, though to be fair it's debatable whether I had a choice.

My second thought was to go to the pantry and steal some non–cabbage juice sustenance (matzo crackers and a 90-percent-eaten three-year-old jar of peanut butter). My third thought was to find Polina, first in her room, which was empty, then in the Red Room, which only held Dennis's mom and a few heart-hole children struggling to maintain the proper lub-dub-lub-dub-lub-dub rhythm, then to the Main Room, stairwells, and bathrooms, which were all empty. This, of course, meant that she either wandered off into the surrounding environment to die in a forest with tree-dwelling critters or she was on the roof. So I wheeled myself back to the stairwell, dismounted from my chair, writhed up the stairs to the top of the hospital, and yelled through the red metal door leading to the roof.

"You look like a boy with a bald head!" I yelled.

No answer.

"If you plan to die up there, at least let me cover you in peanut butter so vultures can get past the bitter taste of your flesh."

Nothing.

Finally: *"Vitas is a homosexual!"*

I could officially be sure she wasn't on the roof. So I went back to the Main Room, found Alex's hair being brushed by Nurse Lyudmila, whom I deftly ignored, and searched on for a viable alternative, like Nurse Katya, who was absorbed in the supernatural task of organizing Tupperware by size and color.

"Where is she?" I asked.

"Now you want to see her?"

"Where?"

"In her room. She looks like the fire went out. I give her two days."

"She's not in her room. I checked."

"Then she's floating around here somewhere."

"The girl could fall dead any second, and you don't know where she is?"

"How far could a dead girl be, Ivan?"

I decided this comment wasn't worth responding to, so I rolled on. I rolled past Nurse Elena, who was oblivious and buried in a toilet, and I rolled past Miss Kristina, who was oblivious and buried in a phone, and I rolled out through the big brown double doors, and I rolled down the ramp onto the trail, and I rolled past my dread, as my insides felt like a fully formed fly pushing its way out of maggot skin.

I yelled her name. I looked around. I was without answer, and sure she was gone. This was it. I wasn't to see her again. This was day one.

In my resignation, I saw a piece of grass shimmer near the tree where two days ago we sat outside in the rain. This, of course, required me to wheel through the grass to pursue it, which, in my current state, required supernatural strength—but, hey, anything for love, right?—and precision eye-tracking. Black. It was black. And shiny. Black, yet shiny. As I inched ahead, I wondered what things are both black and shiny. Obsidian. Onyx. Polished lava. Which of these would be in the area immediately surrounding the Mazyr Hospital for Gravely Ill Children? Probably none. I was desperate, possibly, looking for some hope in nothing at all. But this is the same sort of desperation that lets losing soccer teams come back to win in the last few seconds of a game, so I let go. Which was the right thing to do because eventually I found that the black and shiny thing was a broken piece of a vinyl record, and there was only one reason why a piece of broken record would be sitting amid blades of grass in the hospital courtyard. Furthermore, it didn't take too much squinting to see that between me and the forest that surrounded the hospital in a little horseshoe, there was another black and shiny sliver, which, after a bit more wheeling through brutally tall grass, was obviously another piece of broken record, and up ahead, just a few more meters was another, and it occurred to me that this was Polina's own version of Hansel and Gretel.

A few more jagged pieces later and I could see I was being led to the forest and, more specifically, into a tiny opening that imitated the closest thing to a trail that nature has ever made without the help of a man. By my seventh serrated piece of vinyl, which I added to the puddle of black now collecting on my shorts, I was there, at the trailhead, quivering, with a heart rate of 130. I tried to whistle, but I was never good at whistling. Besides, whistling was never a way in which Polina and I typically summoned each other, so I stopped trying to whistle and instead just called out to her, but didn't hear anything back.

The forest floor was a potpourri canvas of dirt, broken twigs, and soggy leaves, which was not at all conducive to more wheelchair wheeling. Nevertheless, I pushed the wheel anyway, testing new boundaries in disabled locomotion, and of course, looking furiously for more glint. Up ahead, slight right, I saw some gleam, which I laboriously pushed myself toward to discover that it was indeed another piece. This one, however, had some writing—"До свидания, желтая кирпичная дорога"*—which I took to be a sign. A few more meters ahead was another sliver, this one with the track length (3:11). And then another one that was just pure black. But then there were no more. Ten meters of rolling around in every direction and nothing.

So I started to weave new story lines in my head to accommodate the facts. *Polina, one frustrated and lonely night, leaves her room to come outside and shatter old records to release six months of stifled rage, the yellow brick road just a cruel coincidence. No rhymes, no reasons. Just anger.* And I started to believe there was no trail and no bread crumbs and that she was gone again. Until I looked down and saw the thirteen pieces sitting in my lap and thought that perhaps I should put the pieces back together. Perhaps there was a clue in the puzzle. So I began to arrange the shards on my shorts into a vinyl jigsaw. I arranged them like it was the only thing that mattered, and as each one found a partner, I felt a dollop of faith.

But in the end, it was only a record with a mosaic of jagged lines winding through it like spider legs, no secret messages or further game instructions.

Nothing.

Except for the laughing.

---

* "Good-Bye, Yellow Brick Road." Presumably a Soviet bootleg of the 1973 song by Elton John.

"You would, wouldn't you, Ivan?"

Which, of course, came from Polina, who was sitting in a splotch of shade, sporting her hospital gown and dusty bald head, arranging twigs into a model log cabin with crispy leaves for shingles.

"I've been watching you for fifteen minutes," she said.

Stubbornness has no place in dying.

"This wasn't a game?"

"No. It was a victim of rage."

"That was my second theory."

"Astute."

"How did you know I would find you?"

"I didn't think you wanted to find me."

"I didn't."

Polina's eyes gently returned to her miniature log cabin.

"Were you planning to die out here?" I asked.

"Probably. I always imagined I would die against a tree on a cliff in Anapa. Overlooking the Black Sea. Fade out right in nature's bosom. Feed a few bearded vultures with my dead carcass. This seemed close enough."

"Romantic."

"Would you like to hear a story?"

"I would."

"It's about my dad."

"Assistant Professor of Piano. University of Lviv, 1992–2004."

"Yes."

I could see that Polina's eyes were turning luminescent due to some flavor of melancholy.

"Don't waste your time telling stories you don't want to tell."

"No, I want to tell this one."

"You may proceed."

"He taught me how to play piano. He was my hero. He was perfect."

"Standard little girl."

"They sent us home from school early on the day Lviv flooded. When I got home, he was fucking one of his students on our piano. The one he taught me on. She was eighteen. I was twelve. She scrambled to grab her purse and panties. My father scrambled to cover up his *Hui*."

"What did you do?"

"I stood there, shaking. I couldn't look at his eyes. I remember there was a tiny piece of wallpaper peeling off the wall, so I stared at it. He tried to touch me, and I yelled. He offered me anything I wanted. He told me he loved me more than anything in the world. All the standard shit. Though, when you're twelve, it doesn't feel all that standard. He said that there was no limit to what he would do to make it right. I said, tell Mom. He said, except that. That it would ruin the family. He asked me if I loved the family. I said yes. So I let him bribe me. Whatever I wanted for the next two years. I almost started to forgive him."

"Almost?"

"Déjà vu two years later. She was sixteen, and her tits had just started to bud. It was also the day before my fifteenth birthday. The apologies started all over. How he would do anything to make it right. So I pretended that everything would be okay. I would take the gifts. But I kept the panties, which were blue. Then when my mom came home, the words burst right out of my mouth. She didn't believe me. I was dubbed a storyteller. Until I showed her the blue panties. Luckily, neither of us had blue panties."

"What did she do?"

"She left. For approximately three hours. Which was just enough time for my dad to knock a tooth out of my mouth. But the worst part is that my mother died that day. Not her body—she still had a heartbeat and everything—but after that day, she was like a piece of driftwood. And every day since, I've blamed myself for killing her."

"You did the right thing."

"I'm not looking for absolution. This isn't a confession. I was absolved when I got cancer. Dying is nature's purification. You should try it."

"Then why are you telling me?"

"Because we're all going to hell, Ivan. Except maybe you."

"You don't even believe in hell."

"That's irrelevant."

"What makes me special?"

"Because you've been severed. You're a karmic anomaly. It's why I risked everything to tell you. You're free."

"I don't feel free."

"That doesn't make it untrue. There's a safety in the trap. But when Mikhail locked up your file and made a new one, one that says that your parents could be anyone in the universe or no one at all, you were severed from him. You were cut from history. You're not required to live out someone else's sins. That's something I'll never know. But you, you're a vacancy. Starting yesterday, you get to write yourself to life."

"If I'm free, you're free. His sins aren't your sins."

"I played my own part in everything. I participated. Not that it matters much at this point. I just know that after they died, I looked at my father and then at my mother. And it was in their eyes. And then in mine. They seeped into me. I knew we would be tangled up forever."

Polina stopped to adjust a few twigs in her cabin and remove the leaves from the top so that she could see inside.

Then she said:

"You're not tangled up with anything."

To which I said:

"I'm tangled up with you."

To which Polina lifted her head and smiled 12 percent, which made me ask:

"Have I told you how surprisingly pretty you are for a bald person?"

Polina dropped the twig she was fidgeting with and crawled over to me, presumably because that was all she could do. Then she took my face into her hands and kissed me for the second time. But this time felt different from the last. Counterfeit could not live in that kiss. I'm not sure whether at that moment she was possessed by some imperial and selfless charity, or if she, like me, was caught up in the fantasy that I wasn't a hideous creature, but I didn't care. I felt the addictive grandeur. I leaned in and kissed her moist mouth back, even harder. I had no idea what I was doing, but the more primal currents in my body took over and attacked her lips in a way that I can only imagine resembled what a passionate kiss should look and feel like. An impulse arose to pull away and see where her eyes were and attempt to assess her reactions through her facial expressions. Before giving in to it, I considered whom I was kissing, succumbed to the ensuing avalanche, and sucked her upper lip. I got to enjoy that lip for a few delicious seconds, and then the moment soured, literally. I tasted familiar metallic bitters, which probably meant that Polina was bleeding into my mouth. When I pulled away I saw bloody streaks oozing from the corner of her eyes. Without thinking, I used my white T-shirt to wipe them up. Polina looked down in alarm, saw the bloody smears, and cried hysterically.

"Let's go back," I said.

She tried to stand but fell back into the autumn ambrosia.

"When I sat here, I knew I wouldn't get back up again," she said.

"Not an option."

I tried to yank Polina onto my lap, and she tried too. And after a few minutes of flailing, we proved that two halves of a person equal a whole. Eventually, her body fell over mine, and her fingers clung to my bloody T-shirt, while I started rolling at a drip. I didn't know how long my one arm could push two people or whether there were things dying inside of Polina that were going to make her never come back, so I screamed for help. I screamed for Katya and Lyudmila and Elena, even though I never asked them for help before, because Polina taught me that there is no room for stubbornness in death. I screamed for them until I sanded down my vocal cords to nothing and the screams turned into air. And still I screamed some more. We were five meters from the forest when she started to convulse. We were twelve meters from the forest when the bleeding in her mouth turned to a thin little red river Styx accumulating on my shorts. We were eighteen meters from the woods when I saw the blurry blue scrubs burst out of the hospital. We were twenty-one meters from the woods when Nurse Katya and Nurse Elena each took hold of an extremity or two and carried her back half-dangling into the hospital.

"Are you trying to die?" I heard Katya ask her.

They left me back in the field, wheeling away like a one-armed fiend through the six-inch grass. The sky was like solid granite, like on every other November day in Belarus. Flecks of rain started to appear on my face, while I expended caveman-like effort, only to inch along at a speed that was not commensurate with that effort, while my beloved bled out bad blood from most of her orifices.

Three minutes later, I was back inside the hospital, which was like a ghost town. All the mutants were put away into their rooms, and all the nurses were in the Red Room huddled around Polina's bloody gums. I wheeled up close to the door and watched them all do a particular job. Nurse Elena wiped the blood from her teeth and her eyes. Nurse Katya slapped her cheeks. Nurse Lyudmila connected plastic tubes to her. My job was to pay better attention to the process of someone dying than I ever did before. Until that job wasn't enough and I started shouting at the nurses to take more of my blood.

"It won't help, Ivan," one said.

"She'll just bleed it out," said another.

"We took two of your pints in three days," said the last one.

"It'll kill you," said the first again.

And it was true, it might. I felt like a vodka IV was dripping into my bloodstream ever since they took the second pint. But I hated feeling null.

"How long now?" I asked.

"Hours probably," said another.

"Now leave," said the last one.

Which of course I didn't. I wheeled back a few inches so they couldn't see me. And I went into a coma. But really I was listening to everything. All the jargon ricocheting around the room, mixing right along with all the memories in my head. And then the commotion inside the Red Room stopped, and everything was silent except for the chirp of each heartbeat. The nurses filed out one by one, passing my comatose body. When they were all gone, I wheeled back into the Red Room and held her sedated hand. Her eyes were fluttering under the skin of her eyelids again, and I felt brokenhearted because there was no dream she could possibly be having that was happy. So I held her hand tighter, subtly hoping that the pressure would find its way through the neural wires and let her know that she wasn't alone. Then it occurred to me that it didn't matter because dying is the loneliest event in life. Polina could be surrounded by a village, each resident tending to a different need, each one reminding her of why she mattered, and she would still die alone. Because when it finally comes, you take that step into the black by yourself.

Some blurry hours later, Nurse Natalya showed up for her night shift.

"Take more blood," I said, aborting her attempt to pull me into her bosom.

She rolled her eyes.

"Please?" I said.

She crossed her arms.

"I implore you."

"It could kill you."

"It won't."

"You don't know that."

"I feel strong."

"It won't make any difference. She's leaving now, Ivan."

"It could give her another day."

"You will always want one more day."

"Yes, but on this day, I didn't get to say good-bye."

Apparently this touched the right organ, because she was suddenly elbow deep inside of a drawer getting a syringe and bag.

"Give me your arm," she said.

And I did, and the needle slipped in, and she took more blood, and immediately my brain stopped working and my vision blurred. Nurse Natalya gave me a few good slaps on the cheek.

Stay here, Ivan.

Stay here.

I didn't.

The Suitcase Day

I woke up in the middle of the night, shortly after 3:00 in the A.M. The first thing I noticed was a large bruise on my forehead and also my nose, which hurt and felt swollen and slightly crooked according to my fingers. The second thing that I noticed was that I was still in my chair and still in the Red Room. Polina was asleep, or in a real coma, or whatever. I didn't even know if the last transfusion happened. All I knew was that now tubes were coming up and over her ears and into her nose to help her breathe. I also noticed that when I looked at anything for too long, it felt like my head was attached to helicopter blades. So I decided to lay my head back down next to hers and make it stop. I remember feeling her few returning fuzzy hairs tickling my cheek as I laid my face against her otherwise bald head. And then the helicopter blades stopped and everything went black again.

Then I woke up at 5:00 in the A.M., to some jostling by Nurse Natalya.

"Ivan, can you hear me?"

"Unfortunately," I said.

"I have to leave now. Eat this Tula bread. It will help."

"Help what?"

"Help you keep your head up."

"You took my blood?"

"You begged me."

"And you gave it to her?"

"Yes."

"Will she wake up today?"

"I don't know."

"Don't leave."

"I need sleep too, *moya lyubov.*"*

"You can sleep here."

"Where?"

"In my room."

"Never. I know what happens there."

"Will I see you tonight?"

"Of course."

Natalya went home, and I took a bite of Tula bread, which made my head stop spinning for a second. I took the opportunity to look over Polina, who was illuminated by the summer morning light coming in through the barred windows. By now most of her skin was purplish black, as opposed to the innocent porcelain she donned when I first saw her walk into the hospital. And where the skin wasn't purplish black, it was smeared with occasional brushstrokes of blood. Her bones were like tiny hands trying to push through her face and shoulders, and her knees were like the pictures that they sometimes show of Auschwitz residents. Her mouth hung open vulnerably, and her teeth were orange from the slow diffusion of blood from her gums, and incidentally, so were the half-moons just beneath her eyes. Her breathing was short and shallow and sounded like her lungs had been replaced by

---

*   My love.

birthday balloons. I could go on, but as it is I'm sure you'll never get this picture out of your head, Reader. I traced some of her bruises with my limited fingers, laid my head next to hers, and went back to sleep.

The next time I woke up, it was because of Polina, who was trying to kill me in my sleep again. I gasped for air to save my life, and she started laughing like an insane person.

"There's something very wrong with you," I said.

"We don't have much time, so I'm going to have to ask you to go to my room and look under my bed," she said.

"What?"

"Wheel yourself into my room and look under my bed."

"Why?"

"Ivan, I'm going to die waiting for you to do me this one small favor."

"Okay."

I turned around and wheeled my way through the three halls and two turns required to get to Polina's room. When I opened the door, I noticed the faint smell of mold light up my nostrils. As quickly as I could, I dismounted from my chair and writhed under her bed, where I found an old-style portmanteau. I writhed back and awkwardly dragged it out from under the bed. Then I unlatched each of the two latches on either side and opened it up. The first thing that caught my attention was a stack of rubles, which after counting amounted to about a hundred thousand.* The second thing I noticed was

---

* Roughly five hundred U.S. dollars.

a large folded map of the Mazyr metropolitan area, with several key locations circled in red ink, including restaurants, alternative health care locations, and notable city landmarks. Also included were six packets of cookies, some crackers, two bottles of water, a small knife, an umbrella, a combination lock, a watch, a compass, several books by Russian masters, including *Lolita, The Master and Margarita,* and *Crime and Punishment,* and Polina's journal. I put the journal in my shorts, packed up the rest of the suitcase, pushed it underneath the bed, and wheeled myself back to the Red Room.

"Thank you and good-bye," I said.

"You're an odd fuck," she whispered, because now everything she said was air.

"I wanted to make sure I said it now because you almost died yesterday before I had a chance."

Our eyes were mutually soaked, which was nice.

"You're weird," she said.

"I know."

"Perhaps the weirdest."

"I know."

"Are you going to use the suitcase?"

"I don't know."

"That's not a good answer."

"I can't say yet."

"For me?"

"Okay."

I just said it, but I didn't mean it.

"Do you think it's going to hurt?" she asked.

"What?"

"Dying."

"No. There's a lot of morphine in you right now."

"Do you think there will be monsters like the Tibetans say?"

"I think the monsters are already in you."

"How do I kill the monsters?"

"I don't think you need to kill them."

"Then what?"

"I think you invite them. And let them stay. And learn to live with them. Then when you die, they stop being monsters."

"I'm so scared."

Then the dam broke, and Polina started wailing, maybe because she took my advice and let her monsters in. I wiped away the tears as best as I could, but they were coming faster than one hand could wipe.

"So scared, so scared," she said.

"Don't be afraid of scared," I said.

And she just kept repeating herself, and I just kept wiping her tears, which were orange. I kissed her cheeks in spite of the mess of it all. Some of her blood got onto my lips and into my mouth, which I knew because it tasted like tin. Some of it was bad blood, and some of it was my blood.

"I want my mother," she said. "Mommy," she repeated over and over like crying people sometimes do. Slowly the words abated. I thought that maybe it was all over. Maybe she had died. But the little chirp on the heart monitor kept chirping. So I said her name a few times, but she didn't respond. That was the last time I ever heard Polina talk. As suspected, despite my proximity, Polina would be dying alone.

I didn't move for the rest of the day except to run my fingers through her imaginary hair and listen carefully to the comforting ping of her heart monitor. Somehow her face looked peaceful. Occasionally, she would whisper something indecipherable, and I would get excited, imagining that possibly she was coming back from the void. But I quickly realized that she was in her head, probably in negotiations with monsters.

The Day of Delirium

On the second day, she was hooked up to a nauseating machine that dripped morphine into her blood and secured her in a sufficiently dissociated state. My pale partial hand held her little porcelain hand throughout the morning as the usual suspects passed in and out to see if she had died yet. Even though she was hooked up to an IV of saline water to keep her hydrated, her lips began to dry, almost in real time, and I could see the cracks and fissures of a California desert form in front of my eyes.

Nurse Natalya, who was still working nights, somehow appeared this morning.

"What are you doing here?" I asked.

"I wanted to give you this," she said.

It was like a sucker. Except instead of hard candy at the end, there was a moist sponge.

"You can use this to keep her mouth and lips moist."

She demoed the Popsicle sponge on Polina's chapped lips. I watched her carefully dab and spread water over Polina's tongue and around the perimeter of her mouth. Then she showed me how to rehydrate the sponge with a cup of water.

"I will be here," she said. "From now on."

"You don't need to be," I said.

"I want to," she said.

"Are you staying in Polina's room?"

"It's the only available bed."

"Don't look under it."

"Why?"

"Because."

"Okay, Ivan."

Then she leaned in, and turned my face toward hers, and looked at me with her maternal eyes, and said:

"It's even lonelier for you than it is for her. I know."

When she said that, I realized that Nurse Natalya had once been exactly where I was.

"I can take it from here," I said.

"Of course you can," she said. "I'll be cleaning dishes if you need me."

Aside from the occasional nurse strolling in with a clipboard and taking down a few notes from the machine that illuminated her vitals, I was the only one tending to Polina on the second day. I kept her mouth moist, I checked her pulse and also her temperature to compare them to the results displayed on the machines, I gently shifted an arm or a leg this way or that to minimize bedsores (not that it mattered), I carefully monitored the amount of saline in her IV bag and morphine in her blood, I notified people if levels were low, I pushed back on them if they pushed back on me, I wiped the pellets of sweat from her fevered bald head as they developed, I adjusted her pillows, I hummed familiar songs (out of tune so I'm not sure she recognized them). Most of all I waited for signs that she was coming back from a temporary holiday in her mind.

By 11:00 in the A.M. the delirium set in, which was perhaps not a delirium at all and instead could have been the epic battle for her next incarnation, which I knew about from the *Tibetan Book of the Dead*. But then I realized that such thoughts violated the Three Tenets of Ivanism, so I crushed them.

It wasn't always easy to decipher the contents of her whispering, mumbling, moaning, and guttural explosions, but I did the best I could and took liberty to fill in the gaps with reasonable details. At 11:17, she was clearly Cleopatra mourning the suicide of Antony. In the next hour, approximately 12:31, she was her very own seven-year old self in a car with her mom and dad, driving down the trans-Siberian highway, asking her dad why the moon didn't fall to the earth. At 1:00 in the P.M, she was a concubine of Joseph Stalin, and at 2:40, she was inside of her dog Sputnik.

Then, at 3:17, something unexpected happened. Something

that caused a cascade of biochemical reactions from my head to my nubs. Two unfamiliar characters showed up at the door of the Red Room. Both of them were female. One was Nurse Elena's age, and the other was Polina's age. I panicked due to an unacceptable lack of intelligence information. At the Mazyr Hospital for Gravely Ill Children, visitors were rare. They were even rarer when someone was about to die, because we all can secretly smell death and avoid it, quite literally, like a plague, which is why two new characters, at this precise moment, were unusual, and, in my personal opinion, in poor taste.

"Hello," the older one said.

"Who are you looking for?" I asked. "This is the Red Room. This is where people die. I don't think you meant to come here."

"The nurse said this is the room. She pointed right to it," the older one said again. The younger one just looked confused and nervous.

"Well, who are you looking for?" I asked.

"Polina Pushkin. Is she here?" the younger one said.

I wanted to say no. Instead, I instantly stopped swabbing Polina's mouth.

"Who are you?" I said.

The two looked at each other as if to silently decide who should say it.

"I'm Marina Markova, and this is my daughter Katerina. She and Polina were friends in school."

"Best friends," the younger one confirmed. "Is she here?"

"How did you know she was here?" I asked directly to the younger one. "Her parents are dead."

Again the two looked at each other uncomfortably.

"I got a letter from her. About a month ago," the younger one said.

"What did it say?" I asked.

"It said she was here. And that she was sick. Can you please tell us where she is?"

"She's here."

"Where."

"Here."

I pointed to Polina's limp body, which caused the two visitors to lose all the color in their faces. That's when I realized just how devastated Polina's physical body was. According to my day-to-day perspective of Polina's transition, she was still the most beautiful girl I knew, hair loss and orifice bleeding included. This was not so for the poor bastards who got the bona fide before-and-after experience.

"That's not Polina," the younger one said, shaking her head.

"I promise it is."

"What happened to her hair?"

"Chemotherapy."

"And her eyes!"

"Her blood cells don't work right."

The younger one started to cry.

"*Moya lyubov,* you knew she was sick. We talked about this," the older one said.

"Is she going to die?" the younger one asked.

"In a few hours," I said.

The younger one started to cry harder, which made me want to suggest to the both of them that salt water causes spontaneous and fatal reactions in leukemia patients. I didn't want to share Polina's death with them.

"What happened to her gums?"

"I told you, her blood happened."

I thought about what Polina would think if she heard me be an asshole to her friend, while the younger one walked over to the other side of the bed. Polina mumbled a few delirious words.

"Is she trying to talk to me? Does she know I'm here?" the younger one asked, choking all over her own wetness.

"No. I think she is playing poker with Oscar Wilde."

"Huh?"

"Nothing."

"Why were you touching her?"

"I was taking care of her."

"Why do you look like that?"

"The same reason you look like you do—bad genes."

"I don't like you."

"I don't care enough to like or not like you."

"Stop!" said the older one.

The younger one disengaged from me and turned back to Polina. She tried to touch her face in a tender way. It was clear that she thought the right thing to do was to act compassionately to her face, but really I could tell she was disgusted by it. She reminded me of an egg that looked like an egg in every way, only it was undercooked inside, which made it very disappointing when it came time to eat it.

"Mom, we should have come sooner. She's already dead," the younger one said as she reinitiated her sloppy wet mess, then rested her head on Polina's chest. I noticed the tears starting to soak through Polina's gown, and it made me want to leap across the bed and punch the girl in her big puffy wet face.

"You might not want to do that. She is very susceptible to bruising," I said.

"Stop being an expert and let her say good-bye to her friend," the older one said.

"I can't be here," said the younger one. "I just can't."

The younger one lifted her head and tried to look at Polina's face for a few more seconds. It was like she was trying to stare at the sun for as long as she could before she burned her retinas, then turned to the side, wincing.

"Let's go, Mom," said the younger one.

"But we just got here," said the older one.

"I said I can't be here," said the younger one.

"But we drove for—" said the older one, who was interrupted by the younger one unapologetically exiting the Red Room. The older one looked back at Polina for a few seconds, then over to me.

"You love her," she said.

"I don't know what that means," I said.

"Of course you don't."

She was about to leave but added, "You're an asshole. But I'm sorry for you."

She left before I had a chance to respond. Still, I said, "Thank you," in a whisper. Then I sat confused about whether I was happier or sadder that they were gone.

I spent most of that afternoon wondering how long the fuse was, since it was clear that at this point Polina was a time bomb ticking away to a death rattle. Only it was a magical bomb that wouldn't devastate my body physically like most bombs would. More traditional bombs would have been favorable considering my physical body was already fairly devastated and not much more substantive damage could be had. Instead, Polina's bomb would wreak havoc on my emotional body in a way that had never been wrought, and I wasn't exactly sure what that might mean.

After a few dozen minutes ruminating on this topic, I was jostled out by a voice. "But hasn't the fuse already burned away and the bomb exploded?" it said. I looked up and realized the voice was coming from my mother, who appeared opposite Polina's bed, standing in exactly the same place that Polina's friend was standing a few hours ago.

"She's already dead," she said. "Let go."

"She is. But also she isn't," I said.

"In what conceivable way is she not dead?" my mother asked.

"In the way that I can take care of her," I said. "And in the way that, quantum mechanically speaking, something unbelievable could happen."

"For a nihilist, you harbor a lot of hope."

"I've lost my taste for labels, Mother. What is a nihilist anymore?"

"And now a rhetorical question? I don't even know my baby boy anymore."

"I'm not sure I know myself right now."

"Start your mourning, *moya lyubov*."

"I can't."

"Why not?"

"Because I can't."

"Because you don't want to. And in an hour, or tonight, or tomorrow morning, she will rattle. And you will still resist. And you will refuse to accept that it happened. And you will be convinced that they buried a girl alive. So, let go."

"I wish I could."

"It's the only sane thing to do."

"Sanity is overrated."

"It wasn't a month ago."

"Touché, Mother."

"I know best."

"If I don't listen, I lose you, don't I?"

"In this case, maybe."

"More yes than maybe?"

"Yes."

"Where will you go?"

"Maybe to French Polynesia. Or your hippocampus."

"Why?"

"Because you won't have much need for me anymore."

"But I will."

"But according to your brain you won't."

She paused and thought and smirked.

"But do what you need to do," she said.

Then I closed my eyes, and she was gone.

That was the last time I talked to my mother.

Three hours later, I had still not let go of Polina and had no intention of doing so. Instead, I continued to rehydrate her lips and mouth. I couldn't remember the last time I rehydrated myself. When the other nurses left, Nurse Natalya attempted to remedy this situation by providing me with several hydration options, including soft drinks, lemonade, Orangina, and several varietals of bottled water, which is quite rare in the asylum. I largely ignored those drinks and continued to tend to her vitals and sweaty forehead. Several times, I felt my head drop suddenly as the delta waves took over and I was legally asleep. The first seven times this happened, I caught myself plummeting. On the eighth time, I woke up to Nurse Natalya pulling the lollipop sponge out of Polina's mouth because it was blocking her throat, causing a hideous guttural sound, which incidentally was the sound that people have just before they choke to death.

"Please sleep," she said. "You can't help her like this."

"It won't happen again."

"Do as you will. I know you're too stubborn to listen."

And she was right. But she was also clever. She knew me well enough to know that my head would plummet again. So she staked out the Red Room waiting for my eyelids to get heavy like a neutron star, and when they did, she immediately pulled the sponge pop from my hand, turned out the lights, and left my head positioned carefully next to the skin of Polina's neck. That's where I would wake up the next morning. On the last day.

The Death of Polina Pushkin

A Tuesday.

I think it was the smell of cancer that woke me up.

Prior coma reconnaissance has revealed that there are two sides to this debate. Some say cancer has no smell. They say death odors depend on the particular person and the bedsheets, gauze brands, cleaning solutions, and antibacterial soaps used by that particular hospital, mixed with the general city and cultural aromas. Others say that the cancer itself has an unforgettably pungent smell, one that is indescribable yet distinctive. On the morning that Polina died, the debate was settled for me. Her smell was nonclinical. It was not an odor that a soap or a bedsheet or anything chemically based could produce. It was organic. It was alive. And it was dead. It drew you in, and it pushed you away. It was the smell of sweet, but also the smell of rot.

After coughing out the night's worth of sweet-and-sour cancer residue from my nose and lungs, I reinitiated the caretaking process. The first thing that I noticed was that my rehydration campaign was now a lost cause. Her lips now looked like a Martian landscape with red valleys that bordered on tectonic fissures. I felt guilty because when I looked at them I was disgusted.

The second thing I noticed was her tongue, which looked like it was perpetually seizing. I also noticed her eyes, which were all whites and no iris, because they were fighting so hard to roll to the back of her head. I noticed her breathing, which seemed to be only long, wheezing exhales, and I wondered where she was getting the air to exhale so much without any inhales, and then I wondered if she had just stored secret oxygen in her body from sixteen years of breathing and just now her body was giving it back to the universe. Surely, someone more spiritually minded would have been convinced that she was exhaling her soul, breath by breath. And if I were any less rational, I might have thought the same thing.

I noticed her skin, which had almost completed its transformation to purplish black.

I noticed her scalp, which was more cracked than it was smooth.

I noticed her ribs through her hospital gown, which were now carved like the ripples in desert sand.

I noticed her legs poking out from her hospital gown, which now looked more like broomsticks.

I noticed my hand was on her hand because I didn't know what else I could do.

I noticed it was 7:43 in the A.M.

As I was noticing all these things, her tiny little hand grew icier and icier as if to warn me it was coming. Then her skin hit a critical temperature, and her torso leaped up, chest out, exhaling one more long sandpaper breath, while her once adorable breasts were now compressed and stretched over the landscape of her rib cage. Then she lifelessly collapsed back to the bed, and her chest didn't undulate anymore, and the chirping of the heart monitor stopped. I put my face really close to her chapped mouth and felt nothing against my cheek.

Good-bye, Polina.

PART THREE

Farewell Song

The Aftermath

My first thought after Polina died was that I hoped the millions of rubles of medical technology that was attached to her would notify the nurses that she was dead so I wouldn't have to. Instead, I stared with lifeless eyes at her equally lifeless body for at least a thousand seconds before it occurred to me that no one was coming. So I said, "It happened," and then I waited a few more seconds. No one came. Then, it occurred to me that maybe I didn't say it loud enough, so I said it louder—"It happened!" Still there was no stampede of hospital personnel from the Main Room, which usually accompanies a death. It occurred to me that I had lost my ability to judge the volume of my own voice, so I decided to repeat myself one more time because I didn't think I had the gumption to do it again:

"IT HAPPENED.
THERE IS A DEAD GIRL IN THE RED ROOM.
ATTENTION. COLLECT THE DEAD GIRL FROM THE RED ROOM."

This may have also been accompanied by a bit of thrashing about, which may have resulted in several intravenous tubes being yanked from Polina's dead body and a few monitors crashing to the floor, which further resulted in a flood of broken glass spreading throughout the Red Room. And finally, the dead were woken, and the room flooded with nurses, Natalya, Lyudmila, Katya, Elena, to be exact. And Mikhail Kruk, my father.

The next hour passed by in some combination of fast forward and slow motion. Arms and fingers fluttered around with vapor trails, pulling out stethoscopes, then putting them away, then pulling out needles from veins, disconnecting tubes, turning off machines, sweeping up monitor glass, wiping down sweat and bile, disrobing then rerobing Polina, transferring her body onto another bed (one with wheels), which was then rolled off to some undisclosed location. Throughout the whole ballet, I was simply a prop that was worked around, an inanimate object to be avoided, much like I've been for my whole life.

At some point the curtain closed, but I was still there. Natalya was the first one to make contact. *Ivan?* she said. *Moya lyubov?* she said. *Where are you?* she asked. I didn't know. But I do know I found myself in my bed the next morning, quite literally paralyzed. Then three days later, three days ago, I started writing to you, dear Reader.

∞

Currently, the clock reads 5:55 in the A.M.
It is the sixth day of December.

The year is 2005.
I have been writing for seventy-seven hours.

And now it is now. It is hard to imagine that I brought so much of you back to life, my strange love, only to let you die all over again. At this moment, I'm terrified that I failed you. I'm worried that this memorial won't be acceptable to Bulgakov or Nabokov or Tolstoy, let alone you. Part of me wants to rip these pages into confetti and start all over. But I'm tired. I've just completed a complicated surgical procedure in which I've cut a two-hundred-kilo tumor from my soul, and I'm not sure I feel like putting it back in right now. And, if I'm to be totally honest, I'm not sure if this catharsis was for me or for you. Besides, I think I might finally sleep. Really sleep. Sleep made of limestone and granite. The urge is building at the base of my brain and spreading up into my amygdala and occipital lobe. In a few seconds, it will reach my eyes. I hope that's okay.

Nurse Natalya caught me sleeping.

"I measured you in your sleep," she said, barging into my room with boundless enthusiasm, her hands behind her back where she was clearly concealing something.

"How long was I asleep."

"Almost a day."

"And you did what?"

"I measured you."

"For what?"

"To make sure you would fit into this."

Nurse Natalya pulled her hands from behind her back to reveal that she was holding a black suit. The legs were thoughtfully tailored into shorts so that the two long, empty black pant legs wouldn't draw attention to my lack of appendages.

"I'm supposed to wear that?"

"You are."

"Where did you find this?"

"Does it matter?"

"Yes, it does."

"My church."

"Then I'm definitely not wearing it. You should know better by now."

"Oh, stop. You act like the savior himself wove it. Actually, it belonged to a young boy who now studies astrophysics at Heidelberg University."

"Okay."

"Okay?"

"How do we get there?"

"A long time ago, Karl Benz invented the automobile."

"I knew that."

"Then why'd you ask?"

"I've never been in a car before."

"It's like being in your bed, Ivan. Only it moves."

"You're wittier than normal."

"I switched coffees. Now get dressed."

This was when I typically initiated protest behavior, but I was surprised to find the edge wasn't there.

"Okay."

"No countermove?"

"Knowing I can win is enough."

Natalya looked disoriented. Then her face twisted into suspicion and then back to normal.

"Well, then, I'll be back in fifteen minutes to tie your tie," she said.

Natalya left, and I laid out my suit and wormed into it. Then I writhed my way across the floor, while I thought about how I should have writhed across the floor first and then changed into my suit. Nevertheless, I made it to the bathroom and began to pee. And as the long-built-up stream made music into the toilet, I couldn't help noticing the mirror, which was forever positioned above the sink. It was the same mirror I typically avoided at all costs due to my previously mentioned phobia of reflective surfaces. This time, however, while adorned with a suit for the first time, albeit with floor dust smeared over the lapels, I was overwhelmed with curiosity and could not help myself but to look. The first thing I noticed was that my hair was atrocious, so I licked my palm and adjusted some of the dirty-blond madness geysering from the top of my head. The second thing I noticed was that for the first time I wasn't completely disgusted by my own reflection, though I give most of the credit to the suit.

I finished peeing and writhed back to my bed to check the clock. There were three more minutes before Nurse Natalya would return to tie my tie, and she was quite punctual when it came to things involving dressing and funerals. I decided to use these three minutes to open up the folder hiding beneath my bed and take out the top page, which contained the inked-out part. I folded up this paper and put it into the breast pocket of my suit, like I had seen people do in the movies before, but which I had never done myself because I never before wore anything with a breast pocket. This only took two minutes and twenty seconds, so for the rest of the forty seconds, I took rapid swigs of ethanol and then pulled out Polina's journal and read the last page. It said:

Dear Ivan,
Stop reading my journal. You have a problem.
    If it's possible to miss someone as a ghost, then I'm sure I will miss you. Looking forward to haunting your life.
                    Live,
                    Polina.
PS—You'd better use the suitcase. You have no idea how hard it was to steal ten thousand rubles in this cheap hospital.

Then, like a grandmother clock, Natalya exploded back through the door and began wrapping a tie around my neck. Her face was about six inches from mine, so I got to watch the sequence of faces that she made while attempting to get it tied.

"It's been a while," she said.

"Since your husband?" I asked while simultaneously holding my breath so that she couldn't smell the Stoli.

"Yes. Since him," she said, and then after a few more seconds of wrangling and pinching the skin of my neck:

"There. Quite handsome, Ivan," she said.

"I know," I said.

She maneuvered her way behind my chair and wheeled me out of my room, and then down the hall, and past Miss Kristina's desk, and then out the two big brown double doors, and then we were outside, which I hated. She stopped for a moment, perhaps to get me acclimated to my agoraphobia, or maybe because she was tired of pushing. Then she dusted some of the hair off my forehead and continued to push me down a gray concrete ramp to a small parking lot where her car was parked.

"What do you call this car?" I asked.

"It's a Lada."

"It looks old."

"It is old."

She parked my chair near to the door, but not too close, because she needed room to open the door, which swung out like a pterodactyl wing. Then she wheeled me right up close to the seat and started to drag my body into the car.

"No, I can do this," I said.

"Of course you can," she said, relinquishing my body.

And, of course, in my attempt to transition myself from my chair to the car using some combination of worming and writhing, I fell out of my chair and slammed my chin into the car's metal frame, which resulted in minor bleeding. This meant that two of my phobias (agoraphobia and hemophobia) were now being simultaneously activated.

"Sweet Saint Joseph," Nurse Natalya blurted while her hands and legs positioned herself to pull me off the ground.

"I can do it," I said. And I did. Almost. Until I didn't. At which point I slipped, and this time my nose collided with a tire, which made even more blood and several flashes of bright light inside my head.

"Don't," I said preemptively. And she didn't. And after what felt like climbing a small mountain, I was in the front seat of Nurse Natalya's Lada with trembling hands. When it was clear I wouldn't kill myself, Nurse Natalya folded my chair and put it in the backseat.

"Seat belt," said Nurse Natalya.

I watched as she slipped into her seat, attached her seat belt, and started the car all at the same time.

"I have one arm," I said.

Nurse Natalya took a moment to look me over and assess the logistics of her request, after which she made an agreeable gesture with the wrinkles in her forehead and reached over to attach my seat belt herself. And without another word, we pulled out of the long driveway of the Mazyr Hospital for Gravely Ill Children for the first time in my life.

The wordlessness lasted for most of the drive to the cemetery. There were several reasons for this. Reason #1: I turned and looked at Nurse Natalya's face, and it was clear that she was gone, perhaps in a deep trance to some other place and time where her husband still lived, but I was too afraid to ask her if that was true. Reason #2: The paper was burning a hole through my breast pocket. Reason #3: I felt dangerously close to vomiting all over Nurse Natalya's Lada whenever I thought about how the next time the car stopped moving, I would show her the paper.

There were exactly seven turns on the way to the cemetery. I know this because every time we took one, I had to swallow some juices back into my stomach. It only got worse once we pulled into the cemetery, which was filled with snaking dirt roads designed to provide easy access to every tombstone, but also provided an incessant tug at the contents of my stomach. Something about being inside the cemetery shook Nurse Natalya out of her trance, which made her remember that I was in the car.

"It's called car sickness, Ivan. It's common."

"How common?"

"Quite common."

"It's rare, isn't it?"

"Yes, but you've never ridden before."

I let her believe it was car sickness.

"How far is it?"

"Another hundred feet."

"Why did you pick this cemetery?"

"Because it's nice."

"Because it's free?"

"Not free, but cheap."

"Free."

"Not free, but already paid for."

"Who paid for it?"

"My husband."

"Your dead husband?"

"Yes, my dead husband."

"But he's dead."

"He bought it when he was alive."

"Why would he buy a plot that he wasn't going to be buried in?"

"Because I was supposed to be buried in it."

Natalya parked the car, while I sat in a state of confusion.

"Why wouldn't you get buried with your husband?"

"I was supposed to be. He's buried here too."

Natalya pointed at the hollowed-out grave about fifty meters from the car. There was a casket next to it, which I imagined had Polina inside. On the other side of the casket was a tombstone.

"Is that your husband?"

"Yes."

"Polina is being buried next to your husband where you were supposed to be buried?"

"Yes."

Her simple yes made me uncomfortable for several reasons. First, because I was very angry that Natalya would do that to herself and to her dead husband. Second, because levels of generosity such as this did not operate in the machinery of my world. So I responded with a blurt. Perhaps there was no other way.

"Was Dimitri my brother?"

I paid careful attention to Nurse Natalya's face from that moment on. At this particular moment, it had all the makings of confusion. *The Art of Reading Faces* by Sergei Goglinov suggests that the expression of confusion comes in many flavors. The one on Nurse Natalya's face was the *Where the fuck did that come from?* flavor, which is quite different from the *How the fuck does he know that?* flavor. This distinction is quite important and fell in Nurse Natalya's favor.

"Dimitri didn't have a brother, Ivan. And neither do you."

"If you say so."

The confusion in Nurse Natalya's face reconfigured. It was now obvious that she was angry, at least according to the creases in her forehead and the tightness of her jawline.

"Where is this coming from, Ivan? And make it quick because we have someone to bury."

"From this."

I pulled the paper out and handed it to her. I watched her face carefully as she unfolded it. Her jaw loosened, and the wrinkles turned shallow, and now her confusion was back. Her eyes, with slightly blue scleras and irises fading from green to orange, were shifting all over the document like she was trying to see every word at once. At some point, they started moving more traditionally, left to right, top to bottom. Then, when she was done, her eyes went back to the top, to the beginning, the lines that had my name, and started all over again. And when she finished the second time, the hand that held the paper fell into her lap, and her head moved up into the sky like she was curving things out, massaging old memories, letting history assemble, connecting the dots of some secret symphony that she was always just shy of unearthing. Her mouth hung slightly open, and her other hand moved to her lips. And then she turned to me, and the expression became a cocktail of pity, and anger, and sympathy, and forgiveness, and concern, and maternity, and resolution, and I wondered how Nurse Natalya's brain did not explode with so much happening all at the same time.

"Oh, my Ivan, in the name of the Father—"

Little tear streams formed from nothing on Nurse Natalya's cheeks, but the mosaic of expressions in her face didn't change.

"Answers," I said.

Stoically. Firmly. Resolutely.

"Where did you find this?" she asked.

"*She* found it. In Mikhail's office. And you don't get to ask questions."

"Okay."

"Who knew?"

"No one knew for sure," she said.

"But."

"But some of us wondered."

"Why?"

"Because one of us would suddenly vanish."

"But no one asked."

"No one asked."

"Why?"

"Because you just don't ask."

"I deserve better than that. Especially from you."

"I know you do."

The little streams on Nurse Natalya's cheeks got fatter.

"Did you know my mother?"

"I did."

"How do you know you knew her?"

"Her name was Yulia. I know because you can see the *Y* and the *l* pop out from the marker ink."

Nurse Natalya showed me the paper to confirm.

"Was she a nurse?"

"Yes."

"Was she your friend?"

"She was."

"Do you promise that you never knew?"

"I promise," which she could barely say because now Natalya's face started crumbling in on itself like a rotting apple.

"What was she like?"

"She was smart, like you. And she made me laugh. No one else at the hospital could make me laugh."

"What did she look like?"

"She had big blue eyes. Also like you. I remember her hair was starting to gray even though she was young, which made her more beautiful in her own way."

"What happened to her?"

"I never heard from her after she left."

"Not once?"

"Except for a short letter from Leningrad."

"What did it say?"

"It said that she was happy."

"With a family?"

"Yes."

Which hurt my heart.

"How old was she?"

"When she left, or when she had a family?"

"Both."

"Twenty-three when she left. Thirty when she sent me the letter."

"Did you know she was pregnant?"

"I did."

"She told you?"

"No, but I figured it out."

"But you didn't know it was *him*?"

"I suspected. We all suspected."

I waited for my thoughts to catch up with my mouth before asking the next question.

"Why didn't he just end us?"

"You mean in the womb?"

"That's what I mean."

"When you were born, abortions were easier to get than bread. But the Mikhail I know would never allow it. He's the most God-fearing philanderer I know. You don't manage the most Orthodox hospital in the Eastern Bloc otherwise."

"There may be more?"

"Probably."

"Why keep *me*?"

"I can only guess because you were sick."

"So?"

"You would need to be treated. Which requires money and a story—two things that would haunt him like the ghost of Saint Francis. They could lead back to the misses or the church."

She held her breath for a few seconds and thought some things. Then she continued:

"At the hospital, you cost nothing. And he could make it

look like you never happened. As hard as that is to hear, *moya lyubov.*"

Natalya tried to hold me, but I batted her away.

"My baby—"

"I would like to kill him."

"Ivan. You are not his blood."

"There is nothing I would prefer more than to kill him."

"Ivan. You are not from him."

For the first time ever, I looked into Natalya's eyes and didn't believe her.

Because I was.

I was him.

No matter what she or Polina said.

But I knew it wasn't my choice.

So I gave in and put my head in her bosom.

And I lurched and then I heaved.

I couldn't breathe I cried so hard.

And still I pushed my head deeper into her skin, where it was even harder to breathe.

I wept till there was nothing left to weep, and I was thirsty because I ran out of liquids.

And then I remembered that we were here to bury Polina.

And I thought about how much I lost in such a short time.

"I think I loved her," I said when I could say things again.

"She loved you too."

"Maybe."

"She said something once."

"What?"

"She said you made her forget that she was dying. That

you gave her the cure to herself. And maybe that's all love is, Ivan."

"Maybe."

"I think so."

"Let's go."

"Okay."

Natalya wiped up the mess all over the both of our faces, and then she wheeled me to the hole in the ground where Polina was about to go.

II

The Funeral

There were four people at Polina's funeral: Nurse Natalya, the priest, and Nurse Natalya's cousin, Maria, who happened to be a nun, and me. Polina was there also, but she was inside of a closed, no-frills casket, which looked like the plain box they might issue to fallen soldiers. The priest, whom Nurse Natalya introduced as Father Petr, a longtime friend of the family, initiated the ceremony promptly.

> "Thou only Creator Who with wisdom profound mercifully orderest all things, and givest unto all that which is useful, give rest, O Lord, to the soul of Thy servant who has fallen asleep, for she has placed her trust in Thee, our Maker and Fashioner and our God . . ."

And all I could think about was how Polina would have laughed at all the pomp. She would have initiated a discussion of the pros and cons of Father Petr's obnoxious beard and mused about what self-deception would make a man surrender his life to God in exchange for a cloistered life.

With the saints give rest, O Christ, to the soul of Thy servant where sickness and sorrow are no more, neither sighing, but life everlasting.

The words didn't connect. They didn't tie a bow around her life like she deserved. I wondered if I should have arranged a set of quotes from her favorite songs and books. In my opinion, Tolstoy, Nabokov, and Janis Joplin made far better prophets. And I knew Polina agreed from her box.

My soul cleaves to the dust, give me life according to Thy word.

But there was something to the pomp.

Turn my eyes from looking at vanities; and give me life in Thy ways.

It almost tricks you.

Behold, I long for Thy precepts; in Thy righteousness give me life.

Into thinking there could be something more.

Thy testimonies are righteousness forever; give me understanding that I may live.

And I wondered if I could let myself be tricked. Because it tasted so good.

Plead my cause, and redeem me; give me life according to Thy promise.

Then I wheeled over to the casket, and amid fierce protests from Nurse Natalya and Father Petr, I lifted the lid with all my mutant might to reveal a Polina not right for the light of day.

Thank you, Polina. Now, I can't be tricked.

Then, I set the lid back down and let the priest proceed with his sermon. Until the words were over and they lifted the box and put it into the ground.

By now, Reader, I hope you understand that at the Mazyr Hospital for Gravely Ill Children, there is no absence of death. The tiny hands of ghosts emerge from the walls and waft its smell in my face all day long, singeing my nostrils and leaving me with a distinct and uninvited congestion. But somehow this perpetual exposure failed to habituate me to the sight of that limp, lavender, lifeless bag of bones whose kiss was warm only a few days ago. If I'm to be honest, Polina was the only creature I ever allowed myself to make real.

My mother (the one in my head) was right. My resistance to Polina's death gave birth to a terrible little thought. It leaked into my head, uninvited and unapologetic, and immediately established a dwelling: What if my beloved Polina wasn't dead? What if this were an inexplicable coma? A medical anomaly? And what if my beloved Polina would awaken long after she'd been buried? My imagination, which was quite honed after a lifetime of sensory deprivation, played out the scenario with precious immediacy. She would open her eyes in a cold, dark cell with pressure-treated pungent pine several inches from her eyes. And after a few confused moments, where she couldn't be sure whether or not she was dreaming a terrible dream, reality would set in, along with real terror. Perhaps it would begin with transcendental claustrophobia or perhaps the freezing re-alization of transcendental loneliness. She would panic. She would kick and hammer and thrash about and claw, but this would only remind her of how close the walls actually were. Even so, she would continue to fight for a minute, which would feel like hours in her fragile subjectivity. Then she would stop suddenly. The hopelessness of the situation would wash over her. A bereaved sympathetic nervous system would be forced to accept that she could not fight or flee. She would have to re-sign herself to lying there in all her transcendental fear and loneliness—until she died of asphyxiation.

Amid this terrible little thought, came a thought within a thought. A thought that perhaps as my beloved was gripped by this morbid arousal, the thoughts of her last waking moments would flood her, if for no other reason than their proximity, or maybe because they were relatively benign compared to what she was going through. Perhaps our last night together would fill her mind. And perhaps she would again be flushed by the derealization that we felt that night. And perhaps she would think of our kiss. And perhaps all this might become her world as the lesser parts of her were preparing to die. And perhaps the fantasy would continue on further and further into a future that neither of us saw but which she needed to imagine in that frigid, lonely place. And perhaps we would die together after all.

III

The Drive Back

Was silent.

But also not uncomfortable. Silently cathartic, in fact.

I looked at Nurse Natalya's face long enough to realize that while her eyes were on the road, her head was a merry-go-round with me, and Polina, and Mikhail, and her husband, and my mother, whose name is apparently Yulia, spinning around in exhausting little circles. I saw all our absurd faces flicker through her eyes.

I, on the other hand, thought about the mating rituals of penguins, and the pros and cons of circumcision, and how antibiotics have only been around for less than one hundred years, and how awful it must have been for men to get a dose of the clap in the 1800s, and how early hominids could survive the cold in Siberia before modern technology, and anything else that could keep me from thinking about the last one hundred hours of my own life.

Fortunately, by the time I ran out of thoughts, we pulled back into the Mazyr Hospital for Gravely Ill Children. And, almost as soon as I saw its off-white painted brick façade and heard the random sounds of nurses barking and the occasional mutant howl through the open windows, I began to feel gravely ill myself. But ill in the sweetest sense. I breathed through that wave of ill and looked around at the forested, partially manicured open air and didn't want to throw up all over it. This meant that for the first time in my life, I preferred the outside to the inside.

Nurse Natalya, still silent, pulled out my chair and then pulled me out of her car and dropped me into it. She wheeled me back up the dirt path to the big brown double doors, which, for me, meant being immersed in every memory that could ever haunt me, and for Natalya it must have meant something completely different, because her clip was too brisk, and there was something alarming about the waves of intensity radiating from her loose skin as she plowed through those brown doors. When we broke the seal, the intensity didn't abate. She pushed my chair through the hallway, past Miss Kristina's desk—"Morning, Natalya," she said—and on through the linoleum she wheeled me, at least twice as fast as the fastest she ever pushed before, and then through the Main Room, where the gingers were building a castle from hospital pillows, and Dennis undulated like a human timepiece, and Alex smeared chocolate all over his face, and a couple of heart-hole kids sat somberly avoiding any escalation in heart rate, and on past the Red Room, where no one was left to die, and then through to the girls' wing, and right up to Polina's door, which she opened, and then wheeled me inside and shut the door behind me, at which point I said, "Natalya?" but of course she didn't respond because she was too absorbed in the process of rummaging underneath Polina's bed and squeezing more of her physical body through the space between the floor and the bed frame than the space would allow for her and then almost lifting the bed right from the floor as she thrust and thrashed on until she pulled out the suitcase, my suitcase, the escape pod that Polina had built for me, which she then plopped onto my lap.

"Say yes, and we're gone," Nurse Natalya said. "But it has to come from you."

"Where will I go?"

"With me."

"In your home."

"In my home."

"And Mikhail?"

"I will worry about Mikhail."

The room bent and spun while my heart started jamming the blood that remained in my veins (what I didn't give to Polina) into the farthest parts of my body, like my fingers, nubs, and earlobes. Then I wondered why I was so afraid. And as if she could read the prose across my eyes, Nurse Natalya said:

"It's because your life will be yours. Which means your misery will be yours too. It won't belong to Lyudmila, or Mikhail, or the state."

And I knew she was right. It was something my mother (my imaginary one) would have said if she were still here. This, however, came from a real person, which made it problematic.

"Ivan, if you want to give them custody of your misery, I—"

"No."

It shot out of me.

"What?" Nurse Natalya asked.

"I said no."

"No what?"

"Do you have a TV?"

"Ivan, it's 2005. Everyone has a TV."

"And borscht?"

"Every Sunday."

"Okay."

And with an agility that was not congruent with her age or athleticism, Natalya got behind me and started pushing, and I quickly secured my suitcase, which almost fell from my lap due to the sudden acceleration. Once she started pushing, she didn't stop. She kept pushing. She pushed me back through the Main Room, through my carnival of friendly mutants, through the foyer past Miss Kristina's desk—"Bye, Natalya; Bye, Ivan"—through the big heavy brown double doors, through the front seat of her car, through the seventeen miles of road leading to her small apartment in downtown Mazyr, onto a street called Vostok, and through the charming front red door of her apartment, through her adequately but elderly decorated living room, and then dining room, and finally into a guest room, which appeared to be my room, because it was already set up for me, equipped with a large bookcase filled with volumes of Russian, and also French, and also American literature, and various textbooks ranging in topics from medicine to quantum physics, and the walls had posters of things like celestial events, and James Joyce, and Franz Kafka, and then she said, "I expected you would be here someday, just didn't know which one," and then I used my index finger to motion for her to come to me, because I wouldn't have been able to use words, and when her face got close, I kissed her. Then I asked her for a few minutes so that I could pull out this notebook and write down what just happened, which is what I'm doing right now.

Ivan Isaenko
June 10, 1987– September 3, 2008
Mazyr, Belarus

Epilogue

There is a ghost that haunts the descendants of Pripyat. It hides inside of every seed and every cell. It resides in the mind where it sneaks up behind every thought and every hope. A tricky spook that dulls the bliss of every birth and every love. Some call it a ticking time bomb, but no one ever knows when the clock is set.

Ivan Isaenko succumbed to his own ghost on September 3, 2008. Six months earlier, he was diagnosed with non-Hodgkin's lymphoma, one of Pripyat's favorite phantoms. Inevitably, it is hard to overstate the bitterness of this pill given the denouement of Ivan's story.

Beyond his death we know little of Ivan's life after the Mazyr Hospital for Gravely Ill Children with the exception of these few sanguine details. Ivan lived with Natalya Beneshenko for almost nineteen months before losing his fight. Miss Beneshenko retired from the Mazyr Hospital for Gravely Ill Children shortly after Ivan moved in. We know that in the nineteen months Ivan lived outside of the hospital, he published two short stories, one in the *Mazyr Chronicle* titled "дважды,"*

---

* Translated from Russian as "Twice."

and another in the Belarus State University literary journal, titled "клерк."[*] He also visited the grave of his hero Vladimir Nabokov in Montreux, Switzerland, during a trip to Western Europe. When Ivan passed, Miss Beneshenko buried him in the same cemetery as her husband, next to Polina Pushkin.

There are as many themes in Ivan's story as there are pages. It is at once a love story, a revelation of the dark legacy of the Soviet experiment, a conversation on medical ethics, a reproach of religious hypocrisy, and an admonition against choosing fear over purpose. But, ultimately, it is simply the story of a single human life, within which so much can be held. We hope the reader can pause to appreciate that fact.

---

[*]   Translated from Russian as "The Clerk."

Acknowledgments

Had I not met these people, this book either would have never been published or I wouldn't have been the guy who wrote it:

Victoria Sanders, you probably don't realize, but you single-handedly taught me more about how to write a novel than any other person on the planet. I'm so grateful to have you in my corner.

Jen Enderlin, dream editor and co-parent of *Ivan Isaenko*. I couldn't ask for a more wonderful person to share this book with.

Bernadette Baker-Baughman, the supportive spirit who makes me feel perfectly at ease asking the dumbest, most naive questions about this weird new world of publishing.

Linda Stambach, the bold supporter of every pie-in-the-sky dream I've had since the age of five.

Shawn and Nicole, best siblings ever.

The OG Circle: Ryan Degley, Bill Kalish, Danny Trout, Matthew Ellish. Who the hell would I be without all of you?

George and Donna Lightsey, my West Coast parents, you'll never know how grateful I am for the nonstop love and *Big Bang* night.

Stacey Keating, my soul sister, moral compass, co-founder of Noetic, and the 2,349 other things you are in my life.

Cat White, my first reader and dear friend. Thank you for being the most loyal friend in the world.

Anna Chiles, my teaching partner and constant reminder to be my best self.

Lucy Boulatnikov, my lovely Russian-language checker, so much of you is in this story.

Tania Jabour, my wonderful friend, this book would not have happened if not for Six Flags 2013.

Paul Temple, my broham and possibly the kindest human being alive.

Mike Anderson, for the years of inspiration, encouragement, and epic late-night convos.

Jon Yu and Matt Ortiz, my brothers and fellow Sets.

Yuri Shatz for his Eastern Europe expertise and eagle-eyed editing skills.

Many thanks to all my early readers for their feedback and encouragement: Matt Martin, Mike Heyd, Isaac Rivera, Kennadi Yates, Sarah Dear, Ady Sukkar Kayrouz, Isabella Miranda, Samira Kester, Miriam Tullgren, Erin Duarte, Alejandra Torrero, Deborah Kutyla, Daniel Cordello, Jyothsna Konda.

All my teachers for the sum total of what you've taught me.

All the sweet, crazy, and earnest High Tech High, Mesa, City, and Grossmont students I've ever had the privilege of ranting to about physics and space. I'm a better writer when I see the world through your wild eyes.

If I missed anyone, you know I love you. Deadlines make for bad memories. . . .

Reading
Group
Gold

THE INVISIBLE LIFE OF IVAN ISAENKO

by Scott Stambach

About the Author

- A Conversation with Scott Stambach

Behind the Novel

- A Selection of Photographs

Keep on Reading

- Recommended Reading
- Reading Group Questions

Also available as an audiobook
from Macmillan Audio

For more reading group suggestions
visit www.readinggroupgold.com.

W WEDNESDAY BOOKS

A Conversation with Scott Stambach

Could you tell us a little bit about your background, and when you decided that you wanted to lead a literary life?

I'm a bit of a weirdo in the literary world because I have no literary background! Back in college, I was 100 percent determined to become a research physicist or a rock star—whatever came first. In the end, I became a physics and astronomy teacher, which allowed me to be a physicist and a rock star.

Then I made the mistake of reading the book *House of Leaves* by Mark Z. Danielewski. Anyone who picks this book up and fans through the pages will immediately see that it is one of the most unique and experimental pieces of literature ever written. But when I started reading it, I discovered that it wasn't just clever—it was enthralling. I couldn't stop reading. So much that while I was supposed to be visiting Machu Picchu in Cuzco, Peru, I found myself holed up in a cafe for six days reading instead of exploring the city.

When I finished the book, I had this thought: I want to write something that makes people feel the way I do right now. So over the next year, I made a commitment to write five hundred words a day, every day, no matter what. I wrote these really bad short stories and sent them to journals. Then somehow, then years later, I finished *The Invisible Life of Ivan Isaenko*, my first novel.

Would you care to share any writing tips?

God, yes. I learned way too much the hard way. Like...

Tip #1: Learn to love rejection to masochistic proportions.

I received 116 rejections before I ever published a single short story (and if that doesn't seem like a lot, I urge you to count to 116 while imagining a gut punch after every number).

But before I let it shatter my dreams, I did something clever. I reverse psychologized my rejections by making a folder in my inbox called "celebrations." Then I stuffed every rejection into that folder. I trained myself to be exhilarated by every new rejection. This was so successful that by the time I finally read *Dear Mr. Stambach, We are thrilled to accept _____ for publication in _____* I was thoroughly confused about how to feel.

Eight years later, I started shopping *Ivan* to agents. How many rejections did I receive before I got an email from my agent telling me that she loved the book? The answer is ninety!

I'm guessing you get the point—there is no way through this business without experiencing comical amounts of rejection. So…learn to love it. Maybe even enjoy it.

Tip #2: Find a routine that works for you and commit to it like a marriage.

Writing is not a career. It is art and art is a value.

Waiting until you feel inspired before living out your values is a huge trap. Imagine a mother whose deepest value is being a good parent. Would she wait to feel inspired before she decided to be a kick-ass mom? Nope. She'd commit to being a good caregiver even when she felt like holy hell.

The same goes for writing. Art is not about whether or not you *feel like it*. You may not always love what comes out. That's fine. You can always edit later. But the bottom line is that at the end of the day you've made art.

Tip #3: Have something to say.

Writers should consider the investment required to read a book: someone needs to drive to a bookstore, pay money on the gamble that they will like it, and then spend all the hours it takes to flip pages to the end. This is a lot to ask.

So if a reader is going to do all that work, you need to give them something back, something so real and human that they see a piece of themselves reflected in the story. Readers want to feel connected and understood.

What was the inspiration for this novel?

Much like Ivan, the exact birthday of the book is debatable. The only thing I know for sure is that sometime in the summer of 2007, I accidentally stumbled onto a documentary called *Chernobyl Heart*. It depicted way too well the realities inside of the hospitals in Eastern Europe where victims of the infamous nuclear explosion were hidden from the world. By the end, my eyes were soaked

and I was ready to step into the ring and go twelve rounds with Lenin's ghost.

The film was almost unbearable to watch for several reasons. But, one piece stood out, leaving me feeling most helpless and hopeless. It was the fact that even with the acute public interest, these kids had no voice. Yes, they got some camera time on an internationally distributed documentary. Yes, they got to mumble a few words into the cameras. But, it wasn't enough. There was too much pain there, too much history, too much hush-hush. Ultimately, *Ivan* is an homage to those kids.

In the days that followed, the idea of writing a novel chronicling their lives started to assemble. A year later, I was lucky enough to take a creative writing course taught by the brilliant writer of *Madeleine Is Sleeping*, Sarah Shun-lien Bynum. I ended up writing *Ivan* as a short story for that class. Fast-forward three more years, I decided to include it in a collection of short stories I was trying to publish. But, instead of publishing that collection as planned, I was urged to develop *Ivan* into a novel, and found myself back to my original inspiration. After fourteen months of feverish writing, the Mazyr Hospital for Gravely Ill Children came to life.

About the Author

Can you tell us about what research, if any, you did before writing this novel?

Most of my research came from two places. My initial spark and source material came from documentaries like *Chernobyl Heart*. The other was my Ukrainian high school sweetheart who was kind enough to provide translations for all the Russian curse words.

Do you have firsthand experience with its subject or base any of the characters on people from your own life?

I'm happy to say that I don't have any firsthand experience with friends or family being involved in the radioactive fallout of Chernobyl. That said, this book would not have been written without my grandmother, Josephine. When I was old enough to know what was going on, but not old enough to process it, I watched the painful process of her passing away from cancer. I also happened to be in the room the moment she passed. That was when I learned how loud and lonely death could be. I never really processed that experience, but twenty years later, as I was writing this book, I realized that I was writing what I saw on the day my grandmother died into the life and death of Polina, Ivan's love. And for the first time I realized that I was making some meaning out of that experience.

What is the most interesting or surprising thing you learned as you set out to tell your story?

One of the most amazing things I learned didn't happen until much after I set out to write. Actually, it happened after it was already published.

Once *Ivan* was out in the world, I had the odd realization that the book was technically only half done when it was published. Obviously, I don't mean this literally (there's no way you can

get a half-finished book through all those intense copyeditors). What I mean is that so much of the book's meaning wasn't built until readers started sharing their thoughts with me and to the world. As much as I thought I knew what this book was about when I finished writing it, I realized that it wasn't complete until readers had their say. This was both surprising and beautiful. It made the book feel like a living, breathing thing existing in the world. In a way, I had to give up exclusive ownership of my book, my baby. In exchange, I gained a relationship with readers that felt much more collaborative and alive.

Are you currently working on another book? And if so, can you tell us what it's about?

I'm in the process of writing two new novels. One is about a hotel in Rio de Janeiro that contains all of time. The other is about a derelict in New Orleans who finds himself in the strange position of having to raise his infant niece off the grid and hide her existence. I hope to publish one or more of them some day.

About the Author

The following are photographs of Pripyat, the abandoned town where the Chernobyl engineers and their families once lived.

Jennifer Boyer

Ben Adlard

*Behind the
Novel*

Jennifer Boyer

 *Recommended Reading*

House of Leaves by Mark Z. Danielewski

I could sum it up in a sentence: this book is the reason I became a writer. If you held this book in your hands and fanned through the pages, you would find a curious assortment of fonts; pages with words going backward, sideways, up and down; and some pages with only a single word. The book is extremely playful with form. But don't fall into the trap of thinking it's unreadable. I've never been so hooked on a book in my life, largely because of its engrossing premise: a family who discovers (to their horror) that their house is bigger on the inside than it is on the outside.

Kafka on the Shore by Haruki Murakami

Haruki Murakami might be a genius. But not just any genius. A genius whose mind works unlike any other writer I've ever read. *Kafka on the Shore* is a magical and surreal story about a teenage boy who decides to leave home on an epic journey only to later discover that his father's been murdered and the evidence points to his involvement. Along the way, we're introduced to hidden dimensions, a magical crow, supernatural sex scenes, and a simpleton with a telekinetic connection to cats. The story is so addictive that only hunger and extreme exhaustion could get me to put it down. Half of the allure comes from the prose itself. Murakami reads so easily. He's like a wizard in the way he creates complex and charming stories with such simple prose. I remember telling a friend that Murakami's books are like fully functional intergalactic spaceships made out of Play-Doh.

Ultimately, Kafka is my reminder that prose doesn't need to brag to be brilliant.

The Brief Wondrous Life of Oscar Wao by Junot Díaz

I don't know of any book that's shown up on more "Best of the 2000s" lists (and very often in the number-one spot) than *The Brief Wondrous Life of Oscar Wao*. And I couldn't agree more with the hype. *Oscar* is as close to perfect craft as anything I've ever read. It is the literary equivalent of Jackson Pollock. Every element hangs in artful balance. It masterfully juggles historical rigor, humor, and experimental prose with seriously heavy issues like immigrant belonging, masculinity, and the history of the DR's Trujillo regime. Telling a story like this, especially through such an innovative voice, is about as tough as storytelling gets. And yet somehow Díaz does it masterfully. I'm not too proud to confess that whenever I finish writing a novel, it's *Oscar* I turn to as the yardstick to measure my own craft.

Keep on
Reading

One Hundred Years of Solitude by Gabriel García Márquez

This was the other pivotal book that lit my fire to write. It was also the first book that taught me how beautiful words can be. Oh yeah, and it also happens to be one of the most inspired and ambitious novels ever written. This is illustrated perfectly in the story of how García Márquez came to write the book (which may be my favorite author story of all time). Apparently, he was driving his family through the mountains of Colombia on the way to a summer family vacation. However, when the idea for the novel came to him, he pulled a U-turn, drove all the way back home, and sold his car so that he could spend the next eighteen months writing nonstop. As it would turn out, the gamble paid off. The story filled with humanity, imagination, and magic. Not to mention, it scored García Márquez the 1982 Nobel Prize in Literature.

Consider the Lobster by David Foster Wallace

It's hard to imagine any Gen X writer not having a bit of a crush on David Foster Wallace. With that said, most people equate him with his long and dense works like *Infinite Jest*. Most don't know that his nonfiction is a whole other beast, made up of hilarious, accessible, and insightful investigative journalism. *Consider the Lobster* is probably the best example of this. In it you'll find stories about what happens when adult-movie starlets meet their fans, the wars that dictionary writers wage with each other, and the age-old question of whether lobsters feel pain. Wildly weird and enjoyable for readers of all ages.

Lolita by Vladimir Nabokov

Lolita needs to make an appearance on this list for a bunch of reasons. First, it's Ivan's favorite book. Actually, it's more like an obsession. He owns three copies and references it constantly. As for me, what I love most about *Lolita* is the voice. It is simultaneously beautiful and smart and clever

and crude and self-conscious. The main character, Humbert Humbert, might be my all-time favorite unreliable narrator. And it is certainly a voice that inspired Ivan's own brand of intellect, vulgarity, and charm.

Keep on Reading

Reading Group Questions

1. As the last paragraph suggests, there are as many themes in *The Invisible Life of Ivan Isaenko* as there are pages. But if you were to put the author's overall message into a single sentence, what would it be?

2. At the beginning of the book, Ivan gets into a conversation with Natalya about Buddhism. Afterward, he says that he "bear[s] a striking resemblance to the Buddha sitting beneath the Bodhi Tree." What do you suppose he meant?

3. What did you know about the Chernobyl incident before reading this novel? How, if at all, did it teach you about, or change your impression of this event?

4. For seemingly no reason, Ivan bursts into tears after having exerted rigid control over his emotions for most of his life. When Natalya sees this, she comforts him and says, "You'll find, Ivan, that most of the evil in the world is done by men who are addicted to their own thoughts." What does she mean?

5. Ivan has a bit of a potty mouth. He can be vulgar and doesn't seem to know that he overshares a lot (especially as it pertains to bodily functions). What do you suppose was the author's intention for that element of Ivan's voice?

6. Ivan lives a very detached, managed, and curated existence. He does this so he doesn't have to feel too much or worry about any surprises. What is it about Polina or his relationship with her that is able to change his most entrenched habits?

7. Many of the themes of this book have to do
   with our heart's deepest values, those things
   that bring purpose and meaning to life and
   define how we want to be in the world. What
   are the core values that help guide your life?

8. At the Mazyr Hospital for Gravely Ill
   Children, patience and kindness is hard
   to come by. The nurses are impatient and
   ornery, as is Ivan and the director. It seems
   that Natalya is the only exception to this rule.
   What makes Natalya different?

9. Ivan seems annoyed that Ridick is able to cure
   the heart-hole children while the rest of the
   patients are left hanging in the breeze. He even
   quotes his hero Nabokov: "The world needs
   happy endings no matter how unethical." Why
   does Ivan use this quote? What do you think it
   means within in the context of this novel?

10. Ivan seems to be both terrified and drawn
    to Polina because she is someone who can
    reflect his reality back to him. What does this
    mean for Ivan? What does this mean for us as
    human beings?

11. At the end of the day, what can we learn about
    our world—and ourselves—from Ivan's story?

*Keep on
Reading*

Made in the
USA
Middletown, DE